THOUGHT WARRIORS

The Frozen
Saint of Baikal

POULOMI SANYAL

Connect with Poulomi Sanyal

Website: https://poulomi-sanyal.weebly.com/

Twitter: https://twitter.com/sanyal_poulomi

Facebook: https://www.facebook.com/authorPoulomiSanyal/

LinkedIn: https://www.linkedin.com/in/poulomisanyal/

To follow latest updates, insightful blog-posts, book-signings, giveaways and promotions, sign-up to the author's newsletter at:

https://www.poulomisanyal.com/news

ISBN-13: 978-1-7753950-3-4

DEDICATION

"The woods are lovely, dark and deep,
But I have promises to keep,
And miles to go before I sleep,
And miles to go before I sleep."
—Robert Frost, Stopping by Woods on a Snowy Evening

"Long is the way and hard, that out of Hell leads up to light."
—John Milton, Paradise Lost

"It cannot be seen, cannot be felt,
Cannot be heard, cannot be smelt,
It lies behind stars and under hills,
And empty holes it fills,
It comes first and follows after,
Ends life, kills laughter."
—J.R.R. Tolkien, The Hobbit

This book is dedicated to all those who fearlessly seek the light.

PRAISE FOR THOUGHT WARRIORS
BOOK 1
THE COMING OF KALKI

"… this same stylization also evokes the action-film genre, and indeed, Zoya and company would not feel out of place in a movie. Their scenes are easy to visualize, and the mix of science and myth effectively draws the reader in to the story. A cinematic … supernatural adventure."—***Kirkus Reviews***

"I'm a writer & this book intimidated me. I recommend it for everyone. It's a modern masterpiece."—***Amazon Reviewer***

"This book has a very unique blend of science and mythology. The author did an amazing job writing this complex story … This author is very talented. The story held my attention from beginning to conclusion. I'm looking forward to book 2."—***Adriana B (Amazon Reviewer)***

"It is a science fiction of a fabulous thought-provoking escapade enlightened with highest amount of imagination, thrill and breathless excitement. It is an exceptionally fascinating journey of exploring ancient secrets with modern scientific thoughts. Enriched with adequate conceptual training and background in optics in general and photonics in particular, this young promising author has made this science fiction so exciting."—***Dr. Purushottam Chakraborty, Saha Institute of Nuclear Physics***

CHAPTER ONE

It was pushing midnight when a slightly hunched, withered old lady with closely cropped silver hair, walked into the Prohibition Era speakeasy in the heart of New York City, wearing a dark brown winter coat and fluffy earmuffs. A uniformed host greeted her at the door, took her coat and offered his arm to lead her to her seat. They walked past plush couches and wooden tables, arranged in a 1930s style décor, to arrive at a quiet, dimly lit corner of the room. In the darkness, sat a middle-aged man with salt and pepper hair, wearing a grey business suit. He stood up promptly upon seeing them. Bowing slightly, he extended his hand.

"Good evening, Madam Faraday, a pleasure to meet you," he said courteously.

"Evening, Mister Gao, is it?" Wanda Faraday clasped her tiny hands around his and smiled.

"Kevin Gao, that's correct Ma'am. I'm glad you could make it. Can I get you a drink?" Kevin waved at a waiter as he spoke.

"Just water will be fine, thank you." Wanda sighed.

"Are you sure? They make a mean martini here in the weekends."

"Do you think I would need one? To prepare myself for what you have to say?"

A wave of sadness washed over Kevin's eyes. "Perhaps," he said, sitting down.

"Alright, then. I'll have a dry martini, please." Wanda nodded at the waiter.

"So, a dry martini for the lady, and for you sir?" The prim waiter turned to Kevin.

"Jack Daniel's neat, thank you."

The waiter jotted down the order and walked off, leaving behind an uncomfortable silence in his wake. After a minute, Wanda cleared her throat.

"So why here, Mr. Gao?"

"Oh please, call me Kevin," Kevin insisted.

"Alright. Kevin, tell me, must we meet like mafias?"

"I'm sorry you feel this way about … er … our venue, Madam Faraday." Kevin gestured with his hands to indicate their surroundings. "But you read my letter, didn't you? Irene insisted that we keep this absolutely hush hush."

"You mean, Mrs. Kostas?"

Kevin nodded. "She is after all, the sole heir and trustee, and her wishes must be honoured."

"I see that she isn't here—"

"She's still grieving," Kevin interjected a little too quickly. "I'm sure you understand how that is."

"Indeed. Indeed, I do," Wanda confirmed with genuine sincerity. "I presume you've brought it with you then—" Wanda checked herself abruptly, seeing the waiter approach with their drinks. She nodded as he set the glasses down and pivoted on his heels to walk away.

Kevin raised his glass to Wanda and took one long, delicious sip. "I have it all in an USB. I'll hand it to you in a minute."

"Another USB? What for? Isn't it just a password?"

"Mmhm. And the instructions to unlock the encrypted pen drive you received earlier."

Wanda leaned back with her drink and sighed. "I see. It's a shame Mrs. Kostas couldn't make it here tonight. I wanted to speak with her."

"I understand." Kevin searched Wanda's face. "Believe me, I do. It must be hard for you too. I heard you were close—you and Mr. Schmidt. Speaking with her would've helped you share your grief."

"No. It's not that." Wanda shook her head vehemently. "I need to know for certain before I grieve. And it is not yet time."

Kevin reached across the table and clasped Wanda's tiny hand in his. "Denial," he whispered, as a profound sadness flashed across his eyes. "It's the first stage."

"When did you say was the funeral?" Wanda asked, ignoring the commiseration.

Kevin looked taken aback. "I … I didn't say … uhm, Tuesday. It's next Tuesday. You will attend, I hope?"

"I will try my best."

"It'd make Irene incredibly happy if you did," Kevin asserted with a little too much enthusiasm.

Wanda gulped down the last of her martini and stood up. "I better get going." Then, extending her hand, "the USB please, Mr. Gao. If you don't mind, of course."

"Oh yes, certainly." Kevin fumbled nervously inside his pockets and retrieved a small white envelope with Wanda's name typed across it in capital letters. "It's all in here. You …" he lowered his voice, "you have a body guard, am I right?"

"Waiting outside." Wanda's eyes flicked to the exit. "Although, I can't imagine why I'd need one."

"Like I said earlier. What you have access to now could make you some powerful enemies."

"Then I better hope it also makes me some powerful friends." Wanda's lips curled into a sly grin as she turned to take her leave. She did not wait to find out how Kevin Gao reacted to her retort. Instead, she made a beeline for the exit where Amon had been waiting for her, tall and broad shouldered, like a bouncer right outside the entrance.

"Do you have it?" he asked, as soon as she emerged through the door.

"Yes."

"And where's the lawyer?" Amon rubbed his gloved hands together for warmth.

"He's still inside. I left as soon as I could. He's hiding something, and I did not want to stick around to find out what."

"Couldn't you read his thoughts?"

"I tried."

"And?"

Wanda glanced around and lowered her voice. "They are well shielded."

"How is that even—"

"Let's get out of here."

"Okay, I'll bring the car."

"No, I wouldn't advise that." Wanda hailed a cab. The cold dreary night had become suddenly overcast and flakes of snow began to dust the street in front of them. "We can talk at the hotel," she said as the cab pulled over to the curb.

* * *

Nirmala awoke to the sound of footsteps. She was lying on a comfortable mattress on the floor of a cavernous room, surrounded by columns of carved stone. There were no windows anywhere, but a soft blueish iridescence emanated from the walls. Groggily she rubbed her eyes.

"Oh hey, Alejandro? Where am I?" she asked the approaching man.

The intruder coughed before crouching to kneel beside her. "Umm … it's me, Chris. Alejandro isn't here. You're in a healing room. In Lumania."

"I see. How long have I been here?" She struggled to sit up straight and slumped back, groaning in pain.

"About a month. Don't you remember anything?"

"I remember being shot. After that, I can recall stuff in disjointed pieces, like some sort of a montage or dream sequence. Spells of waking. Spells of sleeping."

"You had a fever the whole time. It only went down last night."

"Oh!" Nirmala reflexively touched her forehead. It was cool and slick with sweat. She sighed. "I know … I know that you saved me. Back there. In Moscow. Thank you for that, Chris."

Chris blushed. "Please, no need to thank me. Besides, it was your locket. The locket Alejandro gave you. So, in the end, it was all Alejandro, really."

"Oh c'mon, you're too humble. If it wasn't for your quick thinking, I'd have been long dead. So, I owe you a life debt, whether or not you like it."

Chris chuckled. "Alright, if you put it that way." He reached into his pocket and pulled out a small box.

"Speaking of the life-saving locket. Here it is," he said, extending the box to Nirmala. "The Lumanians were curious about its power, so I had lent it to them. I hope you don't mind?"

"No, of course not. Did they tell you what they found out?"

Chris shook his head. "Not really. But then again, I didn't exactly ask."

"Why not? Aren't you curious?"

"I am. But it's obviously an object of Heka and that's mostly Wanda's expertise. So, I'd rather wait for her to examine it, before starting my own investigation."

"Makes sense. So, maybe I should ask Wanda about it. Where is she, by the way?"

"She left for an important mission in New York."

"Oh! And the others? Zoya? Alejandro?"

"They all left a couple of days ago. It's just you and me here. And the Lumanians, of course. I stayed back to escort you, once you're healed."

"Escort me? Escort me where?" Nirmala shot up to a sitting position and immediately regretted her decision, as her shoulder threatened to explode. "Oww, oww, oww!"

Chris' face sank. "Easy there." He leaned over to give her a hand before sinking down to the floor beside her.

"So?" Nirmala asked, looking him straight in the eyes.

"I ... we're going back to ... your home. You know, in India?"

"What! Why?"

Chris shrugged. "I wish I knew, but I don't. It was Alejandro's decision. With Wolfgang missing, he's in charge now and—"

"Wait, back up. Dr. Müller is *missing*?"

Chris nodded and leaned back against the wall.

"How did that happen?"

"It's a long story."

"Tell me."

"Okay, but not on an empty stomach. You're still weak and need your energy." Chris flicked his wrist and checked his watch. "It's almost time for dinner. Why don't we head to the dinner hall, and I'll fill you in while we eat?" He stood up and held out his hand to her.

"Alright," Nirmala said. She grabbed his hand and stood up.

* * *

Zoya tiptoed into the library in Wanda Faraday's California home, and flicked on her torch. In an alcove towards her right, a man was at a desk, hunched over some documents under a lamp. She walked up to it, pulled out the chair across from him and sat down.

"There you are, Uncle Alejandro." She grinned, addressing him by the pet name she used as an inside joke.

Alejandro jumped from his seat. He looked gaunt and disheveled, his grey-streaked black hair messy and longer than usual. "Whoa, you almost gave me a heart attack! What are you doing up so late?"

"I could ask you the same thing."

"We need to find answers. You know that as well as me."

"True. But if you burn yourself out, then how would it benefit anyone?"

"I'm fine. Go catch some sleep." Alejandro replied, without looking up from his books.

"No, you're not fine! You haven't slept in days. You have dark circles under your eyes. You don't eat. You don't crack jokes. You're a different man, Alejandro. And I hate to see you like this." Zoya slammed her palm on the desk for emphasis.

"Jeez. You're sounding like my mom." Alejandro chuckled, despite himself.

"I know what this is about."

Alejandro cocked an eyebrow. "*Do* you, now?"

"You shouldn't have banished her. It's killing you. I can see that it's killing you."

"I don't know what you're talking about."

"Sure you don't." Zoya pulled out a crumpled piece of paper from her pocket and straightened it out on the table. "Then explain this!"

Alejandro squinted at the note, scrawled in his neat, rounded handwriting. "Dear Nirmala, I'm so sorry I had to do this. I know you will never forgive me but ..." It didn't continue. Alejandro cleared his throat. "Well, it's Lumania. They don't have e-mail there, remember?"

Zoya looked positively furious. "That's not what I meant!" She all but screamed. "Don't deflect the question."

"What exactly do you want me to say?"

"That you'll bring her back."

"You know I can't do that. It's not safe. She nearly *died*, for heaven's sake!"

"But we *need* her. *You* need her, more than anyone else," Zoya implored.

"Now you're just being selfish. We can't just ask her to risk her life again and again for a cause that she has nothing to do with whatsoever. It's bad enough that we've dragged her in this deep. If we continue, we are no better than the adversaries we seek to defeat."

"But it's not your *call*. It's her decision. It was always

her decision. And she *chose* to be with us."

"Only after I got her into a mess in the first place—"

"No! You have to stop doing this! Stop blaming yourself for everything that happened. She's had plenty of time to think, since your first run in with the Aifra, and during that time she has never backed out. Never decided to leave us. Besides, what about the Novo-Hekameses? Who's going to train them in her absence?"

"We don't have the resources to continue that program anymore. Not with all the trouble we're in right now."

"Really? Dr. Müller is going to be sooo unhappy!"

Alejandro's head jerked up and he slammed his fist on the desk. "Doctor Müller ... is *dead,*" he said, slowly and deliberately, enunciating every word.

"Oh c'mon, Alejandro! Surely you don't believe that?"

"It doesn't matter what I believe, Zoya. That is what we've been told. Why do you think Wanda went to New York?"

"I know why she went, but even she hasn't stopped looking. She hasn't given up. I mean, it's Dr. Müller, for crying out loud. He's invincible!" Zoya tried to laugh, but only managed a strangled coughing sound instead.

Alejandro's eyes welled up, as he looked straight into hers. "I'm sorry, Zoya," he said softly. "This must be really hard for you. It's hard for all of us. We're not going to give up trying to find him. I mean, what do you think I've been doing here every single night? But in the end, we must be prepared to accept the truth. Whatever it might be. We've tried everything on our end, but there's still no trace of him."

"There it is again, your fatalism. Being flotsam or whatever. Letting life carry you wherever it does. Not wanting to take control, because you're afraid of steering it in the wrong direction. Even when I first heard you tell me this theory, I didn't agree. And now more than ever, I don't. Sometimes, you *do* have to take control. You *do* have to be in the driver's seat. Otherwise, life will just slip away. Anyway, no point arguing with you, until you're willing to see reason. I'm going to bed, and I think you should too. Goodnight," she said, before turning to storm away.

CHAPTER TWO

Peter studied his reflection in the frozen lake, without recognizing the face that stared back. His hair had grown to shoulder length and was in dreadlocks. His beard looked like it had been carefully crafted by a nesting weaver bird. He could not remember the last time he had bathed or clipped his nails. In fact, he could not remember much at all from the recent past. There were gaps in his memory with chunks of it missing, like rotting teeth having been pulled out. He remembered a home in England with a father he once loved. He remembered a mother who had died when he was little. He distinctly remembered going to University in America. But after that, it was all messy. Like a foreign film he had watched but not quite understood.

There was a tug on his fishing pole, and he snapped out of his reverie, his eyes flicking immediately to the hole he had cut in the ice. The wilderness had taught him many things, including ice-fishing and hunting. But this winter had been harsh. He had barely caught anything in the last few weeks. Today, he seemed to have run into a bit of luck, because the tug was stronger than he had expected. He stood up and reeled in a wriggling Omul, weighing at least a kilo, if not more. Removing the fish from the hook, he tossed it in the sack, he always carried around while hunting and foraging. There, it wedged itself in between some tired looking vegetables—mostly wild potatoes and pine cones. Then, he slung the sack over his shoulder and made his way back to his cave.

He remembered the last few months quite clearly. It was what happened before, that was the problem. He had woken up one fine morning in the middle of the Siberian wilderness with nothing but the shirt on his back. Well, maybe not nothing. Somehow, magically, he seemed to still have his wallet. The cash in it was untouched, but all his identity documents were missing. Did someone want him to forget who he was? Who would want that and why? He had spent the first couple of months trying to figure this out, but to no avail. He had built himself a makeshift hut in a wooded area, not far from Irkutsk. But it did not feel right. Something about his very existence seemed off. Like he had been plucked out of a tree and replanted in an alien land.

Then came the mysterious packages left outside his shack. The first morning after he had scrambled together the roof over his head, there was a bag of groceries hanging from his door. Nothing fancy. Just some rice, lentils, potatoes, a few carrots, a couple of sachets of unfamiliar spices. He had searched frantically for the person who might have forgotten it there, but the entire grove had been deserted. Apart from some tiny furry creatures, of course. He had let the matter drop and enjoyed a few guilt free meals in the following days. But then, it happened again the following week.

This time, it was left in a different place, yet too close to his hut to have been an accident. More groceries and something else. Blankets. Hand woven, it seemed. Also, a soft fluffy cushion. Again, the owner was nowhere in sight. This had been enough to freak Peter out. He had packed up and left his hut. After a bit of deliberation, he did however, take the free supplies with him. He had also stopped by in town and bought himself some more stuff. Things that would be useful on a long trek through the forest. He had walked for miles into uncharted, unforgiving lands, determined to move as far away as possible from his anonymous benefactor. And finally, he had arrived where he was now, settled inside a snug cave in the foothills of the Primorsky Range.

A rustling sound nearby, broke his train of thoughts. There were wolves in these mountains, although he had been lucky enough not to have encountered any thus far. He backed up and instinctively palmed the hunting knife dangling from his belt. The sound was making its way towards him with a scuffling, halting cadence. He removed the knife from his belt and aimed it in the direction of the disturbance, but a nagging dilemma stayed his hand. It was never wise to injure a predatory animal without any intention of killing it. He stuck his knife back inside his belt and moved tentatively forward. What he did next, surprised him entirely.

"Who's there?" he hollered into the bushes, as if a wild animal could actually understand him. His voice sounded hoarse and unfamiliar even to his own ears.

A whimpering sound floated up from the undergrowth to his right, followed by a flurry of hurried movement. The sound was what startled Peter. It was too human to be real in these parts of the world. He reached inside his fishing bag and pulled out a spare sack. Then, he set his supplies down next to a tree and scanned the forest around him, before charging into the bushes, sack in hand. In the dreamy mid-morning light that drifted in through the gaps in the foliage, he saw a distinct humanoid figure scurrying away through the shrubbery.

"Stop, don't move! Who are you?" he yelled, hurrying to catch up. The stranger did not slow down or turn to look back. Peter hurtled past branches and messy bramble, closing the gap between them with every step. There was a snapping of branches, as the stranger tripped and toppled over. In a swift military motion, the crouched figure drew out a gun and pointed it at Peter.

Peter did not stop to think. His body worked outside of his own volition like an antiquated wind-up-toy. Lunging forward, he smacked the gun out of his assailant's hand and shoved the bag over the latter's head. The figure struggled and squirmed against his grip, as he lifted up the bag and tossed it over his shoulder with surprising ease. Then, bending down, he picked up the abandoned gun and pocketed it.

When he returned to the copse where he had first heard the sounds of scuffling, his haul of the day was still lying against a tree. He dragged it along the forest floor behind him, as he made his way back to his cave with the bagged human slung over his back.

The person inside the bag thrashed and wriggled half the way back to the cave. The remainder of the time, they fell silent. Either having tired from all that thrashing or resigned their fate. Peter had no idea why he had decided to take a captive back to his hideout. At first, when he had thought this to be a furry mammal of some sort, he had brought along a bag in the hope of scoring some fresh game. But, as it had turned out, he had chanced upon something much rarer and far more coveted given his current circumstances. He had run into an actual human being.

Peter could not remember the last time he had heard a human voice barring his own. In these long, dreary months of winter, he had lain curled up in the corner of his cave, listening to the sound of his own breathing and counting the fireflies that clung to the ceiling. It was perhaps this months-long desolation that had driven him to his decision this morning. The urge for human companionship had been too powerful to resist. So, he had acted on impulse, following through on a fiercely primal instinct.

He squinted as he entered his cave, letting his eyes adjust to the change in lighting. Against the wall, was the straw mattress he had made for himself when he had first moved in here. He dropped his prisoner on it and turned to the door. There was a large boulder next to the cave opening that he used to block the entrance when he was inside. He got busy pushing it in place to secure his home. Behind him, he heard rustling noises.

"Don't try to run. You won't get very far. Besides, I don't plan to hurt you," he said into the darkness. The scuffling sounds stopped, but Peter did not turn to check behind him. He knew he had great reflexes in battle. He had no idea how, but he did. So, any attack by his unarmed captive would be futile. He knew that, and it reassured him. Once he had moved the boulder in place, leaving only enough opening on the top to let light and fresh air come through, he bent to the side and picked up his lantern. Slowly, he lit it. Then, placing it on the top of the boulder, he turned around to face his quarry.

To Peter's surprise, the prisoner sitting on his bed was a slight young woman with large, dark-brown eyes and messy curls that stuck in patches to her sweaty forehead. What was more surprising was that she was dressed in what appeared to be fighting gear—bottle green tights and a camouflage T-shirt complete with a bullet-proof vest. She had managed to remove the bag from over her head and sat staring at him in wide-eyed astonishment. Her lips quivered, struggling to utter words that seemed to evade her. He took a tentative step towards her. She backed away instinctively.

"No. Please don't. Don't send me back," she muttered, her eyes beseeching.

"Send you back? What do you mean?"

"I ... Peter ... I mean General Cobb, I'm sorry sir. I really am. But if you take me back, they'll *kill* me," she shrieked, while continuing to back up on her hands and knees.

"Wait, General Cobb? How did you—"

"You are ... General Peter Cobb, aren't you, sir?"

"Well, I ... I'm Peter Cobb, yes. But ..." Peter stared blankly into the distance, trying to catch at a wisp of memory that kept slipping away.

"Don't you remember me?"

"Should I?" Peter turned to face her. "What's your name?"

"Urm ... it's ... Julie. I'm Julie, sir." There was hesitation in her voice.

"You don't look like a Julie," Peter challenged.

A wave of horror washed over her face. But she collected herself quickly and sat up. "I don't know what to say to that, sir," she replied, as calmly as possible.

"Just kidding," Peter said, smiling for the first time in

months. "By the way, just call me Peter, alright?"

"Whatever you say, sir … er … I mean Peter."

Peter cupped his chin and studied her intently. Something told him she was intimidated by him, had always been intimidated by him. He figured it had something to do with his past. A past that he barely remembered anymore. "So, Julie, what may I ask, were you running from?"

"Didn't I tell you? I've been selected. So, I had to run."

"Selected for what?"

"For the blood sacrifice, of course!" Julie's eyes widened with shock and beneath that, a vague sense of understanding. "You're not lying then," she whispered after a pause, "You really don't remember anything at all!"

CHAPTER THREE

Zoya stood in the doorway of Wanda Faraday's kitchen, watching Alejandro munch on his breakfast. He seemed to be in a faraway place with only his body staying behind. He didn't hear her entering the room, and only looked up when she coughed to draw his attention.

"Hey, Zoya. Good morning," he said absentmindedly. "Sleep well?"

"Morning. Yeah, I got some sleep, but is there any point asking about you?"

Alejandro merely chuckled, while continuing to munch on his toast.

"Anyway …" She pulled up a chair and sat down. "I wanted to tell you that my dad will be here in five minutes."

Alejandro's head jerked up. "And?"

"Well, I called him last night. And asked him to pick me up. Since Wanda's away and you don't really seem to need me." She shrugged.

"I never said I didn't need you. But if you want to see

18

your folks, I'm definitely not going to stop you."

"I figured as much," Zoya mumbled, her face drooping. The doorbell rang. "He's here. Call me if you need me back."

Alejandro flashed her a weak smile. "I will. Go have fun."

"Thanks." Zoya nodded, before running out the door.

She had already packed last night. Her small travel bag now stood next to the front door, where Dr. Carter was waiting to pick her up. She grabbed it and walked out into the brisk spring morning.

"Darling. Come give me a hug." Dr. Carter grinned, walking up to her.

Zoya scurried down the couple of steps to where her dad was waiting and threw herself into his arms. "It's so good to see you," she choked out, as Dr. Carter lovingly petted her head. Then, he picked up her bag and walked them to his rental car.

The flight back home was fairly uneventful. Zoya made up amusing stories about her college activities to regale her father, and he in turn, filled her in, on every annoying little thing her mom had done in her absence.

"Dad, you gotta stop complaining about mom, you know," Zoya blurted, suddenly finding the courage she had never found before.

"Complaining? Who's complaining? I'm just sayin' that she can be nagging as hell sometimes. Drives me nuts, that woman!"

Zoya rolled her eyes. "But where would you be without her?"

"Of course! She's the light of my life. You know that as well as me. But when did *you* get to be so wise?"

"I'm growing up dad. Everyone does." Zoya grinned

mischievously, knowing that she could never tell him what she had been through, since that day he and her mom had dropped her off at Stanford, for the very first time.

It was afternoon by the time they got home. Mrs. Carter had set the table for a welcome home lunch. Zoya rushed to her bathroom to wash up and slip into a comfy tee and track pants.

"I made your favourite chicken casserole," mamma Carter said at lunch. "And for later, I baked some pies."

"Ooh, pies!" Zoya's eyes lit up. She greedily ladled some chicken and veggies onto her plate and pounced on it like a wolf.

"Whoa there, slow down kiddo." Dr. Carter chuckled. "You're gonna choke if you eat so fast."

Mrs. Carter narrowed her eyes. "You haven't been eating well, have you? What's wrong, sweetheart?"

"Mghh?" Zoya blurted through a full mouth. She swallowed quickly and washed it down with some water. "Don't be silly, mom. I've been eating fine. Your cooking is just sooo good. I missed it, is all." She reached over to grab a bread roll.

"Unh unh, I can tell it's more than that. I'm a mother after all. You look paler than usual and … and …" Mrs. Carter drew back her chair and scanned her daughter up and down. "You look leaner. Not thin, but you know what I mean. Just more wiry and tough. Like you've been on a survival show on TV or something."

This comment cracked Zoya up. She grabbed her tummy and guffawed. "You're crazy, mom. I've been working out more nowadays. Besides, my karate lessons are getting more intense, now that I am preparing for my dan—"

"Be careful not to overdo it, honey. I didn't name you

20

Zoya for nothing, you know."

Zoya's expression tightened. "About that. I've been meaning to ask you, actually. Someone brought it up … I can't remember who … that my name means something in Ukrainian. Is that true mom? Did you guys give me a Ukrainian name?"

"Yes, of course. It means *life* in Ukrainian. It was my idea to name you that."

"But why?" Zoya's eyes widened with confusion.

Mrs. Carter exchanged a meaningful look with her husband and fell silent.

"What is it mom? Tell me!" Zoya urged.

Dr. Carter cleared his throat. "We should tell her, Celina. It's time," he simply said.

"Alright. I guess you have a right to know." Celina Carter sighed. She paused for a breath before continuing. "You were born in Mongolia, as you probably already know." She looked at Zoya for confirmation.

"Yeah, when dad was a doctor there."

"Exactly. Anyway. The delivery … was complicated."

"Complicated, how?"

"We were told … we were told …" Celina's voice choked up. She grabbed the napkin from her lap and dabbed at the corners of her eyes.

"We were told that you wouldn't make it," Zoya's father completed. "Even with a C-section. The umbilical cord had wrapped itself around your throat, and you weren't getting any oxygen."

"Okay. And then what happened?"

"They anticipated that trying to save you might kill your mother. But your mother insisted that we try anyway. She was sure you could be saved. She felt it in her bones."

Celina nodded wearily.

"So, we went ahead with the surgery. It took several hours. And in the end—" Dr. Carter was interrupted as his wife bent over broke down in tears. He looked at her with tired eyes, while Zoya gripped her in a hug.

"Hush mom. Hush. Don't cry. Everything's okay now. I made it, right? I made it!"

Her mother continued to whimper. Zoya looked at her father for support. "Dad?"

Dr. Carter shook his head stoically. "No. No, you didn't," he whispered.

* * *

Wanda Faraday was sitting at the small desk inside her hotel room, re-reading a letter for what felt like the hundredth time, when the knock came. She straightened her glasses and looked up.

"Come in." She had given Amon a spare key to her room, just in case. Amon swiped that key and entered, standing tall in the doorway. "Did ... did you unlock it?" she asked.

"No." Amon clicked the door shut and moved towards Wanda's desk. "They gave us a fake password."

"Sit," Wanda said, waving to an armchair next to the window.

"You don't look surprised. You expected this, didn't you?"

Wanda nodded sadly. "That lawyer. There was something wrong with him. I am beginning to worry about Irene Costas. We need to find her. To make sure she's safe."

"I am sure we can trace her. I can ask Alejandro for help." Amon's gaze flitted to the piece of paper she was holding in her hand. "What are you reading?" he asked.

Wanda extended the letter to Amon. "This was the last letter Wolfgang sent me. He had enclosed the pen-drive with it."

"Where was it from?" Amon asked, grabbing the letter.

"I don't know. It was sent via a military courier."

"Interesting." Amon fell silent. He scanned the letter. "That's it? Cryptic as usual."

"Not really. He did call me, before sending the package. He said the pen-drive contained a message from some US army captain, a certain Alexander Costas, and that I was to receive a password to unlock it, in the event of both their deaths. Upon unlocking the information, I was to make it public as per the last will and testament of Mr. Costas."

Amon eyed the message again. "It's a poem."

"Read it to me," Wanda whispered.

"Okay." Amon cleared his throat. "Be wary of the monster. That hides within the light. We look towards the hawk's head. Missing the eagle in mid-flight. In the letter to a father. Of a vanished son they speak. Hidden in this missive. Is the answer that you seek."

"You are good with riddles, my friend. What do you make of it?"

"I ... who else have you shown it to?"

"No one yet. Just you."

"I think we should show it to Dr. Cobb. The reference to the disappeared son ... I have a feeling it has to mean—
"

"Peter. His lost son. I don't mind showing it to Albert. What about you, though? Are you back to trusting him again?" Wanda smiled her typical motherly smile.

Amon shrugged. "What choice do we have with Wolfgang missing? Besides, he did stand with us in

Moscow."

"Let's show it to him then. I plan on leaving for London tomorrow."

"Oh, aren't we staying for the funeral?"

Wanda shook her head. "It will likely be a trap."

"Fair enough. I'll book us tickets." Amon turned to leave and hesitated. "Do you believe it?" he asked, looking over his shoulder. "You know, that he's really dead?"

"It's highly unlikely. Knowing what I know of him. And I think that's exactly why he sent us this message. So that we don't mistake him for dead and send out a search party instead. I believe the poem holds the key to where we should go looking for him."

"Then we need to bring it to Dr. Cobb immediately."

"Exactly."

"I'll book us on a morning flight to London. Get some sleep. Goodnight." Amon smiled and left the room.

* * *

Zoya tossed and turned in bed all night. What her parents had told her that afternoon kept ringing in her ears like the pit of an echo chamber. Try as she might, she could not switch them off. She remembered the recurring dream that had plagued her of late. The one where her mother always cried inside a shrine with an infant huddled in her arms.

At last, she knew what that dream meant. She was the baby—a stillborn. The shrine belonged to the Frozen Saint. *The Frozen Saint of Baikal.* It appeared, that this had not been a dream at all, but a scrap of memory. A lingering piece of information that had floated around in her subconscious all these years, only to resurface in the form a dream.

Her parents had taken the newborn Zoya to the temple of the Frozen Saint and begged for her life. They had found the shrine deserted. Her mother had collapsed with grief. And then, just as they were about to leave with her lifeless body, Zoya had stirred. Her revival had been a miracle. *She* had been the miracle. The miracle of life— Zoya. They had named her thus, to honour her father's Ukrainian colleague, who had sent them to the Frozen Saint.

Zoya did not know what to do with this brand-new information. Whether to be happy or sad. Was her life really a gift, or a curse in disguise? Was it ever a blessing to have been brought back from the dead? Was it natural? Was it healthy? She remembered what Solaris, the Lumanian elder had said about the Frozen Saint.

"An ancient twisted soul, that one," Solaris had said. Zoya shuddered. For all intents and purposes, she was inclined to believe him. Anyone who claimed to be a necromancer could never be trusted. But her parents had trusted. They had been desperate, and in their desperation, they might have done something unthinkable. Zoya had to find a way to reverse the damage. Otherwise, deep inside her soul, she knew that a life would be owed to someone, somewhere. A life in exchange for a life. For all things must find balance.

She fumbled out of her bedclothes and turned on her night lamp. Her luggage was lying in a heap next to her dresser. Jumping over to it, she rummaged through her stuff. Several minutes later, after having upturned all its contents onto to her bedroom carpet, she finally found what she had been looking for—a crumpled piece of paper with Yuri's phone number scrawled across a corner. She checked the time in Irkutsk. Then, she picked up her phone and dialled.

CHAPTER FOUR

"Are you sure you don't want me to go with you all the way?" Chris asked Nirmala, as they disembarked the Lumanian underground train.

"No, I'll be fine. The Lumanians are sending me an escort."

"Did they tell you they'll meet us here?"

"At the station, yes. We are in Cobalt, an eastern township. It's their transit hub for Asia-Pacific. Delhi isn't far from here." Nirmala searched the platform for signs of her escort.

Chris turned to face her. "I … I hope …"

"You hope what, Chris?" Nirmala smiled, not without affection.

"I hope you're not mad at me." He paused. "For all this." He gestured with his hands.

"Don't be silly. I know it wasn't your idea. I know how stubborn he can be."

"Fair enough. So, you're mad at Alejandro then?" Chris's eyes were quizzical.

Nirmala did not respond. Instead, she continued to scan the crowd for her guide, as if Chris had not spoken at all.

Chris coughed to attract her attention. "C'mon! You are, aren't you?"

Nirmala pivoted around to face Chris. Then scrunching her brows, she said, "Not *mad*, per say. Annoyed, yes. Frustrated, upset, a little let down too, maybe. I mean …" her voice was rising, "he didn't even say goodbye … The gall—"

Chris clasped both his hands over her shoulders. "There there. I thought you said you weren't mad?" He chuckled compassionately.

"I think my guide is here," Nirmala deflected, pointing to a bald-headed woman in a flowing, navy blue robe and silver belt, pushing through the crowd towards them.

"Alejandro means well, you know." Chris looked wistfully into the distance as he said this.

"Good for him," Nirmala responded curtly. "What about you? Will you write to me sometime?"

"Of course! I'll come see you too, if you'll allow it."

Nirmala nodded. "I better get going."

"Good morning. I am here to escort a Miss Nirmala," the robed lady said with a bow.

"That would be me," Nirmala said, turning to smile at Chris. "Goodbye then. Please let Wanda and the others know that I am on my way home."

"I will. Safe journey, and call me when you get there."

* * *

Peter watched Julie sip the root vegetable soup he had made and felt a sense of warmth creep through his skin. It was still bitterly cold outside. So, there was no logical explanation for this feeling. Julie set the empty bowl down by the bed, and wiped her lips on her sleeve. The sun had set outside, and a storm was howling in the wilderness. A biting draft of wind occasionally made its way into their cave, dragging in a smattering of snow with it.

"That was really good. Thanks," she mumbled.

"How long haven't you eaten?" Peter noticed that she was shivering slightly under the blanket he had given her.

"Three days, I think. I've lost track of time."

"I can understand that feeling."

Julie leaned forward. "So, you really don't remember anything?"

"I remember some things clearly. The rest is choppy," Peter admitted.

"What are the things you remember well?"

"Stuff from my childhood and early youth mostly. A huge chunk of years in between seems all muddy. But after that, my memory's intact again."

"Since when did they start becoming intact?"

"From the day I woke up in the middle of Siberia several months ago, with only the clothes on my back."

"Interesting. You think you were attacked? Kidnapped perhaps?"

Peter shrugged. "Seems likely. But why would anyone do such a thing?"

Julie leaned forward and drew a shape into the cave floor with the tip of her index finger. "Do you remember this?"

Peter reached for his lantern. Bringing the light closer to the shape, he squinted to get a better look. "It's … an eye?"

Julie was staring at him anxiously. She nodded. "Do you remember it?"

"It looks familiar. Like I've seen it in a dream," Peter muttered.

"Or a nightmare," Julie whispered.

"Perhaps. What is it?"

"The eye of Ra," Julie stuttered. "Ring a bell?"

"Nope." Peter's expression was blank.

"It's the emblem of a deadly terrorist organization—the Aifra."

"Is that who you were running from?"

"Yeah. And you should too, if you know what's good for you."

"Me? Why?" Peter looked baffled.

"Because ... you were one of them. So was I. And they don't take kindly to deserters."

* * *

Nirmala had followed her silent guide through several dark tunnels and up and down numerous stone steps, before she started wondering about their destination. When she had first arrived in Lumania via an underground tunnel in the outskirts of Delhi, a train had brought her straight to Cobalt. But now, instead of boarding another train to trace their way back, they were getting sucked into the labyrinthine alleyways of the township itself.

"Where are we going?" she finally asked, turning to her guide.

"To the Chamber of Prophecies," was her companion's curt response.

"Wait! Where?" Nirmala froze in her tracks.

"To The Chamber of Prophecies," the guide repeated in a matter-of-fact way. "Actually, we are already here. Look." She pointed at a set of huge brass doors embedded into a tall stone wall in front of them.

As they approached, the doors opened automatically, but at a glacial pace, like they do in movies for dramatic effect. Nirmala imagined that her escort was doing this with her mind. The Lumanians were powerful telepaths, she had learned. Once the doors had opened completely, the Lumanian stood aside.

"I will wait for you here," she said, with a little nod of her head.

Interpreting this as her cue to go inside, Nirmala proceeded with tentative steps, glancing from side to side, like she was crossing a busy street.

"It's alright," her guide comforted. "Mercuriva is expecting you."

"Who?" Nirmala turned to say, but the door had already begun to shut behind her.

The room was much smaller than Nirmala had expected, given the size of its doors. It was dome shaped with glowing crystals of various colours encircling it along the walls. At the centre, was an elevated seat, upon which a smiling elderly lady sat cross-legged. She bowed in greeting and looked up with a smile. "Welcome Nirmala. I am Mercuriva, the Elder."

Nirmala returned the bow and opened her mouth to speak, but before she could utter a single word, Mercuriva began again. "I'm sure, you are wondering why you have been brought here, instead of having been returned to your home."

"I have indeed been wondering that."

"Do not fear, I am not about to harm you in any way. We are Lumanians. Pacifism is our mantra. We do not harm anyone. Not even our enemies."

"Yes, I have heard that about your kind, Ma'am."

"Very well then. Please, do not remain standing. You will tire yourself." Mercuriva said, waving at some cushions that were set out in front of her seat. Nirmala walked over to one of them and sat down. "I have requested your presence here today," Mercuriva began, once Nirmala was seated, "merely to ask a question."

"Ask away, Your Highness."

"Oh, Dear One, no one is called by such a title in our kingdom. You may simply call me, Elder Mercuriva or Wise One, if you so prefer."

"As you wish, Wise One. Please tell me what is your question."

Mercuriva smiled radiantly. "I wanted to ask you, if you would like to stay with us, here in Lumania."

"Oh! For how long?"

"For as long as you wish. You would be one of our citizenries. You will be free to come and go as you wish. Only if you so prefer, of course."

"Wow … okay. That … that is very kind of you Ma'am … I mean Wise One. But why are you offering me this?"

"Because, you are loath to return to your erstwhile home. I can sense it. I have always sensed it. You are being sent away against your will. You seek something greater. You wish to belong. But that is being denied to you. Am I not correct?"

"Bang on! Umm … I mean, yes. Yes, you are." Nirmala blushed.

Mercuriva chuckled. "You are a pure soul. Brave and kind-hearted. You have powers that you have not even come to comprehend. You will do well in Lumania. We seek out people like yourself. That is why, when I heard that you were passing through Cobalt, my hometown, I sought you out."

"I … am honoured."

"You will stay, then? You do not have to decide right away—"

"Are you kidding? I'll stay! Of course, I'll stay." Nirmala blurted out and immediately regretted her impudence.

But the Elder did not seem to mind. Instead, she started laughing coyly like a child. "I am pleased to hear this. We are building a new colony with newcomers like yourself. Someone will take you there in the morning. Unless of course, you want to depart at once."

"I don't mind going in the morning. If that is okay with you."

"You can do as you please, Nirmala. In Lumania, you answer to none but your own freewill. Once you settle down, you will learn all of this—our customs, our values, our prophecies. At that time, you can also decide for yourself, what services you would like to offer our society."

"That sounds great! So, where is this new colony you speak of?"

"It is quite far from here. So, I suggest you rest well tonight. The cartography of your world, places the region in the territory of northern Canada."

"Canada? Wow, that *is* quite far. Are there Lumanian tunnels leading up to it?"

"There had been. Many years ago. But in recent times, they had closed up. We have started re-opening them, as our population grows."

"Wonderful. I look forward to being a part of this."

"As I suspected you would. It is settled then, Dear One. Pala awaits you outside. She will show you to your quarters for tonight." Mercuriva bowed, indicating that the audience was at an end.

Nirmala took the hint and returned the greeting, before

turning to take her leave.

CHAPTER FIVE

It was dark inside the truck, but bright enough to discern the outlines of two captives sprawled across its grimy floor. Their legs were bound with sturdy ropes and arms handcuffed behind their backs. One of them was passed out, or sleeping. It was hard to tell which. The other was wide awake, sitting with his back to the wall, that separated the cab from the backend. It felt like months since they had been captured. Or maybe, it had been just weeks. Time had become of no consequence. From the cargo of one truck to another, they had been tossed around like cattle for the slaughter-house. In between, they had been locked inside stuffy, putrid storage rooms, night after bottomless night, to rot away till daybreak.

Today, for the first time, the bags had been removed from over their heads. Perhaps that meant they were close to their destination, wherever that was.

The truck lurched and braked, knocking the seated man over onto his side. Noticing that the truck had stopped and the cargo door was opening, he quickly shut his eyes, pretending to be unconscious. There was a clicking sound as his handcuffs came undone and slipped to the floor behind him. Slowly, he wriggled his body closer to the door. Someone boarded the wagon, a stout middle-aged man whose face was hidden in shadows. He began shuffling through some scattered luggage. The awake captive seized this opportunity to make his move. Folding his bound legs up to his chest, he released them at full force, kicking his captor to the floor.

"Heya—" the fallen man began, but his attacker was too quick. He used the wall behind him to propel himself forward and lunged at his prone victim with surprising alacrity. Then, he seized his head firmly between both hands and bore into his eyes with a piercing glare. As soon as the attacker made eye contact, his victim fell silent. A minute passed. Two minutes. The pair remained locked in a staring contest. But it was no ordinary staring contest. One of the parties seemed to have fallen into a trance, his eyes rolling into the back of his head.

Then, as suddenly as it had begun, the staring match ended. The fallen man scrambled to his hands and knees and looked around in confusion. Once realization dawned, a look of horror contorted his face.

"Dr. Müller, I'm so sorry," he said, shaking his head in disapproval. "Who tied you up like this?" His hands worked quickly to remove the fetters from Dr. Müller's legs.

"Your partner. Where is he?" Dr. Müller responded, rubbing his wrists where the handcuffs had chafed them.

"Partner? What partner?" The stout man looked around for his missing partner.

"You're right. You didn't have a partner. Must have been a miscreant who attacked me."

"Let's get out of here then. In case they come back." The stout man began to disembark.

"Wait! You forgot my companion. They tied him up as well." Dr. Müller pointed at the unconscious captive lying on the floor.

"Dang. I'll get him. You can go to the cab."

Dr. Müller nodded and got out of the truck. The bright light outside hit his eyes like a pyroclastic flow. He shut them instantaneously, clutching his temples in pain. When he opened his eyes again, two others were standing next to him—the stout man, whose name he had never learned, and the tall and athletic military general he had grown to love, Lieutenant Colonel Alexander Costas.

Alex looked like a deer in the headlights. He too was squinting from the burst of unrestrained daylight that had greeted them outside. A smile passed between them—a silent understanding to follow Dr. Müller's lead and play along.

In the clear morning sun, the stout man's attire became glaringly obvious. He was clad in an US Army uniform, complete with an assault rifle. He had a rounded, ruddy face, pockmarked with large acne patches and scars from battles uncounted. "We should move," he said hoarsely.

The duo followed silently to the cab. Before boarding the front of the truck, Dr. Müller made a quick scan of their surroundings. A rugged landscape surrounded them—arid and deserted. Dr. Müller had a fairly good idea where they were, based on what he had seen inside the stout man's memories. Alex however, looked aghast, like he had expected them to have woken up inside a five-star hotel.

In the distance, Dr. Müller could see the stout man's partner walking back from taking a leak behind the only clump of trees in the vicinity. Dr. Müller crossed his fingers and prayed to the God, he did not believe in, that they could get going before this other man caught up. His prayers were soon answered. The engine started and the truck lurched forward. He glanced towards his friend sitting patiently by his side. At some point he would have to fill him in, on what had happened. How he had gotten them free. But now, was not the time.

* * *

The drive to their destination proceeded in silence, much to Dr. Müller's relief. Through the windshield, they saw a dirt road winding through a barren terrain dotted with rubble on either side. There were collapsed structures all around them, like an ancient city, now in ruins. Yet, the city did not appear ancient at all. Seemingly modern buildings stood charred and crumbling on either side of the road for as far as the eye could see.

Their surroundings elicited no reaction from Wolfgang Müller. He had expected these lands to be like this—war-torn and devastated. Alex however, appeared to be slowly waking up to a knowledge of their whereabouts. His military instincts were strong enough to hone in, on what they were seeing around them, and draw the appropriate conclusions.

An hour or so into the drive, they finally saw a glimpse of their destination. An encampment in the distance that did not look too different from the military base, they had left behind in Ukraine. Alex flashed Wolfgang a sidelong glance in recognition. The truck rolled languidly along the bumpy, unpaved road, before pulling over at a checkpoint. The driver leaned his head out the window and spoke in

Arabic to the guard who immediately let them pass.

From the inside, this encampment looked markedly different from their Ukrainian military camp. There were no overground structures anywhere, nor were there any soldiers milling about. No rowdy occupants huddling together for their meals, singing merry jingles. It was eerily quiet. The scorching sun overhead seared a passage through the centre of the field, leading them to a bomb-shelter entrance.

"Come, the General is waiting," the stout man with no name said, as he got off the vehicle, slamming the door behind him. His companions followed in silence. For a fleeting second, Wolfgang's throat constricted. He wondered what would happen if the man they had abandoned in the middle of nowhere had made it back here before them. He shoved that thought aside and focussed on the task at hand.

They walked down several steps, descending deep into the belly of the earth. At the bottom, blocking their way, was a rounded metal door of reinforced steel, much like a vault opening. The stout man coded in some numbers at this door, before turning the giant wheel which unlocked it. Wolfgang had to duck to enter the passage beyond. They walked in a single file until they reached another, similar door. This one opened into a much wider hallway with a high ceiling. Underground rooms designed like military barracks lined the corridor. A muted chatter filled the air. But despite the obvious presence of people around them, an air of gloom seemed to hang heavily in the atmosphere together with a foul, musty odour.

As they moved forward, some heads poked out of nearby rooms to regard them with a touch of fearful awe. The onlookers quickly averted their eyes upon eye-contact and disappeared into the shadows. The trio turned a corner and arrived at an intersection. Their escort stopped to whisper something into a two-way radio. Then, he nodded towards the passage diagonally across from their current position.

It was a short corridor, at the end of which, was a single closed door. "Wait here," the stout man said, before disappearing behind it. A few seconds later, he re-emerged and pointed at Wolfgang. "General Sapieha is ready for you. Just you." He held the door open for Wolfgang.

Wolfgang cast a sidelong glance at Alex who nodded imperceptibly without betraying any trace of emotion. Then, Wolfgang strode through the open door and closed it behind him. Seated at the centre of the room, was a slightly hunched, wiry man, decorated with military insignia. He looked up, hearing Wolfgang come in.

Wolfgang took in the sight before him and his stomach dropped. There was something surreal about the figure scanning him with piercing, beady eyes. His lean face was all muscle and no fat, the skin stretched across it like Saran Wrap. His eye sockets looked like meteor craters, where a pair of eyeballs had crash-landed from outer space. He had white cottony hair that was sparse and combed backwards to cover the bald patches. Overall, he looked like one of those macabre Body Worlds' exhibits with artificial skin tacked onto it. In his long life, Wolfgang had never seen anyone like him. His gut told him something was terribly wrong with this picture.

Outwardly however, he showed no signs of his apprehension and proceeded with confident steps toward the General's desk. "Good morning, General Sapieha," he said deferentially.

The General did not return the greeting. "Sit," he said,

indicating the chair. Wolfgang pulled up a chair and sat down. "You are a friend of Weilhammer's?" the General asked, getting straight to the point.

"I am. I mean, I was." Wolfgang nodded.

"And you know about the people? The gifted ones?"

"Yes, I have heard—"

"YOU ARE LYING!" The General yelled, standing up suddenly and toppling his chair behind him.

"I ... *why* on earth would I do that? Knowing that my life is on the line." Wolfgang reasoned.

General Sapieha stood motionlessly with his face contorted and shooting daggers at his opponent. Wolfgang took this opportunity to make eye contact. He had minutes, perhaps even seconds to enter the General's mind. He seized the moment eagerly. The General's features began to relax. His eyes lost focus. He collapsed into his chair in a hypnotic state and unclenched his fists on his desk. After about two minutes, he snapped out of it and smiled a sinister smile.

"You will have to find them for us," he said decisively. "And your friend? What are his skills?"

"Why don't we ask him that right now?" Wolfgang volunteered, glancing at the door.

The General nodded and spoke into a two-way radio. "Bring the other one in."

Momentarily, the stout man opened the door and Alexander Costas appeared through it. He entered the room and hesitated. Seeing his confusion, Wolfgang stood up. "Come in Alex. I was just telling the General how we have been planning for years to join them. The Aifra. Isn't that right, General?"

General Sapieha nodded gruffly. "What are your skills?" he inquired without a prelude. "Can you lead a battalion? Fly a plane? What about guerrilla warfare?"

Alex swallowed anxiously. "I … uh, used to be a fighter pilot, before I got promoted, Sir. You can check my résumé—"

"There's no need. Wolfgang's told me all about you. What about equipment repairs? We have a need to repurpose old tanks and aircrafts."

Alex flashed his friend a questioning look. "Tell him, Alex. He will assign us according to our capabilities." Wolfgang smiled reassuringly.

Alex studied Wolfgang for a moment, before opening his mouth to respond. "Well, I've overseen repairs in the past. I could definitely add my inputs."

"Good. I will assign you to your company tomorrow," General Sapieha said, before turning to Wolfgang. "You, will stay in this camp. Right under my nose. We have work to do."

* * *

Dr. Cobb read the letter one more time, before setting it down on his desk.

"Be wary of the monster.

That hides within the light.

We look towards the hawk's head.

Missing the eagle in mid-flight.

In the letter to a father.

Of a vanished son they speak.

Hidden in this missive.

Is the answer that you seek." He plonked a paperweight on top of the sheet, and leaned back in his chair.

"So?" Wanda Faraday asked from above her glasses. She and Amon were inside Dr. Albert Cobb's messy office at Oxford University, huddled around his off-kilter desk.

"I have no doubt this is about Peter," Dr. Cobb began. "As for the rest of the riddle however, I cannot understand it at all."

"Oh!" Amon sighed. "What about about the part about the 'letter to a father'? Don't you think it means you?"

"Of course, it does," Albert grunted.

"We thought so too. So, do you have the letter? The one that speaks about your … Peter?" Amon asked.

"Nope."

"Interesting," Wanda observed. "This *is* Wolfgang's handwriting, isn't it, Albert?"

Albert leaned forward and squinted at the letter. "It very much is."

"Are you hiding something from us again?" Amon asked in a heated tone.

"Amon," Wanda interfered, before Albert could respond. "We must calm ourselves. Albert is not lying. I can tell that he isn't. Infighting isn't going to get us anywhere."

"Hmph," Albert huffed, looking flustered. "My boy is missing," he grumbled. "And you think I'd hide a letter about him, if I had it? Do you take me for a fool?"

Amon crossed his arms across his chest and looked away. "Sorry," he muttered.

"Perhaps we should ask Chris," Wanda suggested. "Has he returned?"

"No. Not yet," Dr. Cobb replied. "He went to drop Nirmala off."

"Drop Nirmala off where?" Wanda asked, appearing confused.

"Back at her home in Delhi. I don't know. Alejandro's idea." Dr. Cobb shrugged.

"And when will she be back?"

"I don't believe she will. Alejandro has disbanded the Novo-Hekameses."

"What on earth for?" Wanda Faraday huffed. "I must have a word with him about this!"

Dr. Cobb shifted uneasily in his chair. "Now Wanda, don't be rash. I think it's for the best. Having someone like her and others amongst our kind—"

"Nonsense! Your prejudice does us no favours at a dangerous time like this."

"Oye, I am NOT prejudiced, Madame Faraday. You know that as well as I!" Dr. Cobb hollered, leaning forward over his desk for emphasis.

"Very well then. I shall speak with Alejandro this afternoon. In the meantime, let's wait for Chris to get back." Wanda rose from her seat. Amon stood up beside her. And then, looking over her shoulder, Wanda added. "Do not blame yourself for what happened with Peter. Unlike you, he was not born with the powers of Heka. But, being raised by a Hekameses parent, is not what made him go astray. In fact, it has made him wiser than he thinks he is. I am sure of it."

CHAPTER SIX

Zoya stepped onto the platform at the Irkutsk Railway Station and nervously searched the crowd. The mischievous redhead she was looking for, was nowhere to be seen. Zoya checked her phone—no missed calls. It was approaching midday. The breakneck rush-hour traffic had eased, and a lazy lull descended upon the station. Zoya yawned, feeling sleepy from her journey.

A tap on her shoulder made her jump. "Hello there, mademoiselle," a boisterous voice said from behind her.

Zoya spun around and nearly bumped into Yuri's lean, smiling figure. "Oh, it's you! You scared me there for a minute."

"Scared or startled?" Yuri teased. He looked taller than Zoya remembered. Careless stubs grew across his chin giving him a rugged, manly look. He was wearing a white polo shirt that accented his tattooed biceps, together with a pair of blue, weather-worn jeans. A hefty backpack was slung across his shoulders. Zoya realized that she had lost herself in appraising him, when he snapped his fingers in front of her face, as if to wake her from a trance. "Hey, where are you?"

"Oh! I … umm just jet-lagged. What were you saying?"

"Never mind. Shall we go? My horse is waiting outside."

"Yeah sure. Wait … *what* did you just say?"

Yuri guffawed. "I was just trying to see if you were paying attention."

"Thank God! I really thought we were going on horseback."

"Well, we might have to. Once we're closer to the site. But for now, we're just taking the bus. Are you hungry?"

"Starving."

"Good. Me too. Let's go grab something to eat first." He pointed towards the exit and started walking briskly in that direction. Zoya hurried to catch up. "I still can't believe you made me send you that fake letter, inviting you here for a project. You know how much trouble I'll be in, if my university finds out that I used their letter-head?" He chuckled.

"You have no idea how thankful—"

"You don't have to thank me. I was just pulling your leg. I understand how important this must be for you. I'd do the same, if I were in your place, to be honest," Yuri interrupted.

"But I *do* want to thank you." Zoya looked up at him and smiled.

"Oh, alright then! If you insist." Yuri threw his hands up in mock frustration. "How 'bout you buy me lunch?"

"Ha! That's a very small thing to ask in exchange for a very big favour." Zoya chuckled.

"Don't worry, this is just the beginning." Yuri winked.

* * *

A week had passed since they had joined the Aifra, and until now Wolfgang had only seen Alex once—during dinner on their first night at camp. That day, they had been seated on inverted ammunition crates at opposite ends of the courtyard, with scores of other soldiers between them. So, for obvious reasons, they had not spoken to each other at all. Alex had been shipped away to Aleppo early the next morning, to work on some damaged Russian fighter jets. Wolfgang had remained in the outskirts of Hama, working on General Sapieha's special project.

Today, Alex was back in Hama. Having flown in with two soldiers on a craft he had helped repair. The lunch bell rang exactly at noon, summoning the zombified denizens of basecamp, to assemble in the courtyard. Wolfgang kept his head down in the queue that led them outside, but his eyes were roving wildly. Someone shoved past him to the front of the line, almost knocking his tray out of his hand.

"Hey—" he started to say when he noticed the grinning face that stared back at him. Alex walked past him all the way to the head of the queue and bent to ask the server a question. Taking the hint, Wolfgang walked up to his side.

"No, you can't smoke around the lunch area," the server was saying to Alex, when Wolfgang arrived.

"What about at the back then?" Alex argued.

The server shook her head from side to side with great disdain. "If you must," she finally said, her voice laced with bitterness, "then go up to that hillock over there. That's the only place where you're allowed to smoke in the camp."

"Thank you so much, my dear. God bless ya." Alex's voice was dripping honey. "Can my friend join for a bit?" He tilted his head in Wolfgang's direction.

The server, a young brunette in her late teens, nodded her assent. "Don't forget your lunch, sir," she said, her voice softening slightly. Alex and Wolfgang extended their plates. With an expressionless face, she plunked a lump of gooey mush onto each of those. They nodded graciously and made their way to the hillock in silence.

The food here was dismal. Yet, they had no choice but to eat it. If they were to even think about getting out of here alive, it was imperative they stayed healthy. Both Alex and Wolfgang seemed to understand this basic fact. So, they spent the first couple of minutes wolfing down the goblin vomit they had been served for lunch. Then, Alex set his plate down on the dry earth beside his feet, and lit a cigarette.

"Want one?" he asked.

Wolfgang shook his head. "You know I don't smoke."

"That was Otto who didn't smoke." Alex chuckled. "What about Wolfgang?"

"Wolfgang is a social smoker. But only when he's happy. And now ..."

"Hmm. Fair enough." Alex took a drag on his cigarette and blew smoke rings through his lips.

"Did you get my letter?" Wolfgang asked.

"I did. How did you manage to get it across to Aleppo, without anyone intercepting it?"

"I have my ways." Wolfgang grinned.

"Did you do some of your Jedi stuff?"

"Ha! I wouldn't call it that. But yeah, I found the courier and tampered with his mind. Made sure he'd deliver it to you unopened."

Alex swerved around to face his friend. "So, you can really do that, eh? Tamper with memories and shit?"

Wolfgang nodded. "That's how I got the guard on the truck to free us."

"I read about that in your letter. It's still all very surreal. I mean …" Alex fell silent. "What else can you do?" he said, after a pause.

"I can open locks. Mess with electronics. Stuff like that." Wolfgang's face became thoughtful.

"I have a question."

"Ya?"

"If you can do all that? Then why didn't you escape much sooner? I mean, you could've just freed us back in Ukraine. Those guys wouldn't have known what hit them."

"Nope. I couldn't have. They put bags over our heads, remember? I can't do anything without my eyes. I need to focus on the person or object I am manipulating, to make my powers work. After that, when they removed the bags, we were inside a moving truck. So, even if I had freed myself, I would've had nowhere to run. Besides, I couldn't have just left *you* behind. And you were out cold." Wolfgang crossed his arms over his chest.

"Fascinating. Your powers, I mean. I wish I could've seen them in action," Alex whispered. There was genuine awe in his eyes.

"Give me something small," Wolfgang suddenly said.

"What?"

"Like a box of matches."

"Okay …" Alex dug inside his pockets for the box of matches and handed it to Wolfgang. "Please don't tell me you're gonna burn this place to the ground right now. Because I'd like to get my ass outta here first, in that case …"

"Ha! Don't worry. I'll warn you if I ever decide do that." Wolfgang placed the box of matches at the centre of his open palm and smiled. "Now watch this." As soon as his eyes focussed on the box, it floated above his palm and hovered in midair for a few seconds, before gliding through the air to land on Alex's thigh.

"Whoa! Telekinesis?"

Wolfgang shrugged. "Sometimes. Only for short distances. I'm the only one who can do this. The others—"

"Speaking of others," Alex interrupted. "I've been meaning to ask you." He lowered his voice and leaned closer." When I found out who you were, you know, back in Ukraine, I had information that you have a team. How big is it? Can they help us?"

"We are … a handful … is all I can tell you. For now. As for your other question … yes and no."

"Care to explain?"

Now it was Wolfgang's turn to dial down the volume. "They can possibly help us," he said, almost in a whisper. "In fact, they are probably already looking for us. But my concern is that, they would have no idea where to look. We didn't know until now that the Aifra was building bases in war-torn countries like Syria and enlisting the local militia into their ranks."

"Well, neither did I. But tell me, when I gave you that confidential USB with my testimony, back in Ukraine, who did you send it to?"

"I sent it to one of my teammates, a very reliable confidante. Why?"

"That is our answer then!" Alex's eyes lit up. "See, I recognized General Sapieha as soon as I saw him. He was my superior in the US Army. And … I have had my suspicions about him for a very long time. He has always been odd. Gone against every high-level directive. Tried to … I don't know how to put it exactly …" He scratched his chin.

"Tried to perpetuate war? Escalate the violence?" Wolfgang added helpfully.

"Yes, that's exactly right. But how did you know?"

"Let's just say, I took a little peek inside his head while we were alone together."

"Oh! Anyway … without getting into too much detail … basically, everything is in that USB. All my theories about the General and things I found out. I'm sure my camp has been told that I died in combat. That news will trigger the execution of my will, and my lawyer will give your friend the password to unlock my USB. Once they make the connection between Sapieha and the Aifra—"

"Let me stop you right there, my friend." Wolfgang held up his palm to interrupt. "As promising as this idea might seem to you right now, I can tell you that it won't work."

"Why not?"

"Because that password of yours will never reach my contact. Aifra will make sure of it. Their nexus is deeper than you can ever imagine. Consider me a bit of an expert on this topic." A bell went off in the distance alerting them that their little rendezvous would soon have to end. Wolfgang stood up and brushed some dirt off the back of his jeans.

Alex scurried to his feet beside him and bent down to pick up his dirty plate. "In that case, we need a solid plan to get out of here quick. We can't just continue to serve the Aifra. I'll work up—"

"For now, we don't have a choice." Wolfgang interjected. "I have something they need. Information about the Hekameses. They won't hurt us as long as I am still willing to help them with it."

"Oh! Do they already know? About your … you know … powers?"

"No. Thankfully not. But they are aware of our organization, the Hekameses. And I have told them I have connections I can use to get them more intel."

"So, you're just going to go ahead and betray your own teammates?" Alex shrieked; sheer shock written across his face. "And how will that even secure our release?"

Wolfgang smirked. "I hope by the end of all this, you will come to trust me," he simply said, as he grabbed his plate and left.

CHAPTER SEVEN

"We need to take you to a doctor," Julie said glumly, after spending another futile afternoon trying to resurrect Peter's lost memories. "But it's not safe to do it out here. We're still too close to camp."

Peter's head jerked up at the mention of camp. "You mean the Aifra camp?"

"Of course." Julie was sitting on the flat-topped rock that blocked their cave's entrance, and Peter was sprawled on the floor, warming his hands by a fire.

"You think they're still looking for us?" Peter leaned back against the cave wall.

"For me, definitely. And you, I don't know. You've been missing a while. Although, I doubt anyone's forgotten someone of your rank. But I'm pretty sure they stopped putting patrols out for you by now. Either way, even if they come looking for me and find us both, they'll kill you too."

"That sounds cheerful."

"Ha! That's rich coming from you, Peter. Given that

you were with them *voluntarily* all these years."

"And you weren't?"

"I … my case was different. I told you already," Julie muttered. "Besides, I wasn't there that long, and then I *left*. See? I'm here, aren't I? I ran. But did you?" She gesticulated with her hands for dramatic effect.

Peter nodded remorsefully. "I wish I could tell ya I wanted to leave as well. But honestly, I don't remember. Maybe, I just wasn't as brave as you are."

"I … I'm sorry. I didn't mean it like that." Julie's face sank.

"I know you didn't." Peter's lips curved into a weak smile. "So, what do we do now? How do I get my memories back? Figure out if I was misguided, trapped or downright evil?"

"Meh, maybe a mix of the three." Julie said after some deliberation. They both burst out laughing. "Jokes aside, I think we need to wait it out," Julie finally said, still coughing and sputtering from her laughing fit. "They'll stop putting patrols out for me in a month or two. After that, we need to get out of this forest and find you a good doctor."

* * *

Zoya took a couple of large bites off her delicious hotdog, before noticing that Yuri was staring at her. "What?" she said, through a mouthful of hotdog.

Yuri chuckled. "Nothing."

"C'mon! It's not nothing. What's on your mind?"

"You look older than last year."

"Well, d'oh! I *am* older than last year, by a year. In case that wasn't obvious."

"Ha! That's not what I meant. It's like … a je ne sais quoi. Something has changed about you in the short time, since we last met. You have aged faster than you should have."

"Hey! Are you saying that I'm getting *old*?" Zoya tried to appear genuinely offended.

Yuri laughed out loud. "Forget it." He checked the time. "If you're done, we should leave. The bus is in five minutes. And the next one is not until the evening."

Zoya wiped her mouth with her napkin and emptied her glass of water. "I'm done. What about you though? You didn't finish your sandwich."

"It was a big one. I'll finish it in the bus," he said, hauling his backpack up from the floor. "We'll have nearly five hours on the bus, and after that lots and lots of trekking. I hope you're up for it, old lady." He snickered.

"We'll see." Zoya laughed. "By the way, you *do* know how to get to the shrine, right?"

Yuri scratched his head. "Well, I have a fair idea. But we'll have at least a week's journey ahead of us. That's why I said—"

"A *week's* journey? Why didn't you tell me? I didn't bring enough supplies. Maybe we should stop by a convenience store first."

Yuri waved away her suggestion. "Don't worry about that. You're forgetting that I grew up on those hills. There are hikers' cabins, hidden away in nooks that I know of. We can stop at those along the way. They usually have some basic supplies. There's no way you can carry everything you need on this hike. It's too treacherous."

"Sounds exciting." Zoya smiled.

"You are an intriguing one, aren't you?" Yuri teased. "An adventurer at heart?"

"Maybe. I'm still in the process of discovering myself."

"Aren't we all," Yuri said, before pointing to their right. "There, I see the bus. We should run, if we want to make it." And with that he broke into a sprint.

* * *

Chris stood in front of Wanda Faraday's office door at the Oxford University, a week after his return from Lumania, carrying the information she had requested. This was only Wanda's secondary office, the primary one being at Stanford University in California. But ever since she had retired from her role at Stanford, she no longer went back there at all, and this had become her primary office by default. He knocked on the polished oak door in front of him and waited.

"Come in," said Wanda's soft voice.

Chris strode into the small but airy room, one that he had decorated himself, when Wanda had agreed to return to her position at Oxford, after her retirement. The desk was set perfectly at the centre of the rectangular room with a tall bookcase against the northern wall behind it. Light trickled in through the only window on the eastern wall, pooling onto Wanda's desk to form a dreamy pattern of light and shadow. A small hunched woman sat behind the desk scribbling on a piece of paper.

"I found the letter," Chris said without preamble, as he made his way up to Wanda.

Wanda looked up. "Finally! May I see it?"

"Of course." Chris unfolded the sheet of paper and flattened it on her desk. Three words were printed across it in bold font.

Wanda squinted her eyes and bent forward. "Where is

Peter?" she read. "Just like in Wolfgang's riddle. In the letter to a father. Of a vanished son they speak."

"Exactly," Chris agreed.

"And you found this letter, where?"

"Last year, when Dr. Cobb was missing, I was inside his office, gathering some stuff to set up your office in the next room. It was then, that Tracy from the admin office came in to deliver it. Since Dr. Cobb wasn't back, she left it with me. There was no stamp on the envelope. It must have been hand-delivered to the department."

"Intriguing," Wanda observed. "And you showed it to Wolfgang?"

"I did. That's when he'd come to the conclusion that someone was looking for Peter. What baffled us both however, was this," Chris pointed at an emblem at the bottom of the page. There, watermarked into the footer, was a tiny eagle with its wings outstretched, housed inside concentric circles. The words "United States" floated like a banner above the eagle's head. The word "Army" was etched below its feet. "US Army insignia," Chris concluded.

"We look towards the hawk's head. Missing the eagle in mid-flight," Wanda whispered. "That must be what he means. The eagle in mid-flight is a symbol of the US Army."

"Makes sense." Chris nodded. "But what about the hawk's head then?"

"Oh, that's easy enough. Have you forgotten who our chief enemy is?"

"Umm … the Aifra?"

"Indeed. And where does that name come from?"

"Aifra stands for the eye of Ra, as in the Egyptian God Ra …" Chris scrunched his face and mumbled to himself.

"Ah! I get it! Ra is depicted as a hawk-headed deity in Egyptian lore, am I right?"

"You're absolutely correct, young man. So, there you have it. The answer to our riddle. We should shift our focus from Aifra and look towards the US Army."

"But how can that *be?* I mean, the US is *hunting* the Aifra. They've *always* been hunting the Aifra. Wolfgang can't possibly mean that our military is suddenly in cahoots with the Aifra now?"

"My dear boy, in everything evil there is a shred of good. So, to balance that, in everything good there must always be some elements of evil."

* * *

Amon had not stayed very long in London, after returning with Wanda from New York. Instead, he had made his way back to his home in Egypt. He had been away from home for so many long months that he was craving to return.

Amon was born and raised in Faiyum, where he had worked all his life in the tourism industry. When his parents had died, his siblings had sold him their shares of the ample family estate, so that he could run his business in peace. He had turned this property into a guest house, with a stable for his tour-horses at the back. He had lived with his family in the eastern-wing, for many years. He had seen his daughter grow up here and eventually go off to college. He had retained most of their household staff, and put them to work in his flourishing business.

But then, the Faiyum scrolls were discovered and everything changed for Amon and his family. The Aifra attacks became more frequent and devastating. The threats to their lives became a living breathing thing, that would not let them steal a wink of sleep in the nights. Eventually, Amon had no choice but to wind his business down, and send his wife and daughter away to live with his in-laws in Cairo. With a heavy heart, he had to part ways with many of his beloved household help.

Naturally, upon landing in Cairo last week, Amon had gone straight to his in-laws' home to spend the weekend with his family. It had felt like a breath of fresh air to have been able to see his loved ones again. But no journey home was ever complete without a trip to one's birthplace. So, come Monday morning, Amon had made the trip to Faiyum by himself.

Now, he stood in front of the wrought iron gates that opened into his orchards and gazed pensively at the sight before him. The garden was a shell of its former self. The date palms were drooping and fruitless. The grass was dry and earth cracked. Even the tall cacti that lined the pathway to his front door, looked utterly forlorn, like the sentries to a dying empire.

As he clicked the gate open, a bent form raised his head from behind a clump of bushes. It was his trusted help, Abu, tending to the gardens alone. Upon seeing Amon enter, Abu came scurrying through the hedges.

"You are home," he said, with a broad toothless grin. "Finally."

"Abu! Good to see you. I'm afraid, I won't be staying long. But tell me, how has it been, lately?" Then, lowering his voice, "Any more problems from the terrorists?"

"No, no problem, sir. All is quiet. But this house is not the same. Not without you."

Amon smiled affectionately. "I am not the same when I am not here, either. My roots have been calling to me for far too long."

Abu nodded. "Come inside. I will make lunch. You are hungry?"

"That would be fantastic. But no need to hurry. I want to go to the stables first and then wash up."

"As you wish," said Abu, before making his way to the pantry area at the back of the house.

Amon walked in through his front door and dropped his backpack on the living room sofa. A cloud of dust rose from the impact. A fine sandy sheen covered every piece of furniture in sight. Abu had been mostly asked to water the plants in Amon absence, since he had been the only help around. Amon sighed and proceeded to look for a duster in the broom closet, which was right next to the back door.

As soon as he opened the door to the closet, he heard a thudding sound. He turned on the lights, hoping to find an overturned bucket or a fallen broom inside the closet. But everything in there looked just fine. He shrugged off the interruption and was about to retrieve the duster, when he heard it again. Louder this time. A sort of thumping noise that was coming not from the closet, but the back door.

Grabbing the duster in one hand like a weapon, he walked cautiously up to the door and opened it. A human form slid against the panel and collapsed to the floor in front of him. "Help," said a feeble, whimpering voice.

Amon jumped back in shock. "Abu! Abu, where are you?" he called.

The man on the floor grabbed his leg with one bloodied hand and looked up. Amon's jaws dropped to the floor. His head started spinning, and try as he might to speak, no words seemed to form between his lips. "Help," the fallen man said again, in a barely audible whisper.

This helped steady Amon's nerves. He knelt to the floor

in a quick motion and heaved the man's body over his threshold. Then, laying him down on his back, he patted his cheeks in an effort to keep him conscious "Seb … Sebastian, my friend," he stuttered. "Who did this to you?"

CHAPTER EIGHT

Wolfgang awoke at the break of dawn, before anyone else in his camp had risen. He shaved and showered in the barrack-styled communal showers that were still empty. He combed his neat, French-cut beard like he always did, with prim, efficient strokes, until it looked exactly like it had before his capture. Then, he put on the well-pressed three-piece suit that General Sapieha had provided him for this particular mission.

He had been told that a soldier would wait for him at the camp gate, at five o'clock sharp, to accompany him to Germany. And that, he had better not be late. He used the data on his pre-paid cell phone to make sure, the new access card he had requested from his lab, had been delivered to his Frankfurt apartment last evening. Then, he walked over to the breakfast area and grabbed an apple for the road.

An armoured jeep was waiting for him outside. And next to it, stood the tall, dark, moustachioed escort, he had been promised. He did not look armed, but Wolfgang knew that the Aifra soldiers routinely carried hidden holsters on the insides of their jackets. There was no doubt that his reticent companion would have been equipped with at least one weapon and several rounds of ammunition. Wolfgang knew that this man was no bodyguard, appointed for his protection. But rather, an enforcer to ensure compliance.

"You are Wolfgang?" he asked gruffly, seeing Wolfgang approach.

"Yes, I am. And you?"

The man did not respond. Instead, with a stern face, he held open the jeep door for Wolfgang to enter. As Wolfgang was climbing in, the jeep's driver, half-turned and smiled. "Lucky. His name is Lucky," he said. Wolfgang suppressed a laugh at the irony and nodded his thanks to the driver.

After they had driven for about ten minutes, Wolfgang spoke, breaking the long and awkward silence. "I guess there's no point asking you, how we are getting to Frankfurt," he said to his companion.

Lucky turned his head towards him and as was expected, did not say a word. Wolfgang cast a tangential look at the driver, who seemed to be smirking, but he too did not venture a response. Then, just as Wolfgang was about to relax back into his seat, there was a sudden movement beside him. Wolfgang swung around in surprise. Lucky had reached into his jacket pocket and pulled out something. Thankfully, it was not a weapon, but a folded piece of paper. He offered the paper to Wolfgang, who accepted it with a shaking hand, like it was a death sentence.

It was, in fact, a plane ticket for two, from Damascus to Frankfurt. Wolfgang nodded and handed the sheet of paper back. They were due to arrive at around six in the evening, which would work perfectly for his plan.

Their flight to Frankfurt did not turn out to be any less boring than their drive to Damascus earlier. Lucky sat so eerily still that Wolfgang began to wonder if he was in fact, carved out of marble. The only time there was any activity from his travel companion, was when the hostess arrived with their meals. Wolfgang used this seclusion to gather his thoughts and solidify his strategy. He was told that he would have less than fifteen minutes inside his office. So, he wanted to meticulously plan his every move.

After a quick stop at his apartment to pick up his new access pass to the lab, Wolfgang took an Uber to the Max Planck Institute with Lucky in tow. They arrived at its locked front entrance at around eight that evening, after all the staff and most of the scientists had left. Wolfgang swiped his pass to enter. Lucky was about to follow, when Wolfgang held up his hand to stop him.

"No. I have to go alone. There are still people inside. And security cameras. Everyone knows me, but not you. The General gave me fifteen minutes inside. The homing device is still on me." He patted the breast-pocket of his suit where the said device was lodged. "So, I can't run. You have nothing to worry about. If you come in though, I can't be responsible for what happens."

Lucky stared at him blankly through the entire monologue. But just as Wolfgang felt convinced that he had made his point, the soldier began to speak. "Take out the cameras," he grunted.

"Huh?" Wolfgang's heart skipped a beat. *Did he know?*

"I said, take out the cameras."

"I have no idea how you think I could do that," Wolfgang ventured.

"You are not one of them? The special people?"

"Ha! I wish!" Wolfgang chuckled sarcastically. "But no. Like I told the General, I know about them. And I have a hunch that one of my colleagues was involved. Not much more. If you doubt me, you can check with him directly," he concluded, with an air or finality.

There was a long silence. And then, "Go. Fifteen minutes," said Lucky, checking the time.

Wolfgang rushed inside the building and made a sharp right to avoid the elevators. He headed straight to the fire escape beside the men's washroom that would take him directly to his office on the second floor. Although it was late, he knew there would still be some researchers around. So, he wanted to avoid any chance encounters that would delay him unnecessarily.

Reaching the second floor, he tiptoed up to his office and punched in the unlock code. The room looked exactly like he had left it. The sight filled him with a surge of nostalgia. He felt a tingling urge to grab his favourite ball pen sensor from the desk, but immediately realized that it would be a terrible idea. Nothing from this office should reach the hands of the Aifra, except for the carefully handpicked pieces that he would select tonight.

He walked over to his desk with a heavy heart and turning on the desk lamp, began rummaging through the drawers. Years of documents lay there in heaps. Some, yellowing around the edges. Others, he had forgotten ever existed.

It took him a lot longer than he had expected, to locate the folder he had been looking for. Nervously, he checked the time. He had five more minutes before Lucky would charge in, guns blazing and turn this into his unluckiest day. With clammy hands, he grabbed a set of sensors from the top drawer and hooked them over his ears. He turned on the base-unit at his feet and plugged a memory stick in its USB port. Then, he sank into his chair and scrunching his face, focussed intensely on remembering everything that had happened in the last few weeks. The clock ticked faster then ever. Just one more memory remained to be recorded. He pushed it out of his mind and into the recorder with all his concentration, before jumping out of his seat. There was one last thing he needed to do. He scribbled a note on a piece of paper and left it on his desk, weighed down by the newly-loaded USB stick. With that done, he looked up at the security camera. It was on. He walked up to it, bringing his face as close as possible to the camera. When he was certain that his face was being captured, he turned slightly and pointed towards his desk, making sure whoever was behind the camera would notice his gesture. He had one minute left. Grabbing the folder he had recovered, he sprinted out the door grinning from ear to ear.

His friend Gunter worked in the camera room. Gunter would be watching.

CHAPTER NINE

Chris was running breathlessly down the narrow alleyways of London, when his phone rang.

"Wanda, thanks for calling back," he panted into the phone. "Can you and Dr. Cobb meet me at the lab in like five minutes?" Receiving a response in the affirmative from the other end, he hung up and continued sprinting like the devil was on his tail.

In a couple of minutes, he arrived at the Department of Engineering Science and headed straight for the stairwell, taking the steps two at a time to his lab on the third floor. It was still too early in the day for the other students to get here, so he fumbled in his pockets for the keys to unlock the door. Finding it, he let himself inside. Once inside, he leaned against the wall for a second, to wipe his brow and catch his breath, before proceeding to the rear of the room where Wolfgang had his desk.

There, lying on the floor next to Wolfgang's dusty desk, was the object he needed right now. He picked up the helmet-shaped device, dusted it and placed it on the table.

Then, he proceeded to open the FedEx envelope he had brought with him.

Voices floated in to the room from its open door making him look up. Two elderly figures had entered and were speaking softly. "Over here, Wanda, Albert. And please, lock the door behind you," Chris said, waving his professors over. As the duo made their way towards him, Chris got busy setting up his workstation. First, he removed an USB stick from the envelope and plugged it into the helmet. Then, he attached a console to it. Finally, he lowered the whiteboard that hung directly across from Wolfgang's desk, to use as a screen for projection.

"What's going on?" Wanda Faraday asked, once she had seated herself across from Chris. "What's the emergency?"

"It's good news," Chris assured. "At least, I think it is." He inspected his set-up one last time, before switching it on.

"So, are you going to tell us what this is all about?" Dr. Cobb gestured with his hands.

"Yeah, of course. So, last night, I got a call from Gunter. He is … you know, in charge of security—"

"At the Max Planck Institute. Yes, we are aware." Wanda nodded. "He is also a friend of Wolfgang and an ally of the Hekameses."

"Correct. He has been monitoring the security cameras there for us, since the very early days of his career. So, last night, he said that he was overnighting me a very important package and asked for the best address to send it. He said that he couldn't share any more details over the phone. This morning, it arrived. The package. It was a memory stick."

"Oh Jesus! Not another useless USB device!" Dr. Cobb

threw up his arms in frustration.

"No, not useless. Not this one. It's from Wolfgang and came with a note in his handwriting. The note told Gunter to send the USB to me, saying that I'd know what to do with it. And I did. I knew exactly what it was, as soon as I saw it."

"Well, if it's from *Wolfgang*, then we can be certain it'll work, can't we?" Dr. Cobb rolled his eyes.

Chris chuckled. "I can understand your frustration, professor. I don't know if the other USB was really from Wolfgang or a dirty prank of some sort. But this ... this is definitely from him."

"And *how*, pray tell, can we be sure? The handwriting again? We have already been down that road and know how it all played out." Dr. Cobb continued to argue.

"Yep, there's that. But this time, it's much more. The USB and letter were found inside Wolfgang's office at Max Planck. On his desk, to be exact. And no one has access to it, except for Wolfgang himself and Gunter. Not even me."

"Oh, alright, very well. What's inside the USB? Have you seen it?"

"No. We are going to see in now. Together. That's what this set-up is for. If this USB is what I think it is, then Wolfgang recorded his memories onto it. The head-gear we designed last year, when we went snow leopard hunting in Siberia, can play back this recording like a movie, which I plan to project onto the whiteboard over there." Chris pointed behind him.

"Go on then," Wanda urged. "The blinds are still drawn and the other students aren't here. This is our chance to watch it."

"Okay, here we go." Chris picked up the console and hit play.

A scene started to play out across the whiteboard on the wall. It was inside someone's office. A military man was speaking from behind a desk. He was saying something to the effect of having found out that a certain Otto, was actually Wolfgang. As this conversation was ongoing, two soldiers in US Army uniforms entered the room, armed to their teeth. There was a struggle. Captives were being taken. And then the scene faded out.

The next scene was dimly lit. It was seen through the eyes of an observer who seemed to be sitting on the floor. A door opened in front, and a stout man entered what looked like the backend of a truck. A kick landed on the stouts man's chest and he tumbled to the ground. Then, a pair of hands grabbed his ruddy face and someone stared directly into his eyes. This scene ended with the observer sitting in the cab of the truck and driving through a rugged, run-down neighbourhood, with the military man from the previous scene by his side.

There were two more scenes. One, with the audience inside another, different office, standing across from a military general who looked like a caricature of a Body World exhibit. Words were exchanged. Sometimes heated. Then, they were joined by the same individual who had been around in the first two scenes.

The final scene was the odd one out. It seemed random and out of place. It was the memory of a phone call. A phone call with Chris, where he was heard explaining that Kazhar had convinced a couple of Lumanians to fight with the Hekameses at the Moscow State University.

"It's true then," Dr. Cobb, said, when the show had ended. "The old fool is really alive!" Tears were pooling around the rims of his eyes. He wiped them with his shirt sleeve and sniffled.

"I told you he was, didn't I?" Wanda said gleefully. She too was dabbing at her eyes with a dainty handkerchief.

"Yeah, I didn't believe it either." Chris smiled. "That he was dead. Anyway, what did you make of the video?"

"Mysterious and confusing as always," Dr. Cobb grumbled. "Why on earth didn't he just record a voice message? If he was in his office, for crying out loud?"

"Ha! I seriously don't think he was there of his own volition. It's clear that he's being held captive. So, I presume, he could only use what tools he had at his disposal. And I don't recall him having a voice-recorder in his office. Even the memory recorder had only been there by accident, because I had shown it to him, before leaving for Siberia last year," Chris explained.

"What about using his bloody phone?" Dr. Cobb grunted.

"Again, I'm pretty sure, whoever imprisoned him took away his phone. And using a phone his captors might have given him, would have been too dangerous," Chris replied.

Wanda, who had not joined in this conversation and seemed to be lost in thought, turned around and grabbed Chris' arm. "My dear boy," she said, "could you please play the first scene for me again?"

"Sure." Chris played the video. "Who is this man?" he said, pausing the first scene at its halfway mark. "He's in three of the four scenes."

"Yes, that's exactly what I was trying to remember." Wanda nodded. "For I have seen this man before."

"You have?"

"Indeed. Albeit, only in a picture. He is Lieutenant Colonel Alexander Costas of the US Army. The man who left me the password to his USB in his will. Wolfgang was with him when he was captured. But the question is, where? Where was he then? And where is he now?"

"I guess, we don't need to ask *who* captured him," Chris mumbled. "It's definitely the Aifra."

"If we correlate this with the riddle Wolfgang sent me, it would appear that the Aifra has infiltrated the US Army. Inserted some of its operatives into their midst," Wanda mused.

Chris nodded. "That General from the third scene looked terribly sinister. He must be one of them—a double-agent for the Aifra."

"Could you look into him, please?" Wanda asked. "If we find him, I think we will find Wolfgang."

"And his buddy, Alexander Costas?" Chris chuckled. "Do you think he knows about the Hekameses? This Costas guy?"

"I don't know. Neither do I know why Wolfgang was with him, to begin with. What I do know however, is that, if we plan to save one, we should save the other."

"Oh, definitely," Chris agreed. "But we have to figure out how."

"Can I see Wolfgang's letter," Dr. Cobb suddenly said. "The one that Gunter sent."

"Sure, here you go. It's signed and everything." Chris picked up the letter and scanned it. "Look here, Wolfgang Müller, dated March 25th—"

"March 25th?" Dr. Cobb exclaimed. "No, that can't be right. Today is the 10th of March. Let me see it." He snatched the letter from Chris' hand.

"He got the date wrong? That's weird." Chris rubbed his chin thoughtfully.

"Perhaps, he didn't get it wrong," Dr. Cobb said, looking up from the letter. "Perhaps, he wasn't dating the letter at all, but telling us to make note of this date. He didn't date his signature. He didn't even place the date where he should have, at the top right of the page. Instead, he inked in a date randomly, right at the bottom. Far from his signature. Why?"

"If he wants us to rescue him, he would need to tell us where we can find him and when. I believe this is the when part," Wanda observed astutely.

"That's brilliant!" Chris exclaimed. "But what about the location?"

"Can we—" Wanda began, but a knock on the lab door interrupted her.

"Shit, the other students must be here," Chris grumbled. "I'll get the door," he added, quickly putting away his equipment. After letting the rest of his lab-mates in, he returned and bent down to whisper into Wanda's ear. "I'll watch the whole thing again and do some research. I think our answer is hidden within his memories somewhere. We already have a date, now if we can just figure out the location, we can rescue him."

Wanda nodded. "Keep in mind that we only have two weeks. Depending on the nature of the operation, we might have to involve Alejandro and Amon and possibly even Zoya. And it will take some time to get them where we need them to be."

"Or in other words, I have a race against time ahead of me." Chris chuckled.

Hearing this, Dr. Cobb stood up and patted Chris on the shoulder. "Don't worry, my boy, it isn't anything you haven't handled before." Then, he turned to follow Wanda out the door.

Once his professors had left, Chris plonked himself into Wolfgang's chair and wiped his brow. Time is such an elusive creature. So hard to find, and yet too easy to lose.

Only if there was some way to stop it. Especially at a moment like this.

Reaching into his pockets, Chris retrieved a tiny object and set it atop the table. It was a magical hourglass of Lumanian origin. The sand in it had stopped flowing due to some prophecy that Chris had yet to comprehend. He stared into it absently, contemplating the meaning of time, when it hit him—Lumania. That had to be the answer! He grabbed the headset and USB from the desk and made his way to his apartment, to view Wolfgang's memories, more closely in the privacy of his home. Somehow, he knew the answer was Lumania, but he would have to find out how and why.

CHAPTER TEN

A five-hour bus ride and a whole day's trek later, Zoya and Yuri arrived at an idyllic log-cabin overlooking the western shore of Lake Baikal. On their first night at the lake, Yuri had pitched a tent, where they had managed to catch a few paltry hours of sleep, before setting off bright and early into the great wilderness. Tonight, would be different. There would be a warm fire. Possibly even a hot meal to prepare. The air here was warmer due to the lake effect. The crescent moon rising above their heads, spoke of untold possibilities.

"It's an izba," Yuri said, as they approached the cabin. "A traditional Russian log-cabin."

"It's gorgeous." Zoya beamed. "And ... we can just use it?"

Yuri shrugged. "It belongs to a ranger. A friend of mine, who's not around this week. He doesn't mind."

"You seem to have wonderful friends." Zoya giggled, stepping inside.

"So do you. How is your boyfriend, by the way?" He

smirked over his shoulder.

"My who?"

"You know, Chris. He was mighty jealous of me talking to you the last time you were here."

"Oh! I … was he?" Zoya stuttered. "He's definitely not my boyfriend though," she quickly added.

Yuri broke into a fit of laughter as he collapsed into an armchair. Silvery moonlight trickled in through the windows making his face appear incandescent, like that of an ethereal being.

Zoya found herself staring at this image, a tad longer than she would have liked. "Why … why are you laughing," she said, her stomach in knots.

"Just the way you jumped up when I suggested that he was your boyfriend. It was too funny."

Zoya crossed her arms across her chest. "Why is it funny?"

"Do you have a boyfriend then?" Yuri asked, becoming suddenly serious. "Or a girlfriend?" he added, after a bit of deliberation.

"Well, that's—"

"Personal? Rude? None of my business?" Yuri asked, making comical gestures with his hands. "You can slap me, if you like," he then suggested thoughtfully.

This cracked Zoya up. She collapsed into the love seat across from him and doubled over with laughter. "You … you are … unbelievable!" she sputtered.

"So, you're going with the slapping then?"

"No."

"Phew!" Yuri mock-wiped his brow.

"I mean, no, I don't have either. No boyfriend or girlfriend," Zoya clarified. "Happy now?"

"Why should I be happy?" Yuri rolled his eyes. "If

anything, you are the one who should be *sad*."

"What about you, Mister Smarty Pants?"

"*What!* You want *me* to be your boyfriend?" Yuri exclaimed with feigned astonishment.

Zoya wiggled her tongue at him and made a face. "There's no point even talking to you. You know what I meant. Now you're just playing games for no reason."

Yuri stood up with a triumphant grin across his face. "No. I'm not playing games. But I *would* like to play something else." He glanced at the sleeping hearth. "After I make a fire." He stood up and began searching around the fireplace for the stash of wood. Having found it, he expertly lit a fire and nurtured it with a poker for a minute or two. Then, he walked across the room, straight to the very back and drew open a cupboard door. He did all of this so effortlessly, that Zoya could tell he had been here in this cabin, many times before.

When Yuri emerged from the cupboard, he was walking towards Zoya, holding a wonderfully familiar object—a guitar. "This is the best part about this cabin," he said, shrugging off his jacket and sitting down in the armchair by the fire. "Are you hungry?" He turned to ask as an afterthought.

"No. Not yet."

"Shall I play then?"

Zoya's face lit up. "What can you play? Other than the Russian songs you played last time."

"Mmm ... quite a few things. What kind of music do you like? Country, jazz, pop? The sound of music is a personal—"

"The Sound of Music. I like The Sound of Music." Zoya interrupted.

"Yeah, I mean, so do I, but ..." Zoya rolled her eyes.

"Oh! You mean the *movie*," Yuri realized. "Cool. I like it too. Okay, here goes then." Flashing Zoya a radiant smile, he began playing a tune and humming the lyrics. He sang 'Doe A Deer' and Zoya clicked her fingers to the beats. His singing voice was a baritone-tenor-mix which beautifully complimented the lyrics. Finishing the song, he paused for breath and then, "You are sixteen—" he began.

"Nineteen." Zoya giggled.

"What's that?"

"I'm nineteen," Zoya clarified.

"Okay. You are nineteen …" Yuri began to sing, but trailed off. "No, that doesn't do it. Breaks the rhyme."

Zoya made a face. "Damn! I was hoping you'd tell me how old *you* are, in the next line."

"Cheeky." Yuri smirked, putting his guitar down and standing up. "I'm feeling hungry." He walked up to the kitchen area and took some cans out from a cupboard. Then, he began pulling out the pots and pans. When Zoya started to feel convinced that she had offended him with her earlier remark, he looked over his shoulder and smiled. "I'm twenty-three. And no, I don't have a girlfriend," he said.

* * *

Amon knew a local doctor who made house-calls, whenever he needed. So, this time he had asked for her help again. It had been too risky to take Sebastian to the hospital, given that he had been attacked by the Aifra, who were probably still on both their tails. Besides, it was a shallow stab-wound to the thigh, which would not require hospitalization. Amon's Faiyum estate had police patrols around it, so Sebastian would be safe. For now, at least.

Sebastian had mostly slept through the afternoon when the doctor and nurse had left. Amon had spent the rest of the day catching up with Abu and getting his house in order. Although he was eager to find out what happened to his friend, Amon did not want to rush it. Sebastian needed rest. So, at around sunset, Amon made his way lazily to the living room, to kick back with a glass of whiskey.

Entering the living room, he was surprised to find Sebastian already there, waiting for him. He was nursing a warm cup of tea between his hands. A teapot and a second cup were set on a tray in front of him. "Good evening. Tea?" he asked Amon, as the latter walked in.

"I was actually looking for something stronger. But sure, tea will do too." Amon sat down next to his friend and leaned forward to pour himself a cup. "Good to see you're up and about," he said, taking a sip of the scalding tea.

"Yeah, Abu helped me get out of bed."

"And how are you feeling? How's the pain?"

"I am too drugged to feel pain right now." Sebastian chuckled. "But I bet, it'll hit me in the morning."

Amon nodded sympathetically. "And what about food? Did you have lunch?"

"Oh, I had a hearty lunch. Abu has been taking great care of me all day. He's really nice, your housekeeper."

"Indeed, he is. He has been with our family forever."

"I know. He told me," Sebastian said between sips of tea.

"Oh, he did, did he? I thought you were out cold, because they gave you all those painkillers. When did he get the chance?"

"It wasn't today. I've been to your house several times since you disappeared. I was looking for you. And that's how I've gotten to know Abu over the last few months."

"Interesting." Amon sat up straight. "Abu didn't tell me anything—"

"I told him not to. I wanted to tell you myself. Since Abu didn't know where you were, I kept coming back. Hoping that you've returned and I can finally tell you what I need to."

"Is that why you were here today? When they attacked you?" Amon looked worried.

Sebastian nodded glumly. "Someone threw a knife. I didn't even see a face. I tried to jump, but it was too late."

"Oh dear, I'm so sorry. If I'd only known. I would've contacted you myself. So that you didn't have to risk coming here …"

"I tried to call that number you left me, but for the last few months it was out of range. I figured you were in some remote area or something."

"I was. I feel personally responsible—"

"Don't. Please don't. I still remember how I had left you and Wanda in Hawara, and you told me not to feel guilty. These things are not in our hands. We are dealing with a terrible terror that puts everyone at risk, even if we try to protect them."

"Thank you. And you're right. Speaking of the terrible terror, what is it that you've been trying to tell me so desperately all these months?"

Sebastian looked nervously around the room, before lowering his voice. "Is it safe to talk in here?"

"Absolutely. This home is well protected. You can speak freely."

"Alright then. Remember when we last met? I told you that they were keeping me here, even though the Hawara site was temporarily closed? That they wanted me to investigate the Red Pyramid incident?"

"Yes, I clearly recall that conversation. But at that time, you did not tell me *who* was keeping you here. I figured it wasn't the Egyptian Government, because I am very close to them. Neither was it the Aifra. Then who?"

Sebastian nodded. "I know you were curious about that. And justly so. But I couldn't tell you at that time. My room was bugged and phones were tapped. Now, I can tell you. And you won't believe me if I did."

"Can I venture a guess?"

"Sure, go ahead."

"Was it someone connected with the US Army?"

Sebastian started. "But how … how did you know?"

"We have only recently begun to suspect this." Amon shrugged. "And today, you have confirmed our suspicions. But tell me, what did you find after researching the Red Pyramid incident?" Amon's brows furrowed and worry lines appeared across his forehead.

"I found out about a legend."

"A legend?"

"Yes, since neither I, nor any of my researchers, had actually seen that incident with our own eyes, we interviewed numerous eye-witnesses. They were mostly locals, and they all told me the same story. What happened that day, meant only one thing. That the monster had returned."

"Monster? What monster?"

"They call it The Monster of Egypt. Legend has it, that he is a powerful and twisted wizard, and the locals believe that he has returned."

"Nonsense! You are a man of reason! You can't possibly believe this legend to be true." Amon's whole body was shaking with emotion.

"Normally, I wouldn't have. And at first, I didn't. But

then I spoke to Abu, who told me the entire story. He told me about a magical gift from the sun-God, Ra, that was given to this being, before he turned into what he is today." Sebastian sighed and hung his head. Then, looking up, he said, "I am an archaeologist. So, I went looking for it. This magical gift …"

"And … did you find it?" Amon nearly rose from his seat with excitement.

"No. But I know what it is. The monster found it, and he's definitely out there. But I know what will defeat it."

"There is something that can defeat it?"

"Yes. The Script of Horus. We need to find the Script of Horus."

CHAPTER ELEVEN

Alejandro walked up the front steps to a neat, detached home in Mountain Lakes, New Jersey and rang the doorbell. The porch was lined with flower pots, growing a variety of colourful orchids. Blossoming wisteria overflowed from the gabled roof and hung around the sides, like plumes of velvety smoke. As Alejandro was admiring the casual beauty of this arrangement, a portly black lady with greying hair around the temples, answered the door.

"Yes, who are you looking for?"

"Good morning, Ma'am. I'm here to see Mrs. Irene Costas. Is she home?" Alejandro asked politely.

"I'm afraid not. She left last evening. Do you want to leave a message?"

"Left? A day before her husband's funeral?" Alejandro raised an eyebrow.

"She … her health was failing." The lady hesitated, twitching nervously. "So, her parents came to get her."

"I see. What about the funeral then?"

"It has been postponed." For a second, the lady's eyes darted to the back of the room, where Alejandro thought he saw a shadow glide by. "Anyway," she continued, turning her attention back to Alejandro, "I'm happy to take a message."

"That's alright. I was just here to convey my condolences. Would you happen to know when she'll be back?"

There was a soft thudding sound from inside the house, but this time the lady didn't turn to look. Instead, she became noticeably cagey. "I have no idea, Sir. Now, if you don't mind, I have some chores to get to." She made to close the door, but Alejandro acted instinctively and placed his hand on the panel to stop her.

"Just one more question Ma'am, before you go. Do you perhaps have a number—" Alejandro couldn't finish the sentence as the lady pushed the door shut without responding. The thud from the closing door was followed by a second, softer but distinct clank and the sound of pattering feet.

Alejandro walked off the porch and slid to the side of the building, making sure to crouch under the open windows for cover. The sound of rustling branches wafted through the air from the backyard, and Alejandro trained his ears in that direction. Keeping close to the building wall, he navigated to the backyard and caught a glimpse of a slight figure ducking behind a clump of bushes, diagonally across from him. On the side-street that lined the house, a black Toyota Camry stood idling, hidden from the view of whoever was in the bushes.

Alejandro took a minute to gather his thoughts, and then without hesitation, he made his way to the Camry. A few minutes passed without anything happening. The birds chirped in the trees and a dog barked in the distance, but the car continued to idle, and no one came to claim it. Just as Alejandro was beginning to wonder if he had made the wrong decision, the driver's door opened and a slight woman stepped inside. Alejandro ducked low behind her seat and waited. The lady stepped on the gas and pulled out of the curb with great urgency, making her way to the main intersection to the west.

This was Alejandro's cue to act. He pulled out his trusty Browning Hi-Power revolver and placed it against her head. The woman let out a tiny squeak. "Irene Costas, I don't want to hurt you. But I will, if I must. Do you understand me?" he said huskily into her ear.

Irene nodded, her neck muscles tensing. While still holding the gun with his right hand, Alejandro tinkered with his phone's GPS using his left. Next, he handed the phone to her and said, "This is where we need to go. Keep driving." They turned a corner and were approaching the ramp to the highway, when Alejandro noticed that they were being followed. "We have a blue sedan on our tail," he said, leaning forward. "Don't take the ramp. Keep going straight. The GPS will reroute you."

Irene did as she was told. But within seconds, the blue sedan almost caught up to them. "Speed up," Alejandro urged. "Don't worry about the cops." There was a traffic light ahead of them. It was still red. This was Alejandro's chance.

Irene half turned in her seat and glared at him. "I can't speed up. Red light ahead."

"Do as I say!" Alejandro shouted, startling her enough that she pressed on the gas almost involuntarily. The car zoomed past the lights, just as it turned green with the tailing sedan slowly falling behind. As soon as they cleared the intersection, the lights turned red again and their pursuers got stopped behind them. Alejandro sighed a breath of relief. He could see that Irene too was sweating profusely. "We lost them," Alejandro said to comfort her.

"Not for long," Irene objected.

"Oh, don't you worry about that. I have a feeling they are going to be stuck in traffic for a veeeery long time." Alejandro chuckled, feeling satisfied with how quickly he had managed to tinker with the lights this time.

Irene however, did not seem to find this comment the least bit funny. "Who are you? And what do you want from me?" she asked with a stern face.

"I am an envoy of Otto Schmidt, your late husband's acquaintance, for whom he had left a password in his will."

"And why should I believe you?"

"Because, I dunno … I have a gun to your head?" Even though he knew this was not a great time for jokes, Alejandro couldn't help himself.

Irene did not appreciate this attempt at humour, as was expected. Instead, she continued with her questioning. "Why have you kidnapped me? And why are we going to the airport?"

"You are a worthy companion to a soldier, Madams Costas," Alejandro chuckled. "Relentless and undaunted in the face of certain death."

"Are you flirting with me?" Irene asked, raising her eyebrows.

"No, of course not. But how about I ask *you* some questions now. Why were you running away from home, the day before your husband's funeral? And don't tell me you weren't running, because I know your luggage is in the trunk."

"I don't have to tell you anything," Irene spat.

"Spoken like a true soldier! Have *you* considered joining the Army? Just curious," Alejandro teased. "Anyway," he continued after a brief pause, "since you're not going to cooperate, and I'm in no mood to compel you, let *me* tell you why you were running. How about that, eh? Have you ever met a kidnapper who was this forthcoming?"

"Forthcoming? Or insensitive? Kidnapping the widow of a fallen—"

"You are no widow, Ma'am. Because your husband isn't *dead*," Alejandro interrupted.

Irene's head swerved around in shock. "Wha ... how ... how dare you ..."

"Oh, c'mon! You know this as well as me. You have always known this. Since the day they brought you the news of his death without sending his actual body. When they didn't tell you how he died, or who killed him. Known it, when he didn't even call to tell you that he was going into direct combat. Didn't you, Mrs. Costas? Didn't you know it all along?"

Irene's lips quivered as she looked blankly into the distance, but she neither accepted nor denied the allegation.

"And that is one of the reasons why you are fleeing," Alejandro added calmly.

For a long time neither of them said a word. Irene kept driving, appearing flustered. Then, shattering the silence, she spoke softly, "How do you know, he's not dead?"

"I have my sources. Reliable sources. But he won't be alive for much longer and neither would any of us, unless you tell us everything you know."

"Okay," Irene said in a small voice, her expression softening. "Who's us?"

"Myself and Wanda Faraday, the lady you sent the password to."

"Are you her lawyer, then?"

"No, just her friend. By the way, *your* lawyer Kevin Gao, gave us a fake password. He … he has disappeared, hasn't he?"

"I know. And yes, he has. I've been calling him for days, but he has stopped responding."

"I doubt that he will. Have you reported this to the police? Or told anyone else?"

Irene shook her head from side to side. "I should have, I know. But I just—"

"No, you did the right thing. There's no need to go to the police. If you haven't already figured this out, we are dealing with very dangerous people over here. Dangerous and powerful. The police won't be able to help."

"But who *are* these people? And what do they want with my Alex? It must be about that blasted USB. I know he recorded some really damning stuff in there."

"We have a fairly good idea who they are. And you're right, in all likelihood, it has something to do with the USB. But until we can open that USB, we can't be sure."

"Perhaps I can help you there. I might be able to guess the password. Knowing him, it would have to be something technical."

"See, this is what I meant. We need your help." Alejandro lowered his gun. "I hope you understand that this is not a kidnapping. I just wanted to get to you, before *they* did. And I didn't have much time to explain in the car, so I had to use the gun, to get you to listen."

For the first time since Alejandro had met her, Irene laughed. "What a great way to break the ice!"

"Hey, look at that—a joke! I always love a sense of humour. Even the sarcastic kind." Alejandro smiled.

Irene pulled into the lane leading to Newark airport and sighed. "Where are we going, by the way? Do you have a plan?"

"Of course! I was planning to take us to Dr. Wanda Faraday's home in San Jose. You will be safe there. And we can work together to figure out how to save your husband."

"And Otto."

"Who?"

"Your friend, Otto Schmidt."

"Oh, yes! His real name is Wolfgang Müller, by the way. He was working undercover with your husband."

"Interesting. Is he a cop or something?"

"No. Far worse." Alejandro started laughing, startling Irene. "Don't worry, we'll tell you all about him too."

"Fair enough."

"So, are you game? If you'd like, we can speak to Wanda together from the airport, to make you feel more comfortable."

"Sure. I'd like that. I've spoken to her before. She seems like a sweet lady. Why wasn't she here today?"

"Because I'm the better marksman, I suppose." Alejandro shrugged.

"Ha! Are you always like this?"

"Yes, I'm quite infantile, thank you very much. But jokes aside, she is currently in London, where she teaches at the University. So, she couldn't make it."

"Understandable. We are almost there. I'll head to long-term parking first, and then we can get the tickets?"

"Sounds good."

CHAPTER TWELVE

Wolfgang paced the corridor in front of General Sapieha's office like a caged tiger, his brain working overtime. He cupped his chin with his right hand and clutched a dusty folder with the other. In his mind, he had gone over the script hundreds of times, yet he could not seem to perfect it. Any minute now, he would be summoned inside and after that, there would be no going back. One misstep this morning, would spell certain death for everyone he loved. He was walking on wafer-thin ice.

A soldier walked out of the room and nodded in his direction. "Your turn," he said, curtly.

Wolfgang flashed him a half-smile, before going in. His heart fluttered so violently that he feared it would escape through his throat. The ghastly General looked up from his seat. As their eyes met, Wolfgang cringed. If ever death could bear a physical form, then this was it, sitting in front of him, dawning the hide of General Józef Sapieha. Taking a deep breath, Wolfgang strode up to his desk and sat down across from him.

"Did you find it?" the General asked, without any prelude.

"I believe, I did. The records are right here. In this folder." He slid the folder he was carrying, across the desk towards the General.

The General flipped it open and shuffled through the documents inside. "These are very old. Are you sure this is the right guy?"

"I'm fairly certain, Sir."

The General narrowed his eyes. "Do you take me for a fool, Müller?" he growled. "Have you seen these dates? Have you?" He pointed at the documents and screamed. "Are you trying to tell me that the man whose research this was, is still alive, a HUNDRED YEARS later?"

"He mostly definitely is," Wolfgang said, as calmly as he could manage.

"And HOW exactly do you know that?" Sapieha slammed his palms against his desk and stood up.

"Because." Wolfgang paused, taking his time to relish the feel of the next words coming out of his mouth. "Because, I've met him."

Sapieha's eyes jerked up to Wolfgang's "How?"

"As you can see from these files, General, he was once a visiting faculty at Max Planck, many decades ago. Back then, he started to work on a project which was later passed onto me. During the course of this research therefore, I had to reach out to him from time to time. He is no longer at Max Planck of course, so I—"

"Where? Where is he?" Sapieha almost roared.

"He has returned to his home university. In Moscow."

"That's ridiculous! I don't believe you! How can he still be alive?"

"That's exactly what I had also wondered, and what ultimately led me to suspect that he is no ordinary human. Like I've told you Sir, I've done my share of research on these gifted individuals you seek—the telepaths." Here, Wolfgang lowered his voice conspiratorially. "And, I have reason to believe that they can live exceptionally long lives."

"Yes, I've also heard the same." Sapieha sat down, looking slightly calmer. "But something's still not adding up about this … this Dr. Makarov."

"And what might that be?" Wolfgang smiled, feeling emboldened by the validation.

"How does no one question his age? Or his existence? How can he still work at a university without anyone suspecting foul play?"

"Oh, there are many ways to conceal oneself from the public eye, of course. Dr. Makarov is not known to lecture courses or take on any students. As far as I am aware, he attends to his research only on select days and mostly after-hours. Perhaps he has other means of concealing his identity as well. Using his special powers, for example. I don't know for sure. But I do intend to find out. And that can only be done in a face-to-face encounter. At the end of it, I can trick him to come back to the camp with me, where you can interrogate him directly."

"No, not trick him. We must nab him." The General's eyes were shining with a growing enthusiasm. "I will send you with some soldiers."

"If you'd excuse my impertinence, I'd like to caution against sending too many soldiers. It'd be in our best interest to be as discreet as possible. With the war ongoing, the university is heavily guarded."

"I see. What would be your recommendation then?"

"I think we should have just one soldier, preferably a highly battle-ready individual. Might I suggest, Mr. Costas? He is, after all, a much-decorated Lieutenant Colonel—"

"Yes, I am aware of his qualifications," Sapieha interrupted curtly.

There was a moment of silence, wherein Wolfgang tried to gauge the volatility of the General's current mood. Having picked up no visible indication of a particularly murderous disposition, Wolfgang spoke again. "Besides, I trust him. We will have great chemistry."

Sapieha checked the time. "I'm late for another appointment." Understanding this as his cue to leave, Wolfgang got up. But just as he was about to turn around, "Give me a time and place for this mission, and I will consider it," the General suddenly said.

* * *

Chris rushed out of the shower with only one thought on his mind—he had to call Wanda. Immediately. He had spent the entire day, watching and re-watching Wolfgang's memories, without getting any closer to deciphering their meaning. But then, at around six that evening, right after he hit the shower, everything started to fall in place. This was hardly unusual, since all his best ideas till date, had come to him in the shower. Running over to his desk, while still clad in his bathrobe, he started searching frantically for his phone. Finding it finally underneath a stack of papers, he dialled Wanda's number.

"Hello Chris. How can I help you?" said the soft-spoken professor from the other end.

"I have it, the … I mean, answer. I figured it … figured

out," Chris stuttered.

"Are you alright, young man? Please, do calm down. I had no doubt, you would figure it out. So, tell me, what have you learned?"

"Thanks! As I was saying; I had a hunch back when I was at the lab, that somehow the answer would be Lumania. But there was nothing concrete that pointed to this conclusion. Then, I re-watched all the memories Wolfgang had chosen to send us, and something didn't add up. The first three memories in there were relevant, because all of them were about his capture and captivity. But what about the fourth one? It was a much earlier memory and had nothing to do with his present circumstances. Then, why did he send it?"

"Perhaps it was a clue," Wanda supplied.

"That's exactly what I thought as well. So, I began to wonder, what could Wolfgang be trying to tell us, if not where and when to come save him?"

"Interesting observation. Since we already figured out the 'when', could this be the 'where'?"

"Absolutely! And I believe that's precisely what it is. As you will recall, the fourth memory was also the only one where a distinct location was referenced. That was my first clue. The second clue was Lumania. We all know about the Lumanian secret passages. So, if only there was a way for Wolfgang to slip into one of them, he could easily disappear from his captors." Chris paused to catch his breath.

"So, you put two and two together and tied up the clues," Wanda supplied.

"Correct. In Wolfgang's fourth memory sample, I am speaking to him over the phone and mentioning that the Lumanians agreed to come with us to the Moscow State

University. That's two locations referenced in just one sliver of memory, and both these locations are tied together, because several Lumanian portals exist under this very same university."

"That's brilliant, Chris. Bravo! Now, all we need to do, is alert the Lumanians that Wolfgang will probably be appearing at the Moscow State University on March 25th. And I am confident they will agree to watch out for him."

CHAPTER THIRTEEN

Several days had passed since Nirmala had moved to Amethyst, the new Lumanian colony underneath Canada, and she was settling in just fine. The Elder, Mercuriva seemed to have taken a keen interest in her and was visiting often to assist with her instruction. Nirmala spent her mornings learning Lumanian lore and staring into Seeing Crystals, under the expert supervision of district seniors, and from time to time, Mercuriva herself. The afternoons were mostly dedicated to reading in their vast libraries, and towards evening she would learn a trade or other from the various craftsmen of their society.

This afternoon, she had volunteered in the kitchen, for the preparation and distribution of her district's afternoon meal. She was walking into the Dining Hall, carrying the huge platter of pakoras she had made using her mother's recipe, when she noticed Pala running towards her from the far end of the hall. Lumanians never usually run or show any visible signs of panic. Naturally, this scene shocked Nirmala, who stumbled and nearly dropped her tray of pakoras.

Pala walked breathlessly up to her and spoke so rapidly that a jumble of incomprehensible sounds emerged from her lips. Lumanians always look ageless, neither young nor old, almost like immortals. So, Nirmala could never tell exactly how old any of them actually were. Nevertheless, quite early on, she had realized from certain behavioural traits, that Pala was a relatively young soul. Perhaps a teenager or young adult at best. Nirmala grabbed her shoulders to calm her and smiled affectionately. "What is it Pala? What's the matter?"

"Someone is looking for you. You must go to the Seeing Room at once. I can stay in your stead to help with the meal." Having grown up in Lumania and never seen the world beyond, Pala spoke in a peculiar sort of way, just like many others of this realm.

"Sure, I'll go right away," Nirmala said. Then looking up at Pala, "Sure you'll be okay?" People were starting to trickle into the hall by now, and the children had already begun to line up.

Pala nodded confidently and took her place in the stall. Thus assured, Nirmala hurried away through the crowd. The halls and passages stood empty at this hour, since all their occupants were gathering around in the Dining Hall for lunch. So, Nirmala was at the Seeing Room in no time. A guard at the door lead her inside.

There were no Seers in the room right now, so their abandoned Seeing Crystals lay strewn about the floor in a cornucopia of colour. At the centre of the room sat Mercuriva, as was customary, and in front of her a writhing, struggling figure floated in mid-air. As this floating person's face came into clearer focus, Nirmala's head began to spin out of control.

"Let me go! Put me down! Oof! This is not funny!" The suspended person was saying.

Nirmala ran across the room to him. "Haresh! Oh my God! What are you doing here?"

"Ask *him*," Haresh said, pointing at the Lumanian guard in front of him, a tall man Nirmala had not noticed until now. "All I wanted was to see you. And this dude locked me in his gravity beam or whatever."

Nirmala turned to Mercuriva with a pleading look in her eyes. "Wise One, please. He's my student."

Mercuriva smiled and nodded, before turning to the guard, who held Haresh captive. "You can release him."

Nirmala watched as Haresh was carefully lowered to the floor, where he landed with a thump and immediately regained mobility. "Ouch. The floor is cold," Haresh murmured a complaint.

Mercuriva looked down at her former prisoner with compassion in her eyes. "Have you eaten, Young One?" She asked gently. "You look pale."

Haresh shook his head from side to side, not daring to accost the Lumanians with any further spoken words. "Please, bring our guest some food," Mercuriva ordered her guard, who bowed and walked away.

Nirmala walked cautiously up to Haresh and sat cross-legged on the floor across from him. "What has happened, my friend? Why are you here?"

Haresh quivered slightly as tears burst forth from his eyes uninvited. He dabbed at his eyes and face with the corner of his sleeve and whimpered.

Nirmala placed a hand on his shoulder comfortingly. "There, there. Tell us. You are among friends here. We can help you." As she was saying this, the tall Lumanian guard had returned with a companion, both carrying trays of food from the lunch room. They stopped in front of the duo and gently floated the plates down to the floor, using their trademarked telekinesis.

Haresh greedily snatched an apple from the nearest plate and bit into it. After finishing the apple, he seemed to have calmed down slightly. He straightened his back and began speaking. "I was travelling with Dr. Sinha last week. He said he had found a new lead in his research and needed to go to Mathura to pursue it."

"Mathura, as in the city? The birthplace of Lord Krishna?" Nirmala asked.

"Correct. Since you were away, he asked me if I'd like to come with him. He said that he was getting old and frail and too shaky to travel alone. I agreed right away of course, and we set off to Mathura. The journey was mostly uneventful. We stayed at a hotel close to the temple and met with some other historians on the first day. Dr. Sinha wanted to examine the ancient temple, before we left. His plan was to take some pictures there and study them later. So, on the second day, I packed all my photography equipment and together we headed to the temple." Haresh fell silent and stared pensively at the floor.

"Go on, Haresh. What happened at the temple?" Nirmala urged.

Haresh's eyes shot to hers. "We didn't make it there."

"Oh! How come?"

"The auto rickshaw Dr. Sinha had hired to take us to the temple, did not take us there at all. But instead, to an abandoned store at the back of a dingy alley. Two thugs were waiting for us inside that store. They looked like foreigners and they wanted us to hand over the weapon of Krishna."

"The weapon of Krishna?"

"Yeah, that's what they said. When we told them that we didn't know what they were talking about, they snatched Dr. Sinha's satchel with all his research inside. I grabbed Dr. Sinha's hand and tried to make a run for it. But I guess that was a mistake." He bent his head and started sobbing again.

Nirmala patted his shoulder. "Oh dear," she said. "Did they attack you?"

Haresh nodded. "We had made it out of the store and quite a bit into the rundown alley, when they started shooting at us. We dodged the first few bullets, until one of them found its mark."

Nirmala gave out a short squeak and covered her mouth with her hands. "Did Dr. Sinha get hit?"

"Yes."

"My God! I should go see him—"

"You can't. Because he's dead." Haresh was sniffling again. "He died in my arms, before I could get him out of there."

"Oh no!" Nirmala leaned forward and wrapped her student in a warm embrace. "I'm so sorry Haresh. So, so sorry." For a moment both of them remained silent, with Haresh sobbing into Nirmala's shoulder. Then, she pulled away and wiped her eyes. "How did you manage to get out of there after that?"

"Someone on the street must have heard the commotion and called the cops. Because just as Dr. Sinha fell, I saw cops running towards the scene. A crowd of other people also started to arrive. The perpetrators stopped shooting and fled, with the police rushing behind them.

But the crowd descended on me. I was too scared to face their questioning. So, I too started running in the opposite direction. While I ran, I called Dr. Sinha's home and told his son what happened and asked him to get there immediately. I saw some of the locals taking Dr. Sinha's body to a hospital, but I couldn't manage to get to the ambulance in time. I knew right away that my life was still at risk. Since I was a witness, and the one that got away. They'd come after me, the Aifra."

"So, you came here, to Lumania." Nirmala completed.

"I wanted to tell you what had happened, but you weren't picking up your phone. So, I imagined you would be here, or at least the Lumanians could tell me where you went. Besides, what better place is there than Lumania for someone who needs to go into hiding? With this in mind, I traveled to the Lumanian secret entrance, the one we had used when we had come here last time, and they let me in."

"You did the right thing Haresh. You will be safe here."

"But I can't stay here. Not forever anyway. I have a life outside this world. And you do too. We need to go back as soon as it's safe again. Everyone's looking for you. Xianbin has been calling me every single day. You can't just abandon the Novo-Hekameses." Haresh pleaded with her to see reason.

"I ... don't want to abandon ... it wasn't my decision, Haresh. You must understand ..." Nirmala looked at Haresh and then at Mercuriva beseechingly, hoping for either one of them to feed her with the appropriate words that should come after this.

Mercuriva did in fact, do that. "You know, Nirmala, you do not necessarily have to go back to your team to continue with their training. There is another way."

"And what would that be, Wise One?"

"You could bring them here to Lumania. If they agree, that is."

"Really? Are you sure your people will be okay with this?"

Mercuriva smiled mysteriously. "If we follow procedure and examine their minds for corruption, before we admit them, then I do not see why not."

Nirmala turned to Haresh. "Well, what do you think?"

Haresh shrugged. "I'll have to ask the others. But I'm sure they'll agree to come, at least temporarily. The question is, do we have to stay here forever?"

"No. In Lumania, you can come and go as you like, once you're accepted," Nirmala clarified in true Lumanian fashion, eliciting a small chuckle from the Elder.

"In that case, I have no problem. And I don't think anyone else would mind either."

"Very well then," Mercuriva said. "Since your communication devices will not work inside our tunnels, you will have to go outside to contact the others. Nirmala will show you the way. In the meantime, please feel free to roam around, while we find you a suitable lodging." She bowed in the traditional Lumanian way, signalling their dismissal.

Nirmala grabbed a large plate of food with one hand and Haresh's arm with the other, leading him out the door. Once outside, she walked up to a stone bench, set underneath a miniature hanging garden, less than fifty feet away. She set the plate down on the bench and sighed. "It's a bad omen, all of this. Dr. Sinha's death. The Aifra stealing all his research. Everything."

Haresh, who had sat himself down and was now munching on a massive slice of handmade Lumanian bread, nodded. "I agree. The Aifra didn't get everything though."

"What do you mean?" Nirmala looked surprised.

"When I ran, I still had my backpack with the camera and a bunch of pictures and footage. It also had a notebook with some of Dr. Sinha's recent findings scribbled into it."

"Oh? So, where is it?"

"When I came here, the Lumanians took it. But I'm sure, we can ask for it back."

CHAPTER FOURTEEN

Zoya and Yuri's quest to find the shrine of the Frozen Saint was on its fourth day, when the weather began to turn violently against them. Wet snow and sleet pelted them from all directions, as the wind cut through the steep ridges of the Primorsky Range, stabbing them like a million little knives. Zoya pulled the hood of her jacket lower, to cover as much of her face as possible and trudged through the icy, gravelly path, trying to stay right behind Yuri, who was lumbering on ahead of her.

They had walked like this for two hours now, but there was no sign of any possible shrine or any shelter in sight, anywhere near them. Zoya did not know how much further she could continue like this, without going limp from the cold, like a felled log. She rubbed her gloved hands together for a warmth that escaped her all the same. "Yuri, are you sure this is the right way?" she yelled at the top of her lungs, cupping her mouth with her hands.

"I don't know. But right now, this is the only way," Yuri turned to shout. "If we turn back now, we'll be drawn into

the eye of the storm. If we keep going, it'll clear up ahead."
He stopped to allow Zoya to catch up.

"How do you know all this?"

Yuri shrugged. "Years of experience. So, do you want to
keep going?"

"Might as well. Not like there's a hotel waiting for us
back there either."

"Good. The place I'm trying to find shouldn't be far. I
can't be sure that it's the shrine you're looking for, but my
guess is that, it could be. In any case, if it isn't a shrine, it's
still a cave, where we can take shelter for the night."

Zoya, who was sitting down on a boulder, stood up.
"Okay, let's go then."

"Grab my hand," Yuri offered. "That way, you won't
fall behind."

Zoya grabbed his hand and stepped forward into the
driving snow. Just as Yuri had predicted, the storm seemed
to die down, as they winded further and further up the
mountain. Their progress was slow at first, but improved
with the abating gusts of wind. In another half an hour or
so, they were completely clear of the storm and a rosy pre-
sunset sky greeted them in its full splendour.

The view from here was breathtaking. The crystalline
waters of the Baikal sparkled below the cliffs like a
ginormous natural mirror. Gleaming its way all the way up
to the horizon, endless like the universe. For a moment,
Zoya forgot why she was even here. That she was on a
mission. That her life had any specific goal at all. Instead,
all she wanted right now, was to be alive in the moment,
floating through the fabric of existence like a cottony
cloud, drifting through the sky. She thought about
Alejandro, and his weird logic of living like driftwood, of
going where the tide carried him. And for the first time

since they had had this conversation, she began to see the beauty and simplicity of that philosophy.

Yuri's voice broke her trance. "You see that ledge over there?" he was saying, pointing at a flat area of rock down a steep rocky path from where they stood. "That's where we need to go. Where the cave used to be."

"What are we waiting for then?" Zoya smiled. "Let's go!" She hurried ahead without him, but he quickly caught up. Zoya skid along the path, stumbling over loose rocks and gravel, arriving at the bottom, on her haunches.

"Ha! Vey graceful," Yuri teased, as he alighted next to her as elegantly as a ballet-dancer.

"Very funny!" Zoya scolded. "I'm not used to these mountains. I'm from California. Be nice."

"I know, I know." Yuri extended his hand to help her up, which she accepted graciously and stood up.

The ledge dropped steeply down the far end and was bordered by the mountain wall on the other. Yuri scrunched his face and scanned the area. "This way," he then said, walking east. Here, the mountain wall was slightly concave and covered with layers of compact snow. Yuri ran his palm up and down the wall of snow, as if searching for something, before turning around to face Zoya. "Huh, I was sure it used to be over here," he huffed.

"Maybe we have to open it with magic, like in a fantasy movie," Zoya offered. Although she was joking, given what she now knew about otherworldly things, a part of her realized, that there was a hint of truth in that statement.

Yuri, however, found it funny and laughed. "I don't know what to do. Maybe this is not the right one. We could find a cave to rest in tonight and keep looking tomorrow."

"Hmm." Zoya furrowed her eyebrows thoughtfully. "This snow doesn't look like it has been here very long. I mean, it doesn't look dirty."

"But that's impossible. It'd take time for snow this thick to accumulate and solidify."

Zoya shook her head. "Perhaps this snow didn't accumulate at all. Let me try something." She removed her backpack and placed it against the mountain wall. Then, she stepped back a few steps and bent forward like a puma about to pounce. In a second, she had lunged at the wall of snow, landing a perfect karate kick right at the weak spot around the centre.

What happened next, surprised them both. The wall of snow collapsed partially in on itself, with chunks of it falling on Zoya and burying her underneath them. Yuri shrieked and rushed to her side. Shovelling snow with both his hands, he dug her out from under the chunks, that broke off the wall. "Are you crazy? What were you thinking? You are so rash!" he berated, while pulling her up from the ground.

"I know," Zoya said in a small voice, dusting snow off her jacket. She had landed directly on top of a cluster of rocks that could have split open her skull, had it not been for the padded hood of her down-jacket. "I've been called that before," she added meekly, blushing as she spoke.

"Called what? Rash? Crazy? Reckless?" Yuri grilled.

"All of the above."

"By whom? Chris?"

"And others. But yes, also Chris," Zoya admitted, without any sense of embarrassment this time. She knew there was no need to blush at the mention of Chris' name, because he was nothing more than a brother to her. Someone who had saved her life. Someone who she looked up to and respected deeply, but as a friend, mentor and guide.

"And you didn't care to listen? To any of them?"

"Well, I tried but … I'm sorry, okay? Can we focus on the problem at hand now, please?" Zoya pleaded with genuine sincerity. Then, she crawled up to the cave wall to inspect her handiwork.

Yuri grunted something inaudible, and walked up to stand by her side. Despite all the snow that tumbled out of it, the through-hole Zoya had made in the wall with her kick, did not appear to be very large. The snow that had fallen, was mostly the outer layers of the wall, coming loose in large patches.

Yuri plunged his fist into the opening and began to scrape out the snow from around it. Zoya came over to join him. Soon, they had made the passage large enough for the two of them to crawl through; which they did. Inside, they found the cave, they had been looking for. Yuri stood up and fishing a flashlight out of his backpack, lit it. If this had once been a shrine of some sort, no evidence still remained of its existence.

Yuri sighed and sat down on the floor. "Seems like this was a waste of time, after all. It's an ordinary cave. Nothing special about it."

"But then, why would someone block the entrance to it with layers and layers of packed snow?" Zoya asked, coming over to sit next to him.

"How do you know they did that? That this was not natural snow?"

Zoya rolled her eyes. "I thought you were the pro when it came to understanding nature. Do you honestly think that a cave you had visited on your treks, not that long ago, would get blocked up by *this* much snow, in such a short period of time?"

Now it was Yuri's turn to blush. "I … well, if there's a

really nasty winter … nah, you're right, it has to be man-made," he reasoned with himself. "But why?"

"That's exactly my point, isn't it?"

Yuri smiled. "You may be rash, but you definitely are smart. By the way, I'm sorry that I yelled at you. I didn't mean to. I just wanted you to understand that the wilderness is unpredictable and unforgiving, and no place to pull a stunt like that."

Zoya edged closer to him and gently placed her hand on his. "I know. And when I said that I was sorry, I meant it." Outside, the sun was setting rapidly and an eerie reddish light creeped into the hollow of the cave, turning the setting inside into a portrait in sepia.

"But you know something, this is also what makes you interesting. From the moment I met you, I was impressed. You're so brave, adventurous, unpredictable."

"Am I now?"

Yuri nodded. "You are … what do you call it … an enema."

Zoya did a spit take on the water she was drinking. Then, she bent over double and clutching her stomach laughed like she hadn't in a very long time.

"What's wrong. What did I say?" Yuri asked, when she had stopped laughing.

"Enigma. The word you're looking for is enigma. Enema, on the other hand, means a whole different thing. And believe me, you don't want to go there." She reached out and squeezed his arm lovingly.

Yuri nodded, a crooked smile across his face. "How about we have something to eat and rest tonight? We can continue our search tomorrow," he said, yawning.

"Sounds like a plan!" Zoya said, hurrying to her backpack to rummage for the food items she had pilfered from the last hiker's cabin they had occupied.

They made a light meal out of the bread and cheese and slices of ham, Zoya found in her bag, and hit the sack early, for some much-needed rest. Although they were completely exhausted from the last leg of their hike, Zoya struggled to fall asleep. There was something about this cave that disturbed her. As darkness fell, she felt a presence in their midst, not a fear of darkness, but something else— an energy so profound, that it reeked of ancient magic.

She wanted to wake Yuri up and tell him about this. But she was afraid that he would think she was merely scared of the dark. Yuri, after all, was not privy to much of the things she knew about magic and supernatural powers. About the Hekameses and the Lumanians. About forces much stronger and darker than the two. The energy she felt tonight, was definitely of the latter variety, dark and ominous, unyielding, and potentially dangerous beyond their imagination.

Zoya tossed and turned, contemplating whether she should contact the others, Alejandro or Wanda perhaps, and ask them to come here. They would have a better understanding of what it was in this cave, that she felt so acutely with her senses like a living, breathing thing. But before she could act on this impulse, the sun rose, slowly lifting the gloom that had encompassed her all night.

Zoya stood up, finally abandoning any hope of catching some sleep. In the pale, pearly light that trickled in, the cave walls came into clearer focus than last night. There were engravings on them, words etched in a strange runic language. Words that called to Zoya with such conviction, that she could not help but walk right up to them. Reaching out with the palm of her right hand, she touched a rune and yelped in pain.

"What happened?" Yuri grabbed her wrist and turned it over. Zoya had been so engrossed in her trancelike walk up to the engraved runic message, that she had failed to notice him coming up to her. There were red welts where the rune had seared into her skin and scorched her.

"I don't know," Zoya mumbled, and before she could stop him, Yuri flattened his palm against the wall tracing the outline of the said rune with his fingers. "Nooo!" Zoya screamed. "It's scorching hot!"

Yuri turned to her in surprise. "No, it isn't. Look," he held up his palms for inspection. They were flawlessly white and unmarked.

"Oh?" Zoya reached out and touched the wall again, jumping back so hard this time that she nearly knocked Yuri over. "Owww! Oww!" She stared at her palm, where a fresh blister was beginning to raise its nasty head.

Yuri rushed to his backpack and brought out his first-aid kit. Then, while applying Polysporin to her bruise, he whispered, "I don't understand. Why does it hurt you and not me?"

Zoya was silent for a bit, staring blankly at her hand, as Yuri wrapped a bandage around it. "I think, I understand," she finally said, looking up.

"I'm sorry?"

"I understand why it hurts me, but not you. I also understand what these runes are."

"You do? What are they?"

"They're not runes at all, but hieroglyphics—the text on the wall is an Egyptian script of some sort."

"And how may I ask, did you come to that conclusion?" Yuri quizzed, standing with his arms akimbo.

"It's a hunch," Zoya lied. "I do know someone, who can tell us for sure though."

"Who?"

"My department head at Stanford. She's a bit of an expert on hieroglyphs. Don't ask me how. Could you take a picture of the script with your phone?"

"Sure." Yuri took out his phone and started clicking pictures. "But this still doesn't explain why it hurts you, but not me."

"I think, it might have something to do with the fact, that my parents brought me here, to this temple, to beg for my life. Hieroglyphics can have some sort of weird memory or something." Zoya shrugged. "I dunno. They are strange! I only know bits and pieces from what Dr. Faraday, my prof, has mentioned from time to time. And I could be way off. We have to ask her."

"Wait, so you *do* think this is the temple? The shrine of the Frozen Saint, where your parents brought you, all those years ago?"

"At night, I couldn't really tell. But now, having seen the interior of this cave more clearly and especially after what just happened with the runes, I'm fairly certain that it is. I've seen it in my dreams over and over again."

"Wow! Interesting." Yuri plonked to the floor. "So, the question is, where is the man to whom it belonged? The Frozen Saint himself?"

"Not sure. And I have a feeling, that we don't want to stick around to find out. If this *is*, in fact, his shrine and he *has* indeed raised people from the dead, then he is a man of terrible and wicked power, that we should avoid meeting at all costs."

"I agree. Let's head out then. We have at least a day's journey ahead of us, before we reach the izba we had been in earlier."

"Here." Zoya tossed Yuri a granola bar from her stash.

"This will help us hold out for a while."

Yuri ripped the wrapper and tossed it aside, biting into the juicy blueberry flavoured treat. "Let's go," he said, through a mouthful of granola.

It was a clear morning outside, with tiny globules of frost hanging from the empty branches around them. Zoya trudged along absentmindedly, her mind still buzzing with a million questions. She pulled out her phone to see if she could get a message over to Wanda, but as was expected, there was no signal on her phone.

Last year, they had searched Siberia in vain looking for a possible Aifra hideout. But instead of finding it, they had stumbled into a whole new civilization—the kingdom of Lumania. Zoya knew that their failure to discover the Aifra hideout did not necessarily mean, that it was not nearby. It just meant, that they had missed it for whatever reason.

Now, she had a nagging suspicion, that whoever had blocked the entrance to the Frozen Saint's shrine, belonged to the Aifra or had deep ties to their organization. What did this mean for the Frozen Saint's identity? If Aifra wanted to hide the clues to his existence, then he was no sacred soul, but an evil entity, capable of wreaking havoc upon the world. Her parents had told her, that they had not seen the Frozen Saint with their own eyes, just felt his presence. Zoya had come back to life miraculously inside this cave, and her parents had attributed this to the magic of the Frozen Saint. This did not prove one way or the other, that the Saint was still alive. In her heart of hearts, Zoya prayed that he wasn't.

As she was lumbering along thus, lost in thought, tired to her very bones from a severe lack of sleep, the sound of a gun shot halted her motion.

"What was—" she was about to say, when Yuri grabbed

her by the arm and tugged hard.

"Run!" he said, "Someone's shooting at us!"

Zoya flicked her head around at these words, and surely enough, she saw two people behind them, guns raised. "Stop!" one of them said in a male voice. "Or we'll gun you down where you stand."

Zoya instinctively raised her hands over her head and stood still. From the corner of her eye, she noticed that Yuri hesitated at first, before following her lead. Their attackers were behind them, and Zoya was too scared to turn around and look. From the sound of footsteps behind her, however, she realized that they were approaching quickly. Within a minute, the distance between them had been closed and the cold, hard muzzle of a gun touched the back of Zoya's head.

"Move," said a hoarse male voice. "And don't you dare look back."

CHAPTER FIFTEEN

Chris walked in to the stunning Duke Humfrey's reading room of the Gothic Bodleian Library at Oxford University, with its high, painted ceiling and searched around for a familiar face. Being a Saturday morning, it was relatively deserted, with most students still in their dorms, hungover from their Friday night revelries. Chris passed one oaken-bookshelf after another, scanning all the reading tables in-between, as the faces of the founders stared sternly down at him, from the many portraits along the walls.

Finally, at the very back of the room, tucked away behind a huge stack of books, he found the elderly lady he was looking for. "Wanda," he said, coughing to clear his throat. The nook Wanda had chosen this morning, smelled wonderfully of moth-eaten covers and crisp parchment.

Wanda lowered her glasses to her nose and looked up from above them. "Ah, my boy. What brings you here?"

"It's just," he pulled up a chair to sit beside her, "I tried contacting Nirmala. To see if she got home safely."

"Tried?" Wanda furrowed her brows. "Did you not reach her?"

Chris shook his head. "No matter how many times I dialled, her phone seemed to be switched off."

"That's odd."

"It is. It could be that, she's mad at us. I mean, she wasn't at all happy about being sent away."

"Hmm. I do not blame her. If I was here when Alejandro made this decision, I would have stopped him. Nevertheless, I do think, Nirmala is a sensible young lady, who would not suddenly avoid all her friends, due to the folly of just one."

"You're probably right. What do you suggest we do then?"

"I think we should contact the Lumanians, to see if they know anything. They are, after all, far wiser than all of us and have powerful Seeing Crystals, that can look into the past and present and sometimes even the future."

Chris nodded. "I agree. But the problem is that, there's no quick way to reach them. No phones. No internet. The only way I can think of to get a message through, is by snail mail to a PO Box address in Moscow. They send someone to check it, once every few days. That's their only link to the outside world, as far as I'm aware."

"Sometimes, being expedient is better than being expeditious," Wanda said sombrely.

"I Iuh? Never mind. I'll get that letter out to her then. And in the meantime, I'll try to see if there's any other way, I can trace her. Perhaps, Marshal Panday could help." Chris began to rise from his seat, but Wanda grabbed his arm to stop him.

"While you're here, there is something I wanted to

show you as well," she said.

"Oh okay, what is it?"

"Look at this. Do you recognize this man?" Wanda slid over a black-and-white photograph that was yellowing around the edges. Chris picked it up and saw a princely young man standing by an antique marble table, decorated with a brass flower vase. The man's face looked oddly familiar, yet Chris could not put his finger on where exactly he had seen him. "No?" Wanda asked again, noticing his confusion.

"Umm … I wanna say, yes. But … it can't be. The guy I'm thinking of, is much younger."

"And who might that be?"

"Well, he looks a little like that angry General from Wolfgang's memories."

"Yes, Irene Costas was able to identify him. His name is Józef Sapieha."

"I see. So, I wasn't wrong. Is the man in the picture an ancestor of his?"

"No. It *is* him."

Chris' eyes widened with shock. He flipped the picture around in his palm, and saw a handwritten note at the bottom, Józef Sapieha, 5th October 1932. Oh my God! What is he? A child of Heka? A Lumanian?"

"Possibly worse."

"How so?"

"That is what I came here to find out this morning. And this is what I have discovered so far; the gentleman whose picture you hold in your hand, was a Polish-Lithuanian noble, one of many who had rebelled against the German and Russian occupation of Poland, around the time of the Second World War. He was caught and exiled in Siberia, where he died in a Russian gulag, without leaving any heir."

"So, he can't possibly have any direct descendants," Chris mused. "Is it possible that he is an uncle of his modern-day namesake?"

"Namesake and doppelgänger," Wanda corrected. Then, after a brief pause, "Could be, but it's unlikely. These records seem to say that his family line has died out, having participated in the revolt against the Polish occupation and been captured and killed."

"But then, how?"

"I don't know," Wanda said, grimly.

"Do you think Wolfgang would have figured this out by now?"

"Being that he is currently a prisoner of the Aifra, I do not think so."

"Maybe, I should request a meeting with the Lumanians, when I write to them about Nirmala. They are ancient enough to be able shed some light on—"

Wanda raised her hand to stop him. "No. Not yet. The Lumanians are an aloof race. If we involve them in our problems, more often than is necessary, then we might alienate them, which is not what we want."

"So, what should we do then?"

"Nothing. Other than planning for Wolfgang's escape on March 25th. To that end, I suggest you add a note to Kazhar, when you write to him. Ask him to expect Wolfgang at the Moscow State University on that date. Although, I am fairly confident, that they would let him in, even without any prior information. They know that he's one of us, and the Lumanian Seers monitor that campus constantly. They would surely spot him and let him through. But we cannot leave these things merely to chance. So, go on. Please, send along that message, and let us wait till we find Wolfgang, before delving further into the General's mysterious past."

"Got it." Chris nodded, standing to leave.

* * *

Wolfgang found Alex, smoking at his usual spot on a hillock near camp, the morning after he arrived from Aleppo. He walked up to his friend and took a seat on the boulder beside him. "There you are!" he said.

Alex turned his head and smiled. "What's the plan? How do we get outta here? Did you figure it out?"

"Well, yes and no."

"Please don't tell me, we have to kidnap your teammates first."

Wolfgang sighed. "Not you. Just me."

"Hang on, you gotta be kidding me. You can't really be handing them over in exchange for our freedom!"

"Don't worry, I'm not a monster. Everything's going to be fine. But the reason I came to see you is, because I have some bad news."

"Let's hear it."

"When I told the General about my plan, the one that will help us get away, he insisted that I take another Aifra soldier with me. Someone who can fight. Which was perfect and played right into my hands. I wanted him to say that, so that I can get you to join me. Naturally, I suggested your name. You are the most suitable choice for this operation, because we need a military veteran, who can fly Russian crafts, and someone who can work well with me—"

"Let's cut to the chase," Alex interrupted. "My break is nearly over. He refused, didn't he?"

Wolfgang nodded gloomily. "This morning he assigned someone else."

"That piece of shit!" Alex cursed under his breath. "I could've told you; he'd do that. He doesn't trust anyone. Especially not *me*. Mark my words, the guy he's sending with you, will also be strapped with explosives. If either of you go astray, then both of you go kaput!"

"Hmm. A suicide bomber?" Wolfgang looked like he saw a ghost.

Alex nodded glumly.

"I believe you," Wolfgang muttered.

"Why didn't you play your little tricks on his mind? That was the only way, we could've gotten assigned together."

"I thought I did … I mean … I had, on the day we discussed this in person. I need to have eye-contact to plant a memory. But somehow, after I left, he overcame it. Which is unusual. Not unheard of, but unusual. It would take an individual of incredible mental strength to overwrite the memories, I plant in their heads. If only, I had a little longer with him that day, I could have planted a stronger memory." Wolfgang rubbed his chin thoughtfully.

"Interesting. Could he be one of your kind, perhaps? And therefore, more difficult to manipulate?"

Wolfgang shrugged. "I don't know. I'll have to look into it. But for that, first, I need to be free. So, back to our original issue—the matter of our escape—it seems extremely likely, that you may not be joining me that day. Your only role in this mission will be, to train your substitute to fly a Russian craft."

"And? How do we get around this?"

Wolfgang didn't respond. Instead, he looked up at his

friend with weary, remorseful eyes.

Alex suddenly stood up. Beads of sweat were pooling around the crook of his neck. With a single finger, he pulled at the collar of his tee, as if to free himself from its stranglehold. "What are you saying Wolfgang?" he whispered, horrified. "You're going to leave me here, aren't you?"

"Not for long. I'll come back for you." Then, after a pause. "It's the only way."

Alex let out a dry chuckle. "Huh! And what do I have as an assurance? A gentleman's promise? Is that all you've got? After everything we've been through?"

Wolfgang stood up to his full height and looked him straight in the eyes. "Look, Alex, try to be reasonable. This is no time for a fight between allies. As a military man, I thought you'd know this better than me. If you can't get yourself to trust me, then how about this," he paused a second, before continuing, "how about you trust your leverage? Your leverage over me."

"What do you mean?"

"There are things you know about me. You know who I am, my true identity. You know about my team. You know how my powers work. All of this is information. And information is leverage. You can exchange it for your freedom, when the time comes. The only reason you haven't done so already is that, you trust me. Trust me because I freed you, when I didn't have to. Because, I never used my powers to bend you to my will, although I easily could have. Because … because, we are *friends*." Wolfgang fell silent. "So, if I ever I do anything to betray that trust, I am yours to betray in return."

Alex scratched his head. "Okay. And how long do you want me to wait, before I act?"

"One month. Give me one month to get you out."

Alex sat down on a boulder and scrunched his face, deep in thought.

"Do we have a deal?" Wolfgang prodded.

Alex looked up slowly, his eyes swimming with faceless fears. "Fifteen days. You'll have fifteen days, before I start raising hell."

CHAPTER SIXTEEN

That night, Alex lay awake in his bunk, under a barren concrete roof inside the underground camp in Aleppo, contemplating his options. He did not want to doubt Wolfgang, whom he had grown to understand and love. But as a military man, he knew better than to trust a stranger completely, especially in a hostile situation such as this.

He stared blankly at the bunks across from him, where about a dozen other lowly soldiers of his battalion lay fast asleep. Stripped of his former rank and position, here he had been relegated to the bottom-most level of the military pyramid. This was not even the real military by any stretch of the imagination. It was a dangerously powerful terrorist organization. Thus, he had never really invested any time, getting to know any of his comrades here. Neither had they, in turn, shown any interest in getting to know him.

All the Aifra soldiers he had met so far, were like zombies—grim and reticent, mindlessly following orders and never stopping to think twice. Nothing about their demeanour had interested him in getting to know them better. Every morning, he had woken up, brushed, shaved, showered and participated in the morning drills. Then, he had reported to whatever duty was assigned to him that day, from assisting with combat training for new recruits, to overseeing repairs of military aircrafts and tanks.

He had never asked, like he used to in the army, why he has doing all of this, or what was their end-goal or strategy. Here, he had never bothered to learn these things, because in his heart, he had always known that he was never really an Aifra soldier—only pretending to be one, until they could secure their release. Wolfgang had assured him that he had a solid plan for their escape, and he had been working on it, ever since they had gotten to Syria. Today, all of that had fallen apart with Wolfgang's announcement that he was, in fact, planning to escape, but without Alex.

Alex mentally cursed himself for not having done his due diligence from day one. He had feared that he would be killed, once his decision to call off the attack on Moscow at the last minute, was discovered. And that is exactly why, he had recorded his confession in an USB and left it for Wolfgang in his will. So that the world would know, how he had stood up against the bloodthirsty and warmongering General Sapieha and ultimately laid down his life for the greater good, having exposed his machinations to the public.

Everything changed when he did not die, but continued to live as a captive of the Aifra. Now, he wished dearly that he had, in fact, died that day. Death would have been undoubtedly a better fate than the torment he was going through right now. The only caveat to this was Irene. Every time he closed his eyes, he could see her innocent, beautiful face staring up at him. He desperately longed to see her again. So terrible was his longing, that he was afraid to fall asleep, lest her memories came back to haunt him in his dreams, as they did in the hours of his waking, for then he would have no distraction to drive them away.

Alex's train of thought was broken as the door to their stark room opened with a bang and two hefty men barged in. In the coarse yellow light, that streamed in through the open door, Alex could see that they were Aifra soldiers armed with assault rifles.

"Caleb! Caleb! Which one of you is Caleb?" the soldier on the right yelled, while the other one turned on the lights.

Alex sat up in his berth and squinted. Around him, he could see ashen faces poking out from the other bunks, their darting eyes taking in the unfolding scene with horror. No one identified himself as Caleb and neither did anyone give Caleb away. For seconds, there was a deathly silence, and then a soft scurrying sound from close to the door, drew Alex's attention. A skinny young man in his underwear had slipped from his berth and was edging towards the door.

The soldier closer to him turned around and grabbing the escapee, tackled him roughly to the floor. "Are you Caleb? ARE YOU?" he hollered.

"Please … please, Sir, I'm sorry," the young man mewled, writhing and contorting on the cold cement floor. Upon closer inspection, he did not appear to be any older than in his late teens.

The other armed soldier stepped forward and with the butt of his rifle smacked him across the face with force. There was a cracking sound, like a jaw breaking and blood pooled onto the floor, forming dark glistening puddles. "We asked you, if you were Caleb," the attacker said through gritted teeth.

The young man nodded meekly in response, his shattered face swelling rapidly. Alex averted his eyes to prevent himself from throwing up. With his peripheral vision, he could see the soldiers drag the boy to his feet and shove him roughly towards the door. "Come," one of them said, "you have been chosen." He walked out with his captive.

The other soldier turned to face the room and said in a low, menacing growl, "Try something funny like he did, and you're gonna be next." Sticking his index finger out, he pointed randomly at the various occupants of the room. Alex heard someone next to him swallow nervously. Then, the soldiers were gone.

A chilling silence descended in their wake. No one stirred. Not even to switch off the now blaring lights. Everyone was awake, sitting cross-legged on their bunks or wiping the sweat off their brows with the sleeves of their shirts. Some stole furtive glances at one another. Alex caught one of them in the act of sneaking a peak at him, a lanky black man named Ahmed. He held his gaze for a moment, before twitching nervously and turning away. Alex took this opportunity to strike a conversation.

"What was that about?" he asked, looking directly at Ahmed, but Ahmed did not venture a response. Instead, he glanced around the room, to gauge the reactions of the others.

The man from the berth just below Ahmed's, a stocky white fellow with dense body hair, looked up at Alex. "Caleb's been chosen," he said simply, like it was a process, as natural as sleeping or waking.

"Chosen for what?"

Ahmed stared at him like he was from outer space. "The

blood sacrifice, of course," he said at last.

The stout man turned to Ahmad. "He's new. He doesn't know."

Ahmad nodded with understanding. "It happens when anyone steps out of line. You know, like disobeys orders or tries to run."

"The worst is betrayal," someone said from the bunk below Alex's. "The chick from the women's camp last week was caught trying to contact the cops."

"Oh yeah?" the stout man asked. "Did they ship her to the Commander in Chief?"

"Last week," the other man replied.

"Who's the Commander in Chief?" Alex asked, rather stupidly.

All eyes turned to him. "Our leader, of course!" Ahmed explained. "He conducts a blood sacrifice once every month. It's a huge ritual. Several bad apples are chosen for each, and a public execution takes place. You're chosen to watch, if you're lucky and chosen to die, if you're not." Alex cringed involuntarily. "It's not a pretty sight," Ahmad continued, noticing Alex's reaction. "If you want to avoid going through it, then you better stay loyal, Sergeant."

"Lieutenant Colonel, actually," Alex corrected.

Low chuckles erupted from across the room. "Nobody cares about that here," the hairy white man remarked.

"What *do* you care about then, Comrade?" Alex asked, trying to lighten the mood.

"The same things we all want. To overthrow this corrupt world order, and build our kingdom of peace. To restore everything that science and greed has destroyed." The stout man glanced around the room at the others. "Isn't that right, boys? We're sick of these money-grabbing, world-destroying oligarchs!"

"Aye," grunted the man in the berth below Alex. Several other murmured agreements were heard.

Then, turning to Alex he asked abruptly. "What about you? What do *you* want?"

For a moment, Alex's heart stood so still that he feared it would fail to start up again, like a car left out on a winter night. Then, gathering his wits about him, he responded in a measured tone. "I joined the US Army when I was very young, because I had to. My mom died when I was fifteen. Soon, my dad remarried, and my stepmom wanted me to find my own place. I desperately needed a job, to be able to afford the move. The Army was hiring. So, I signed up. It was my road to salvation."

He paused to study his roommates' reactions. He knew that his life depended on being able to tell them a convincing story tonight. Everyone seemed to be listening attentively, so he continued. "But then the assignments began. One war after another that destroyed entire nations." He stopped to catch his breath. Murmurs rose up from around him.

"You regretted it, didn't you?" someone was saying.

"We can just look outside to see what they did here in Syria," someone else chimed in.

Several other voices rose up, all speaking at once and seeming to blend into one. Alex finally began to figure out what these people were all about. What Aifra was all about. It was about luring the lost and the wronged with the promise of a brighter future. It was about taking in the broken and offering to make them whole. No wonder, the helpless and the hapless were drawn to them like moths to a flame. "Yes, I regretted joining the army. And everything that followed." In his heart, he knew that this wasn't actually very far from the truth. A white lie, at best. "So, when my friend told me about the Aifra, I was determined to join, to redeem myself for what I had done." As Alex finished, a roar of applause rose from his audience. He had not realized, that what he had just recounted, would resonate with them so deeply. He had not even meant to give a rousing speech. He simply wanted to make his lie sound convincing enough to ensure his survival.

"Bravo! You did the right thing," the hairy man said, his face flushed with pride. Alex wondered if he saw the irony of what he was saying. Joining the Aifra did not and could not cure the world of its evils. In fact, it was as much a solution as dousing a burn wound with acid was any cure. Nevertheless, he kept his thoughts to himself for his own safety and smiled graciously instead.

"I think we should turn in." Ahmad yawned. The others nodded in agreement. Ahmad proceeded to turn off the lights without taking a second look at the still-warm rivulets of blood crisscrossing the floor. But even with the lights switched off, Alex's brain would not. Despite having seen a hundred horrors during the course of his long military career, Alex could not get his battle-hardened heart to condone what he had seen in this room tonight. No matter how much he wanted to mistrust Wolfgang therefore, he knew that he could not. Betraying him to the Aifra would be a sin from which no penance could ever redeem him.

CHAPTER SEVENTEEN

Alejandro was making breakfast in Wanda Faraday's kitchen, when someone walked in through the door. Ever since he had half-kidnapped, half-rescued Irene Costas from outside her home in New Jersey, she had mostly kept to herself and ordered take out from her room, only coming out to eat at the kitchen table or answer any questions the Hekameses had about her husband. But today, she walked in and sat down at the kitchen table, a broad smile across her face. Perhaps the assurance that her husband was still alive and might soon be rescued, had finally set her heart at ease.

"Good morning!" she said to Alejandro, who had turned around at the sound of her feet.

"Morning. Would you like some eggs? I'm making eggs."

"Sure, why not. It's a nice day, isn't it?"

"Mhm. How do you like your eggs?"

"Over easy, please. Thank you! Let me make some coffee." She got up and started pouring water into the

130

coffeemaker.

Alejandro brought over two plates of eggs and set them on the table, before going over to check on his toast. "Toast?" he asked over his shoulder.

"Just one. Is it brown bread?"

"Multigrain. That okay?"

"Yep, thanks." She filled two cups with the freshly brewed coffee and walked over. "I don't know if there's any cream or sugar—"

"There's half and half in the fridge and sugar is in the cupboard." Alejandro pointed above his head, while removing his bread from the toaster. "I'll take mine black, but feel free to help yourself."

Irene left Alejandro's coffee on the table and added some sugar to her own, before coming to sit down. Alejandro joined her momentarily, carrying a plate of toast. He bit into his toast, while flipping open the morning paper, that was lying next to his plate. He did not want to be rude, but at the same time did not really know, how to strike up a conversation with his normally withdrawn and mostly unfamiliar breakfast companion.

Irene watched him attentively as he read the paper, as if he was the subject of a psychological experiment. "You remind me a lot of my husband," she suddenly said, in an effort to break the ice.

"Hmm?" Alejandro looked up, slightly startled.

"I said … you are like my husband."

"Oh really? How so?"

"Well, you're silent, brave, often reckless." Holding her half-bitten toast at an angle away from her face, she chuckled.

"Believe me, I'm not that silent." He paused. "Nor that brave," he added, almost as an after thought.

"So, you admit that you're reckless then?" Irene continued to quiz.

Alejandro shrugged. "You miss him a lot, don't you? Your husband?"

Irene took a sip of her coffee and set the cup down. "We were on our honeymoon when he got called away."

Alejandro reached over and gently patted her hand. "I'm so sorry. I didn't know. Did you at least get to complete your honeymoon?" Alejandro could see that her eyes were moist when she looked up at him.

"Yeah, but we had to rush it." Then, after a pause, "You have no idea how happy I was, when you and your friends told me that you could bring him back. I never really thanked you for that properly."

"Hey, you should thank Wanda. She was the one that never really believed they were dead. I had almost given up …" Alejandro got up to wash his empty plate.

"I will. When I see her." Then after a brief pause, "Is there someone *you* miss? A wife or a girlfriend perhaps?"

Alejandro looked over his shoulder. "Why do you ask?"

"It's probably none of my business, but you just look like you're kinda … sad."

"My wife died a long time ago."

"Oh, I'm so sorry. But if it was a long time ago, you must surely have dealt with your grief by now. So, why do you still look so miserable?"

"I'm not miserable," Alejandro replied curtly.

Interpreting this as a signal to back off, Irene grabbed the newspaper from Alejandro's side of the table and began browsing through the headlines. "Ughh," she said after a minute.

"What?" Alejandro returned to his seat and sat down across from her.

"Some of these headlines are so morbid. Look at this." She flipped the paper around and pointed to a news item.

"Dead body stolen from a New York morgue, suspect at large," Alejandro read. "Hmm. Why would anyone steal a dead body?"

"I don't know," Irene said, but Alejandro didn't hear her, being deeply preoccupied with what he was reading.

"The rest of the article is inside," he mumbled, as he rapidly turned the pages. "Oh my God!" he shrieked upon opening that page. He placed the paper flat on the table and showed it to Irene. "This is the man, whose body went missing." He pointed to the said man's picture. "See if you can identify him."

Irene's face contorted with horror. "No! It can't be! Kevin's dead?"

"So, it *is* your lawyer, Kevin Gao then?"

"Of course! When did he die, and how? Does it say?"

"It doesn't say how, but it does say when," Alejandro said in a low voice. "And the date is what frightens me the most. Because … according to this, he died at least a week before he supposedly met with Wanda in New York."

Irene stood up and snatched the paper from Alejandro's hands. "But that can't be! I spoke to him even that morning."

Alejandro leaned towards her. "You are certain it was him? Was it his voice?"

"Unmistakably! I … I don't know what's happening here," she muttered, while staring wide-eyed at the article.

Just that minute, the doorbell rang, startling her enough that she dropped the paper. "Who is it?" she whispered with a hand over her heart.

"Oh, it's probably my friend Zoya. No need to be scared." Alejandro dismissed her concern with a wave of his hand and got up to answer the door. Irene however, did not seem at all comforted by Alejandro's assurance. The news about Kevin had rattled her deeply. So, she followed Alejandro out to the living room, sticking as close to him as possible.

Alejandro arrived at the front door and was about to open it to welcome Zoya, when something inexplicable stayed his hand. He peered into the peephole before answering. Standing on the porch, ringing the bell was no woman of nineteen, but a man. With his head bowed, he seemed to be inspecting something on the floor. Alejandro thought it had to be Zoya's father, Dr. Carter, here to tell him, that Zoya would not be coming back to stay at Wanda's place.

But then, the man looked up and Alejandro's heart nearly jumped out of his chest. He turned around slowly, almost in slow motion and looked at Irene with dread oozing from his eyes. Irene opened her mouth to speak, but Alejandro quickly silenced her with a finger to his lips. He grabbed her upper arm and ran towards the stairwell at the back.

Once at the top of the stairwell, Irene tugged on his arm to stop him. "Wha … what's wrong?" She panted; panic written across her face. "Who was at the door?"

"You wouldn't believe it, if I told you."

"Who?" Irene urged.

"It was Kevin Gao. We need to run!"

"But *where*?"

Alejandro did not respond. Instead, he scrambled down the stairwell leading to the basement, dragging her behind him. When they reached the landing at the end of the first flight of stairs, Irene stopped again. "Wait, stop!" she begged. "How are we going to escape from the basement?

Shouldn't we have used the back door?"

"No," Alejandro replied, while continuing down the steps without her. Then turning, "Are you coming or not?"

Irene followed reluctantly into the dark cavernous belly of the building. Arriving at the basement, Alejandro hurried over to a bookcase against the back wall. Moving aside a couple of books on a mid-level shelf, he pulled a lever. Immediately, the bookcase began to slide to the side and expose the entrance to a dark tunnel.

"A secret passage, huh?" Irene blurted out. "Like in a movie."

Alejandro flashed her a crooked smile, before reaching for a flashlight from one of the shelves. "C'mon. This passage leads to a safe-house. There's a car there, we can use to get away. Kevin will never be able to find us in time."

CHAPTER EIGHTEEN

Zoya walked along a narrow mountain path bordering a deep gorge, for what felt like hours. But it had probably not been that long. The silence and the cold, coupled with the gun to her head, made the minutes stretch on, longer than normal. They walked in a single file, with Yuri separated from her by several yards and her captor walking in between them. So, there was no way she could gauge his reaction.

Zoya knew that their captors were most likely the Aifra, and this calmed her in a weird way. After all, what man fears most is the unknown. Aifra being the known devil therefore, did not elicit that kind of a fear from her. Yuri however, did not have the same advantage. He would be scared out of his mind. Zoya hoped in her heart of hearts, that this did not drive him to do anything foolhardy.

A part of her regretted having brought him here, to begin with. Especially, without telling him, what they might be up against. Endangering his life was definitely not her goal. Now, she feared that Yuri would never be able to forgive her, once he realized that she had known about the Aifra being on her tail all along, and dragged him into it regardless. She did not quite understand why she cared so deeply about what he thought. They had not known each other for long, but in that short duration, perhaps they had grown closer than she had expected.

As she was thinking this, her captor turned a sharp corner and emerged into a wide valley. It was deeply wooded, a sort of dell. The man prodded her with his gun and led her into the pine forest. She stumbled, but caught herself. And in this fleeting moment, chanced a glimpse at her captor behind her. His face was completely hidden behind a dark face mask, but the outfit he wore was unmistakably Aifra gear. Immediately, she was reminded of her last encounter with Aifra soldiers in Iceland, the one where she had seen her beloved friend Nancy in very similar attire. Her heart ached at the thought.

They walked for several minutes more, with the crunching of dry leaves under their boots the only sound around, barring the occasional chirping of a bird or the whooshing of wind between the trees. The mid-morning sky was darkening rapidly, heralding another nasty storm. Zoya prayed that they reached wherever they were headed, before the sleet and snow hit them.

At the end of the dell, was a pebbly forest path, that curved away from the trees into the core of the mountain. They followed it silently like a death row procession, until at last, they arrived at the mouth of a cave. It was nothing like the Aifra cave behind a waterfall in Iceland. Neither in scale nor complexity nor level of fortification. In fact, it was just an ordinary cave, akin to a castaway's shelter in a forlorn island, in the middle of the raging ocean.

Zoya was not particularly tall, but still she had to duck to go inside. The tall man behind her followed and after him, Yuri was shoved inside. The second Aifra soldier did not enter, probably choosing to stay outside to keep watch. The inside of the cave was dark, except for the pale wintry light trickling in through the cave's opening. The man lit a match and crouched to pick up a lantern. Zoya noticed that his gun was no longer in his hand, as he focussed all his attention on lighting the lamp. Nevertheless, she knew it would be futile to run, because the other soldier undoubtedly stood guard outside. She never noticed what the other terrorist carried as a weapon. It could be a Kalashnikov for all she cared. There was no running from two armed Aifra goons, in a desolate place like this, and that she knew for a fact.

The man set down the lamp and removed his mask, his wild eyes scanning Zoya's face and Yuri's, in rapid succession. He was a scary-looking fellow with a scarred face, thick beard and shoulder-length, dreadlocked hair.

"Who are you and why have you brought us here?" Yuri growled, advancing towards the stranger. Zoya placed her hand gently on his arm to stop him, but he had already advanced a couple of steps, before the tall man bent down and retrieved his gun from the floor.

"Stay back!" he shouted, pointing the gun at Yuri.

Yuri raised his hands above his head and tentatively took a step backwards. "Look, we don't want any trouble, okay? You can take our stuff." He shrugged his backpack off his shoulders and stepped away from it, with his hands still in the air. "Here, take it. Take it all."

"Don't talk. Sit down," the fierce man said, indicating a spot on his right with his gun. There, against the rocky wall, Zoya saw some flat-topped boulders, lined up side-by-side like a caveman's couch. Yuri cautiously made his way towards that area. "You too," the tall man said to Zoya with a sidelong glance in her direction. The way this man spoke, reminded Zoya of Tarzan from the movies, like one who had long since forgotten how to speak with humans and was trying to find his voice anew.

Zoya stumbled through the dimly lit interior of the cave, nearly tripping over a straw mattress lying on the floor and found herself a seat on the bench next to Yuri. A rustling noise from the mouth of the cave distracted their captor, who turned to look over his shoulder. Seeing this, Yuri was about to shoot up from his seat, but Zoya pulled him back down. "Don't," she mouthed silently. And her judgement was sound, because their other captor had entered the cave and was standing over them now.

This individual, carried a large and heavy sack slung over the back. The two looked at each other and a silent gesture passed between their eyes. "I found it," the second person said. The voice sounded female. "It was where we had left it, at the bend of the path." She was probably referring to the sack, which she set down against the wall as she spoke. Zoya wondered what could be in it. Ammunition? More weapons? A bomb? Or perhaps even a dead body? She shivered at the thought.

Then, as if sensing her thoughts, the female looked directly at Zoya with piercing blue eyes. She advanced one step towards her, then another. Yuri instinctively extended his arm in front of Zoya to protect her, but this was far from necessary, because of what happened next. In a swift, fluid motion the woman in front of them removed her mask, making Zoya gasp audibly and rise to her feet quicker than a bolt of lightning.

"Nancy," Zoya choked out, as the rest of the sentence vanished inside her throat. Nancy advanced with deliberate steps towards Zoya, the hint of a smile playing across her lips. Zoya too made her way towards her childhood friend, but with halting, inadvertent steps, as if she was being dragged forward against her will by some unseen, inexplicable force.

When they were hardly a foot apart, the two women stopped in their tracks and stared at each other for about a minute or two— one with awe and longing and the other with cautious trepidation.

Zoya was the first to speak, her lips trembling uncontrollably. "You ... they sent *you* to capture us?"

"No," Nancy replied, a sob welling up inside her. "Not to capture you." She dabbed at the corners of her eyes with her palm.

"Hang on, what's going on here? Do you *know* these people?" Yuri, who was watching all of this with growing confusion, now asked, turning to Zoya.

"Just her, not him," Zoya clarified. "She's Nancy, my childhood friend. They belong to the terrorist group—"

"Not any more," Nancy interrupted her mid-sentence, to clarify. "We left. Both of us." she nodded at her companion, who nodded back in acknowledgment. Then, she opened her arms wide and threw herself at Zoya in a giant embrace. "I'm sorry ... I'm so sorry, Zoya," she seemed to say, incoherently between whimpers.

This simple act broke down Zoya's resolve. She could no longer keep her own tears at bay. She clasped her friend between her arms and bawled into her shoulder like a baby. The tall man's voice behind them brought them back to reality. "Did either of you eat?" he asked gruffly.

Zoya pulled away from Nancy and shook her head. "No, not really. This is Yuri, by the way. My friend."

"And I am Peter. Peter Cobb. Nice to meet you."

"Peter *what?*" Zoya swerved around to ask, her eyes widening.

"Peter Cobb," Peter repeated. "Look lady, I don't remember much. If you're gonna accuse me of something, I can tell ya right off the bat, that I probably did it, and I am sorry for it. But at that time, I didn't know what the hell I was doing."

Zoya stared at him in awe, not knowing what it was that shocked her more—the fact that Tarzan was suddenly so articulate or that he was actually the long-lost son of Dr. Cobb, her professor. "I … wasn't going to accuse you," she stammered. "I was just going to say that I know your father, Dr. Cobb. He is my teacher."

Peter furrowed his eyebrows like he was having comprehension issues all over again. Noticing this, Nancy jumped in, to defend him. "He really doesn't remember anything at all. In fact, he didn't even remember me. At first, I told him that my name is Julie, and he didn't even question it," she said, somewhat apologetically.

"I know." Zoya said. "And I also know *why* he doesn't remember."

"Whaaat? Why?" Nancy asked, and Peter looked on with surprise.

"I'll tell you. But first you have to tell me everything. How you joined them, why you left? Where is Jake? Everything."

"Not until we eat," Peter said, hurrying to the sack Nancy had brought in. "We caught a lovely wild fowl this morning. I'll make us a stew." He removed the said fowl from the sack and grabbing his hunting knife, walked outside to clean and prepare the meat.

The rest of the morning passed with all four of them pitching in to cook their afternoon meal. It appeared that Nancy and Peter had gotten quite a haul this morning. While cooking, Nancy recounted how she had run from the Aifra when Jake had fled, because they had blamed her for his escape and sentenced her to death.

She told her how she and Peter, both fugitives from that terrible organization, had been hiding out in this cave and hunting and foraging for days. How this morning, they had gone on one of their hunting expeditions and seen two strangers coming down a hilly path in the distance. Since they rarely encountered other humans in these parts of the world, they immediately took the newcomers for Aifra patrols. Peter had suggested that they ambush the Aifra, before they found their quarry.

So, they had moved closer and hidden behind boulders, searching for the right moment to attack. But, as Zoya and Yuri came nearer, Nancy had recognized her friend and immediately changed her tack. She had convinced Peter to capture them and bring them back to the cave, so that they could warn them of the Aifra patrols in the area. By the time this story was told, their lunch was almost ready. Peter ladled large helpings of stew into the metallic bowls, he had bought from a fair at Irkutsk, before he had arrived at this cave. Then, they sat down on the floor to drink the soup, directly from the bowls and rip into the meat with their fingers.

"I still don't get, how you know a bunch of people from the Aifra," Yuri said through a mouthful of stew.

"I don't!" Zoya objected. "I mean, I don't really know Peter, only his father. And Nancy wasn't always part of the

Aifra. Speaking of which, how on earth *did* you end up joining that vile and reprehensible organization, to begin with?" she asked, turning to Nancy.

Nancy swallowed some soup and looked up. "Well, you know about my boyfriend Jake, and how he was suffering every day, right?"

"Yeah, I do remember that. I also remember having told you to take him to a therapist."

"I know. And I should have listened to you. I regretted it so badly later. Anyway, I didn't want to go to a shrink because I thought they'd medicate him, and then he'd get addicted to the meds or something. So, I joined an online group to discuss about our issues. Someone there, told me that they had the exact same problems and had found relief from a spiritual group called the Church of Ra."

"Shit!" Zoya exclaimed, immediately guessing where this was going. "Go on."

Nancy took in a deep breath. "The Church had meetings on Wednesdays and Saturdays in the basement of an abandoned temple. They were apparently dedicated to practicing ancient Egyptian healing or shit like that. They were a bit weird, almost like a cult, but Jake said, that their rituals were helping. He felt a lot calmer after the first couple of weeks and his hallucinations had stopped. But then, the sacrifices began, and I was starting to feel queasy."

Zoya gasped. "Sacrifices? What kind of sacrifices?"

"Small animals mostly, mice, chicken, sparrows."

Yuri spit out the fowl he was chewing and gagged into his bowl. "There, there," Zoya said, patting his shoulder. "Go on," she urged Nancy.

"When I told the Church leaders of my inhibitions, they suggested that Jake and I travel abroad to train with their Masters for a bit, before making up our minds. They said that they would arrange for all the travel and accommodation and that it would be a life-changing experience. So, after a bit of thought, Jake and I agreed. Mostly for Jake's sake, of course. But there was one problem. How would we explain it to our families?" Nancy sighed and hung her head.

"And, what did the Church say to that?" Zoya quizzed.

"They told us not to worry. That they would handle it. They just wanted to know where we were staying. So, we told them. Before we left, they made us swear a blood oath and drew some of our blood to bind the oath. Later, I figured out that the oath was hardly binding, but just a form of blackmail to condemn you to death later, if you stepped out of line." Nancy broke down in tears, and seeing this, Zoya leaned forward and wrapped her arms around her.

"It was also the same blood, that they must have used to make us believe you were dead," Zoya whispered, as she cradled her friend's head in her arms.

"They did *what*?" Nancy's head shot up.

"They broke into our dorm-room and left your bloodied clothes all over the floor."

"Noooo!" Nancy cried out. "You weren't home, were you?"

"No, I wasn't."

"Good. They must never find you, or even *see* you. Never! Never!"

"Why not?"

"Because, they are looking for you. And it's never a good sign, when the Aifra is looking for someone specifically."

"Wait, they are looking for *her*? Her as in Zoya? *This* Zoya?" Yuri intervened, pointing to Zoya for emphasis.

"Yes," Nancy said dourly. "And others. Some specific individuals. They hunt them constantly. Don't ask me why, but they do. I was told that the leader of the Aifra needs to find them. *Especially* Zoya. Zoya is the key to some sort of ancient magic that he has been trying to tap into, apparently. He's a total weirdo. So, I don't know where he got that ridiculous idea—"

"No," Zoya interrupted. "It's not totally ridiculous." Three pairs of shocked eyes turned to her. She paused a breath before continuing. "I know that they're looking for me. And I know why."

Yuri tapped his fingers on the floor. "Well, are you going to tell us, or no?"

"Give me your phone," Zoya said abruptly.

Yuri took out his phone and placed it on the floor between them. "I'm pretty sure there's no signal."

"I don't need any signal. Do you have any songs on there that you like?"

"Really? You're going to reply with a song? That's so …"

"Tacky," Nancy completed, seeing Yuri fumble.

"I'm *not* replying with a song," Zoya protested. "Jeez! Okay, how about the song we recorded on your guitar that evening?" she asked Yuri.

Yuri shrugged. "Sure, it's in there." He extended the phone to Zoya who took it and placed it back on the floor again.

"Now watch," she said, as she eyed the phone like it was a puzzle to solve.

"Nothing's happening." Yuri rolled his yes.

"Shh!" Zoya placed a finger on her lips. A couple of seconds went by and then the phone abruptly burst into song in an amalgamation of Yuri and Zoya's voices.

Yuri jumped back, as if the floor suddenly scorched him. "I ... wha ... how did you do that?"

"With my mind," Zoya said quietly.

Yuri backed up further, until his back was against the wall. "What *are* you?" he asked horrified. Nancy sat in her spot without moving, like an ice sculpture in her likeness. Only Peter seemed to be handling this revelation calmly.

Now, he got up and walked up to Zoya and sat next to her. "I have seen this before. What you just did. I don't remember where, but I have. Where did you learn this?" he asked.

"From your father, amongst others," Zoya replied. "And that's where you must have seen it."

Peter turned to the others, "Don't be scared," he said softly. "Believe me, when I say that I've seen evil. And this is definitely not it. What Zoya just did, is a gift. It's beautiful and divine, and that's why the Aifra is hunting her. We must keep her safe." All of a sudden, this wild, reticent man had spoken such words of wisdom, that pierced through the fear and apprehension hanging like a cloud over the room.

Nancy stirred, as if waking from a dream. "But how ... where should we go to hide?" she asked.

"I know where we could go. Where we could all be safe—" Zoya began.

"No, we aren't going anywhere. Not until the coast is clear, and the patrols for us have ended. In the meantime, we stay here and keep up the vigil. Okay?" Peter asserted.

Zoya nodded. Nancy followed. And then, after a bit of hesitation, Yuri too consented. "I guess that's as good a plan as any." He breathed.

For the rest of that day, the four of them went out in pairs—Yuri with Peter and Zoya with Nancy—to stock up on supplies for at least a fortnight. It had been decided, that since they were now harbouring Zoya, a much-coveted quarry of the Aifra, their frequent foraging expeditions would have to be curtailed. Yuri's team, aided by his knowledge of the area, brought in some incredible finds, but Zoya and Nancy had no such luck. In fact, after returning to their cave, they realized that they had gathered even less than they had expected, with Zoya having mistaken the poisonous mushrooms for the edible ones.

That night, Zoya went to bed on Nancy's pallet, which the latter had graciously offered up, with her friend curled up in a sleeping bag beside her. But the sleep that her body desperately craved, continued to evade her. She lay awake, watching Nancy breathe in and out softly, as she floated into the land of dreams. Across the room, she watched Yuri bundle up under Peter's blankets, as the former sat watch outside their door.

They had decided that they would take turns keeping watch at nights, now that they were four. Soon Peter would return, and it would be Zoya's turn to sit outside in the cold. Being a night owl, she had offered to take on the late-night shift. She wanted to put in a couple of hours of sleep before her guard-duty began, but it didn't seem likely. All she could think about, was what she had learned today from the Frozen Saint's Shrine, and later, from Nancy. The puzzle was finally beginning to piece itself together. She was somehow the key to unlock the Aifra's true power, so she would have to be the one, to turn that power against them. The question was; how?

As she was deliberating this, a few mushrooms spilled out of the bag that she and Nancy had brought in. She reached for one and twisted it between her fingers, like Yuri had taught her to. It was the poisonous variety. How ironic that two innocuous looking mushrooms would appear so similar, but be so very different in their properties. She slid the mushroom underneath her pillow and closed her eyes, meditatively pondering this question.

* * *

Meanwhile, in faraway London, Chris was sleeping in late, in his studio apartment, when a distant sound awakened him. He had returned rather late the previous night, after having completed a hectic trip to Germany, to visit their Max Planck lab. So, this morning, he was barely coherent and immediately thought that his mind was playing tricks on him. But then, the noise came again—it was a sort of ringing sound like an alarm or a phone or a doorbell. Chris sat up and rubbed his eyes. It had got to be the doorbell, because his phone was under his pillow and the sound came to him from across the room. Groggily, he got up and opened the door.

"Good morning. May I come in?" said the smiling face of Wanda Faraday.

"What time is it?" Chris squinted.

"It's nine thirty, a terrible time for a young man like you to be still in bed," Wanda admonished.

Chris rolled his eyes and stood aside to let her in. "I came in from the airport at two in the morning."

"Ah, yes. How was your trip? Did you see Gunter?" Wanda asked, sitting down at his kitchen table.

Chris merely nodded, not being in the mood for much conversation, before his morning coffee.

"Good and everything's well? Any more suspicious activity?" Wanda asked.

"Nope. Coffee?" Chris said, walking up to his coffeemaker.

"I do prefer tea, but why not? I'll have some coffee with you."

Chris made the coffee silently and brought it over in two mismatched mugs. "Sugar is on the counter, but I'm out of milk," he said, after inspecting his fridge.

"That's all right, I'll take it black. Thank you."

Chris took a sip from his cup and sat down at the table. "No problem. So, tell me, why are you here?"

"Yes, about that, do you want the good news first or the bad?"

"Yikes! Okay, let's start with the good news then."

"The good news is that Alejandro is on his way here. He's bringing Irene Costas with him."

"Oh! And how did that come about?"

"Well, that's the bad news. At least part of it. It seems that my home in California has been compromised. It is no longer safe from the Aifra."

"I see. What about Zoya? Is she coming here too?"

"That's the second part of the bad news."

"What do you mean?" Chris' face lit up with horror.

"Well, she's gone missing."

Chris rolled his eyes. "Huh! Why did I not see this coming? Where is she this time?"

"While on the run, Alejandro had called to warn her not to return to my home and remain with her parents instead.

But her phone was out of range. So, he called at her parents' home to inquire. Her father told him, that she had left a couple of days ago."

"Left where?"

"Apparently, she has been invited to a project at the Irkutsk State University. Her father has seen the invitation letter in university letterhead. I asked him to send the letter to me, so that I may examine it, and he has already mailed it to my address. I should receive it shortly. If this indeed is a real project, then it is certainly not one that I am aware of. Are you?"

"Nope. I highly doubt that it's a project. Knowing her, she's probably off on one of her harebrained adventures again. She never learns." Chris shook his head in disapproval.

"Perhaps the fact that none of her previous adventures have gotten her into any real trouble in the end, has given her a false sense of impunity," Wanda agreed.

"That's only because I've always come to her rescue." Chris chuckled dryly. "And that's probably why we should've never told her about the Faiyum scrolls and her involvement with it. Just like you had wanted."

"Agreed. But the question is, what should we do now?"

"Hmm." Chris became thoughtful. "Do her parents know if she really went to Irkutsk?"

"Yes, she did. Her father got her the tickets himself."

"Okay. In that case, I have a fairly good idea, who would know about her whereabouts. I should go to Irkutsk tonight."

"No, not tonight. I suggest that you take Amon with you. He will be here tomorrow."

"I thought Amon was supposed to arrive this evening." Chris looked at Wanda questioningly.

"He was. But he has gotten detained. You see, he needs to escort our friend Sebastian to a safe house first, and it took us a little longer than expected, to find the appropriate host."

Chris got up from his seat and started pacing around the kitchen. "I don't know … what if she's in grave danger? I'd go right away if I could … but I doubt that I'll find any tickets before tonight at the earliest—"

Wanda reached out and placed a hand on Chris' arm to stop him. "My boy, do not worry yourself too much. At the end of the day, Zoya is the master of her own destiny and none of us can either prevent or facilitate it. All we can do, is act according to the best of our abilities. After that, it is no longer in your hands or mine. Right now, we must be prudent. And going there alone would not be wise. Zoya acted on her own, without consulting anyone, so I could not stop her. But you, I can."

"Fair point. Alright then. I'll speak with Amon and fill him in. After that, I can try to get us the earliest plane tickets. We'll head to the University first. Someone over there is sure to know something, if she was able to forge a letter in their letterhead."

"I do believe you are correct. She must have had insider assistance."

"Good. Since we're both in agreement, I'll get busy making arrangements. But tell me, are you sure you won't need me on hand, on the day of Wolfgang's escape?"

"I do not believe that we will, since Alejandro is also going to be here shortly. Besides, we have very little to do at our end. The Lumanians have received your correspondence, and they will take care of most of it for us."

"But we can't really be sure that they've even checked—"

"They have," Wanda assured calmly.

"Oh? How do you know?"

"Kazhar wrote to our lab this morning to say, that they have received our missive and promise to stay on high alert for Wolfgang, throughout that day. And, as you know, the Lumanians do not take such commitments lightly."

"No, no they don't." Chris grinned. "This is great news, Wanda! Why didn't you lead with this, when I asked you for good news earlier?"

"As they say, one should always save the best for last." Wanda chuckled, before rising to leave.

CHAPTER NINETEEN

It was a bright afternoon in Aleppo, when Wolfgang arrived at the airfield behind the Aifra camp. Two men were waiting for him in front of the newly painted, Sukhoi Su-34 Russian bomber—the square-jawed, broad-shouldered Alexander Costas and with him, a lanky younger man, with a long unruly beard.

"Meet Jeremy," Alex said, by way of greeting, seeing Wolfgang approach. "I've taught him everything I know. He'll be a joy to work with."

Jeremy nodded curtly without betraying any trace of emotion whatsoever. By now, Wolfgang had realized that this was the trademark style of greeting for most Aifra soldiers. With his Hekameses senses, Wolfgang picked up the signal from a bomb strapped to his companion's body, just as Alex had predicted. Despite his customary Aifra demeanour however, Jeremy was not wearing their traditional and easily identifiable uniform. A clever move, considering that they would probably have to blend in with civilians at some point.

"Why do we need a bomber? It's just a kidnapping mission." Wolfgang asked tentatively.

"The General's rules," Jeremy replied in a deep, grating voice. "Always be prepared."

"It was one of the downed crafts that I got to work on myself," Alex boasted. "It's in tip-top shape now. Should take you all the way there and back in a jiffy."

"Get in," Jeremy said, not wanting to waste any more time on idle conversation. Wolfgang nodded at Alex, and while doing so, made eye contact, long enough to slip him a short, brain-to-brain message. "Keep your head down and wait for my message."

Alex nodded his understanding and waved them goodbye. The bomber cut effortlessly through the pearly Syrian skies, without anyone questioning their trajectory. Russian bombers were a common sight here on their way back to Moscow and could travel without hindrance. But the trouble would begin, when they arrive at the university. With the war ongoing, perhaps they could still land within the campus, yet Wolfgang was doubtful.

The best compromise would be to arrive there at night with the campus deserted and pretend to be a military patrol. That way, they could get away with landing on the roof of a building for a few minutes. And a few minutes was all Wolfgang needed. He had explained this strategy to the General earlier, but now, with every passing minute, he became increasingly doubtful, that his suggestion had been accepted.

The plane weaved and tilted between the white fluffy clouds, performing unnecessary acrobatics in mid-air. Wolfgang's stomach lurched. He knew that there was no need for these stunts at the moment, the skies were clear and they were not under attack. So, Wolfgang figured, that the pilot was merely trying to scare him into compliance—a tactic for which the Aifra were notoriously famous.

Nevertheless, this time, Wolfgang knew better not to ask the Aifra soldier any questions. They were trained not to respond or be curt and dismissive at best. This was too critical a mission to jeopardize by antagonizing the walking-talking time bomb sitting next to him. So, he tried to hang tight and not retch his guts out for the next couple of hours.

As they approached Moscow, his apprehension began to coagulate into a physical thing, baring its claws to lunge at him. He only had a vague knowledge of where the hidden entrances to the Lumanian realm lay within the university campus. There was one in the lobby. Another, under the little artificial lake. A third, outside the main entrance to the grounds. He had no idea about the other three.

Ideally, he would need to get close enough to any of these three entrances and hopefully the Lumanian Seers would let him through. If Chris and Wanda were able to decipher his memory burst and send an advance message to the Lumanians, then even better. They would be expecting him. But what of Jeremy? If he was not dealt with effectively, then many lives could be at stake. Letting a live bomb loose inside a university campus, at the heart of a crowded city, was a terrible move.

As the main building of the university loomed over Sparrow Hill, right across their field of view, Wolfgang calculated his options. There were several military vans around the building—the legitimate patrols. They did not, under any circumstance, want to land near them. The grounds inside were relatively empty, so in theory, they could land there, but that would mess up Wolfgang's plan.

He swallowed in a dry throat and opened his mouth to speak.

"The main entrance will be locked at this hour," he simply said.

Jeremy turned to him angrily. "Your point?"

"I don't have after-hours access to the building, sadly."

"Ask your friend to let us in then." He extended his phone to Wolfgang, not trusting him to call using his own.

Wolfgang shook his head. "He is already waiting for us in the lobby and being an old-fashioned man, he does not use a cell phone."

"Okay, I'll kick the door in."

Wolfgang wanted to snigger at his insolence, but checked himself quickly. "You could try, but it's an ancient door, very solidly built."

"Why did you bring us here then? What kind of a trap is this—" his voice was rising and his cheeks turning strawberry red.

"Because," Wolfgang interrupted. "Because, we can enter from the door on the roof. It has a flimsy lock that we cam easily pick."

"Why didn't you say so before?"

Wolfgang had a biting retort at the ready, but he held back with much effort. There was no need with this mindless moron. Especially, since he had already turned the plane around and was getting ready to walk right into Wolfgang's trap. In a minute, Jeremy lowered the bomber and hovered over the roof of the student dorm wing, as if, deciding whether to land there.

"You can land here," Wolfgang assured. "It's the dorm wing, but there's a path inside, connecting it to the lobby. The only catch is that, there will be students inside. So, we need to enter one at a time, in order not to arouse suspicion."

Jeremy did not respond, but he followed Wolfgang's advice nonetheless, landing on the dorm roof, only a couple of feet from the door. Then, he switched off the engine and looked at Wolfgang. "You know how to pick a lock?"

Wolfgang wanted to say that he did, but resisted. "Nope."

"Stand back then." Jeremy got out of the cockpit and kicked the door in.

"Yikes! What if someone heard you?" Wolfgang asked in a panic.

"If they did, then I'll kill 'em. Now go!" Then, after a pause, "And remember, you have the tracer on. So, don't do anything funny."

Wolfgang nodded and raised his two-way radio. "I'll call you as soon as I get to him, and you can come right down. There'll be signs for the lobby—"

"I'll find it. Hurry up!" Jeremy said, giving Wolfgang a little nudge towards the door.

Wolfgang walked into the dark landing and fumbled his way down the steep stairwell. His heart beat at a thousand cycles per second, as he passed landing after landing and arrived inside the dormitory wing. Inside, it was fairly quiet, which Wolfgang had expected, since most of the students had cleared out due to the war. The brave ones that still remained, were nowhere in sight. Not tonight, anyway. Probably, because it was after seven, and there was an ongoing curfew in town. Regardless, Wolfgang found it relatively easy to find his way to where he wanted to go, although he had never actually been to this campus before.

The main building's lobby was dark and deserted when Wolfgang walked in. If he had been expecting to find someone waiting for him here, then that person was either late or not planning to come at all. Wolfgang's heart sank. Time was not his friend. He would have to act quickly, but had no idea, how. The Lumanian hidden entrances are hidden for a reason, so that no one can actually stumble into them. Naturally, Wolfgang would not have any luck milling about the room, looking for a mystery lever that opened a hatch or a stairway that descended into oblivion.

As he was wondering what to do, his two-way radio buzzed and crackled. "Hello."

"Did you find him?" Jeremy's voice roared.

Wolfgang sucked in his breath. "Not yet. He must be late."

"I'm coming down!" the other man growled. more vehemently than earlier. Before Wolfgang could respond, he hung up, leaving Wolfgang standing there holding the silent walkie-talkie in his trembling hands. There was no point calling back to dissuade this man, because Wolfgang knew that any discouragement would undoubtedly have exactly the opposite effect. It would take Jeremy at least a couple of minutes, to find his way down here, but that was hardly enough. Running was not an option from a human bomb. Hiding would have worked much better. But the lobby was large and sparsely furnished, like most university lobbies, and only a child would find it prudent to hide here. He could hide somewhere else of course, only if he knew the campus better.

In the distance, he heard the definite sounds of heavy footsteps. His heart stood still. There was a door to his right, across from the one he had just come through, and he wondered where it led. Perhaps there would be a classroom in there, with a cupboard where he could hide. Crossing his fingers, he turned towards that door. But he did not make it far, because a hooded figure suddenly rose from the darkness and stood before it. The figure advanced towards Wolfgang, making him back away, ever so slightly. But then, the figure, a man in a flowing robe, smiled— a wry and cryptic smile. Immediately Wolfgang knew. He smiled back in greeting.

Just then, Jeremy burst through the opposite door, a gun raised in front of his face. "Where is he? Is he the one?" He screamed. His cheeks were flushed and his eyes seemed to be popping out of his head.

"Yes, he is," Wolfgang said softly.

"Hands over your head," Jeremy instructed. The robed man complied, raising both his hands at a glacial pace. And then, instead of raising them all the way over his head, he stopped midway. In the blink of an eye, Jeremy's gun floated out of his hand and hung in mid-air.

"What the—" Jeremy began, lunging for his weapon. He never got to complete the lunge, but froze on the spot, like a movie paused right in the middle of an action sequence. He writhed and struggled against the artificial bonds that held him, all to no avail.

The hooded man turned to Wolfgang. "Shall we?"

"Yes, please. Are you …"

"Kazhar, I'm Kazhar," he replied with his hands still stretched in front of him.

"Thank you Kazhar. Let's go, if you're ready."

Kazhar bowed his head politely, and in an instant, the floor began to descend, sucking all three of them into the deep belly of the earth, where nothing entered without the blessings of the Lumanians.

CHAPTER TWENTY

C hris and Amon arrived at the Irkutsk University, bright and early in the morning of the same day, that Wolfgang was expected in Moscow. Nikolai was there to meet them, right outside his lab.

"Good to see you again, Chris, Amon," he said in greeting. "Please, have a seat while I get you some coffee."

"Oh, that's not necessary, we just had—" Chris was about to say, but Nikolai interrupted him.

"How about tea, then? It's our tradition to share tea with guests."

"I do like tea," Amon said. "Sure, I'll have a cup, if you don't mind."

"Excellent! And what about you?" Nikolai turned to Chris with a smile.

"Why not? If it's your tradition." Chris chuckled.

"Good. I will be right back."

Chris and Amon seated themselves around Nikolai's desk inside the lab. It was overflowing with papers and lab equipment. In one corner, was a large computer monitor attached to a laptop. Under the table were a pair of rugged, weather-worn winter boots and next to them lay discarded footwear fit for a cleanroom. Both pairs of footwear looked like they were of Nikolai's size. A few other desks were nearby, most of them empty, apart from the one diagonally across the room, where a pretty blonde lady was staring intently into her phone. As she looked up, Chris' eyes met hers and there was instant recognition in them. She smiled and waved in greeting. Chris waved back, remembering her as Nikolai's girlfriend, Hana.

Nikolai retuned with two paper cups full of tea and set them on a stool in front of them. "I'm sorry my desk is really messy. But you can use this. Would you like some cookies? We have cookies."

"Sure, I don't mind," Amon said.

"None for me, thank you," Chris replied.

Nikolai walked off to fetch the cookies. In a minute, he returned with his own mug of tea and a jar of handmade biscuits with a gooey jam-centre. "On second thoughts," Chris said, reaching for one, "these look delicious."

"Ha! They are my favourite. My mom made them."

"Mmmm, really good," Amon said, taking a bite.

While they were busy sampling cookies, neither of them had noticed Hana walking up to stand behind them. "Where is Zoya? Is she coming too?" she asked, enthusiastically.

Chris remembered that Hana and Zoya were around the same age and had struck up an easy friendship, the last time. However, the other person Zoya seemed to have connected with on their previous visit, was conspicuously absent from the room. Chris swallowed down his biscuit with a gulp of tea. "No, she isn't coming. Speaking of which," he eyed Amon through the corner of his eye and found him to be twitching nervously, "have you, by any chance, heard from her?"

"Us? Here?" Nikolai asked surprised. "Should we have?"

"Well," Chris hesitated, before reaching into his backpack and pulling out an A4-sized brown-paper envelope with the Irkutsk University emblem on it. "She received this, a few days ago." He handed the enveloped to Nikolai.

Creases appeared across Nikolai's face as he read the letter contained within it, with an additional fold appearing with every new word he read. "This is odd," he finally said. "It is signed by our professor, but she never told us anything."

"Is it really, though? Signed by your professor, that is?" Chris asked, appearing doubtful.

"I … well it looks like—"

"Give me that," Hana said, snatching the page from her beau. "Hmmm, hold on." She turned around and hurried towards her own desk. She returned a minute later fetching another, similar letter, from a stack on her table. "Look at this." She pointed at the signature at the bottom. "*This* is her signature. She always loops her y's at the bottom. Look here."

"You're right," Amon observed. "The y's are definitely different."

"Someone forged this," Hana said decisively.

What Chris wanted to ask next was a very touchy question, so he wondered how he should frame it. "Umm … well, Amon and I were thinking—"

"It wasn't one of us," Nikolai hastily cut in, preventing Chris from completing his awkward question.

"Oh no, we didn't suggest that you did. But we were

hoping that perhaps you could venture a guess?" Chris quickly clarified.

Nikolai studied Chris for a very long time before opening his mouth to respond. "Why do you want to find the culprit so badly? Is Zoya alright? Did she respond to this message?"

Chris let out an audible sigh. "Unfortunately, she did. And now, we have no idea where she is."

"Oh my God!" Hana squeaked, covering her mouth with her hands. "We should go to the police. Did you report it yet?"

"Please," Chris grabbed her arm to calm her, "there's no need to panic. We have every reason to believe that Zoya wasn't tricked into this, but it was her plan all along. It's best we don't get the police involved in whatever childish fun she's planned with this."

"But how can you be sure it was *her* idea?"

"It's just a hunch. But I know her well enough to say, that it wouldn't be unlike her, to pull such a stunt," Chris explained. Adding, "Maybe your colleague, Yuri would know something. Where is he, by the way?"

"Yuri! That's a good question," Nikolai said looking baffled. "Where the hell *is* he? I haven't seen him in a few days. Have you?" he asked, turning to Hana.

"Nope."

"Let's call him." Nikolai pulled out his phone and began searching for the number. In a minute, he cancelled the call and returned the phone to his pocket. "Out of range." He sighed.

Chris and Amon exchanged a meaningful look between them. "Would your ... professor know?" Chris hesitated.

"She would. But she's at a conference in England. It'd take a while to get in touch with her. I think it's better that we ask his roommate," Nikolai said.

"That's a great idea. Why don't we do that?" Amon chimed in.

Nikolai checked the time. "Let's go right now. He should be home. He sleeps in late." Nikolai tossed the empty tea cups into the trash and made his way towards the door. Amon got up to follow him. Chris turned to Hana, "Are you coming?"

"I'd rather not. We don't want to scare, Mikhail, his roomie. He's a bit of a loner." She chuckled. Chris nodded and followed his friends out the door.

Yuri's apartment was a short walk away from the university and the three of them nearly jogged there, in their haste to catch Mikhail at home. Yuri lived in a low-rise building in the picturesque little city, surrounded by the high spires of colourful churches, built in the Russian Revival style. The concierge buzzed Nikolai in immediately, seeming to have recognized him from previous visits.

They made their way quickly to the third floor, where Nikolai knocked on the second door to their right. No one answered on the first knock, so he tried again. Then, a second time. Finally, on their fourth knock, a sleepy voice answered. "Who is it?"

"It's me Nikolai."

"Yuri isn't home," Mikhail replied without bothering to open the door.

"Yeah, I was worried that he wouldn't be. Can we have a word?"

"Come back later. I have work," Mikhail replied irritably.

Chris rolled his eyes. "Talk about being aloof!"

"Look, Mikhail, we won't take much of your time. But

if you don't come out and talk to us then we have to go to the police."

There was silence, and then, the door opened a crack and a mousy young man with bedhead, poked his face out. "Why? Who are these people?"

"These are friends of Yuri. They are looking for him," Nikolai replied calmly.

"Oh, that's why you were speaking English. I should've guessed." He moved away from the door and tried to shut it in their faces, but Nikolai stuck his foot in through the gap to stop him. "What *is* it?" Mikhail asked, his irritation growing. "What do you want?"

"Like I said, we want to know where Yuri is."

"He's fine. He's on holiday."

"On holiday where?" Chris asked enthusiastically.

"I don't know. Somewhere in the mountains."

"Oh, I see. When did he leave? And have you spoken to him since then?" Chris tried to squeeze in all his questions, before Mikhail slammed the door again.

"He left several days ago. Don't remember exactly. And no, he hasn't called …" He paused and became thoughtful. "But maybe, that girl will know," he added after a bit of hesitation.

Chris' heart summersaulted like a circus clown. "What girl?"

"The one he was meeting at the airport … I forget her name." He tapped his head with a forefinger, like he was trying to jog his memory by poking at the source.

"Was it … Zoya?" Chris quizzed.

"Yeah, that's it. You should ask her."

"If we can find her," Chris said under his breath.

"I have to go, sorry," Mikhail said, and this time he succeeded in slamming the door with an air of finality.

The visitors turned around and made their way down to the lobby, feeling disheartened. The scraps of information that had emerged from the conversation upstairs were useful, yet they only helped to confirm their existing theory and did not throw any additional light on the situation.

"Well, that was a complete waste of time," Chris grumbled, as they walked out into the wintry morning. A light drizzle of wet snow had begun to fall on their shoulders, adding to the gloominess of their current moods.

"I wouldn't call it a complete waste," Nikolai, who had been quiet for a very long time, remarked out of the blue.

"Oh? And why not?" Chris asked. "If you're implying that we now know, Yuri is in the mountains and Zoya is probably with him, then we have to tell you, that we already guessed—"

"No, there's more to it than that," Nikolai interrupted. "You see, I know Yuri loves the mountains around Lake Baikal. He grew up there and visits often. If they're in the mountains, I bet that's where they went. Give me a second, I think I can verify it for you." Nikolai took out his phone and dialled a number. He spoke rapidly in Russian to whoever had picked up on the other end, before hanging up with a big grin across his face.

"What? What did you find out?" Chris asked anxiously.

"Yuri knows a ranger up in the mountains, who owns a Russian log-cabin on the slopes. Sometimes, we used to go there to stay with him. I called him just now, and he says that he is travelling, but he did in fact, let Yuri stay at his cabin a few days ago."

"Brilliant! We should start our search there," Amon said. "Could you tell us where it is?"

"Of course! Also, you would need a four-wheel drive to

go up to it. I can lend you mine."

"Oh, you don't have to—" Amon started.

"No, I *do* have to. Yuri is my friend too. And so is Zoya. I wish I could go with you, but I have my qualifier next week, and I have faith in your skills. But please, please do keep me informed. I'll be worried."

"We definitely will," Chris assured. "We'll start this afternoon, if that's okay with you."

"Perfect. I'll make all the arrangements for you and bring the car to your hotel, when it's ready. How about that?"

"Works for us," Chris said and Amon nodded in tandem.

CHAPTER TWENTY-ONE

For the first couple of days after his arrival in Lumania, Wolfgang had neither been allowed to leave his room nor see or speak to anyone. This was standard procedure in this realm, to allow for a period of quarantine and screening, before letting an outsider mingle freely with the locals. Nevertheless, being a Hekameses, whose friends had vouched for him wholeheartedly, he was not at all treated like a regular intruder.

Once they had descended to the bottom of the shaft, that had opened up under their feet at the university lobby, a couple of other Lumanians had rushed to their side. They had immediately turned to Jeremy, the Aifra soldier, and guided his floating body away with practiced ease. Kazhar, on the other hand, had hung around with Wolfgang and chit-chatted for a bit, before leading him into a hexagonal room, carved out of stone. Once there, he had been asked; to which city he wanted to travel.

Wolfgang had a very rough idea of the layout of Lumania, and that too, only from the verbal descriptions of his friends. So, he had suggested that Kazhar escort him to the city, he deemed most appropriate for a person, such as himself. They had relaxed on embroidered cushions inside the hexagonal room, and Kazhar had arranged for refreshments. Then, they had boarded a super-fast underground train, propelled by sound, and had travelled for what had felt like hundreds of kilometres.

They had disembarked the train at a stunning station, carved out of glittering purple crystals. Kazhar had then escorted him past fountains, creeper-laden trellises and glowing clusters of fireflies, to the residential area of town. There, at the end of a winding stone stairwell, were rows of stark living quarters. Escorting Wolfgang into one, Kazhar had sealed the entrance with a wind vortex, promising to have food and drink delivered to his room at regular intervals, until the hour of his release, two days hence.

In Wolfgang's mind, this was less like a prison sentence and more like a house-arrest—a sort of confinement you would impose on a high-profile political prisoner, for example. He did not mind it at all. In fact, it felt like paradise, after his long days and nights at the hostile, grim and squalid Aifra camp. Kazhar, being the friendly soul that he was, had joined him for a couple of meals whilst in confinement. He had taught Wolfgang the secret Lumanian handshake, and the correct way of bowing before the Elders. He had also introduced Wolfgang to Ishin and Larvo, who fought alongside the Hekameses at the Moscow University last year. Thus, his captivity had passed quite enjoyably for Wolfgang, which was rarely ever the case.

This morning, Wolfgang was to be released, and Kazhar was to see to it personally. At six in the morning, a nightingale flew into his room and sang the morning alarm, waking him from a deep and dreamless sleep. Kazhar had promised to be here at eight, but Wolfgang had lost all sense of time inside this ancient timeless kingdom, that defied all parameters of time and space. He assumed that it would be close to sunrise when the alarms were sounded, so taking that as a reference, he proceeded to clean-up at the small wash-area inside his room.

By the time Kazhar was at his door, Wolfgang was ready and waiting for his arrival. Kazhar waited outside, with his back turned towards the doorway, as was customary, and seeing this Wolfgang walked forward. "Is it safe to pass?" he asked, before stepping further beyond the door. He had no idea what the whirlpool blocking the door, would do to a living human. But he surely did not want to find out. Kazhar did not respond, and Wolfgang stood there for a moment, utterly confused. Then, he remembered what his escort had told him earlier, about privacy in Lumania. How all the doors to the residences were soundproof. He could yell at the top of his lungs, if he wanted, but Kazhar would hear absolutely nothing, while still on the other side of that door.

Bracing himself for the consequences therefore, Wolfgang boldly made for the exit. One long stride and he was across it in a heartbeat, unharmed and completely intact. He chuckled to himself at the potency of the Lumanian magic—*on* when you needed it, *off* when you didn't.

Kazhar whisked around at the sound of Wolfgang's feet. "What are you laughing at?"

"Our inadequacy in comparison to your power," Wolfgang replied humbly.

"I would not call it power. Not in the sense that people of your world call it, that is. But tell me, is there any place within our kingdom that you would like to visit, now that you're free?"

Wolfgang shrugged. "Like I said before, I don't know much about your kingdom. So, I must trust you to be my guide. If that is okay with you," he added, after a brief pause.

"Of course. It would be my pleasure. In fact, I do have a location in mind, where I would like to take you today. But first, we should have breakfast. Properly, like the Lumanians."

Having heard from Chris, about the community meal areas in Lumania, Wolfgang had a fairly good idea what Kazhar meant. So, he smiled and said, "Please, lead the way."

The breakfast buffet they attended was a small one, belonging to District One of this city, according to Kazhar. They ate quietly with a handful of others and cleaned their plates before leaving. Once outside, Kazhar said, "Now, we will go to District Two. It's only a short distance away and the walk will help us digest our food better."

They walked down paved, broad tunnels, all underground, just like the Aifra camp had been, yet so unlike the latter in every other way. The walls that lined the tunnels, were moist and laden with flowering vines and lichen. Sometimes, tiny waterfalls trickled between them, gathering in sweet-water pools at the base. At intervals, the tunnel broadened into an underground piazza of sorts, with a central fountain, lit by dancing glow worms. Lamps of bioluminescent bacteria hung from stalagmite like structures that lined the walls. Wolfgang gazed all around him in awe, wondering how a fairy-tale-like kingdom such as this, remained hidden from prying human eyes for millennia. Just as he was about to ask this, Kazhar spoke instead.

"We are here," he said, with a wide grin across his face. "Follow me." They made a sharp right into a narrow corridor that ended in a large room. A dreamy blue light and a low humming sound rose from its interior. Wolfgang determined that it was probably a meditation chamber of some kind. Kazhar stepped lightly as they got nearer, before almost tiptoeing inside. Wolfgang followed his lead and did the same.

In the dim light of the room, a few figures could be seen sitting in yoga positions and lifting small pebbles with light and breezy hand gestures. One young woman had suspended several pebbles in mid-air and was now busy, arranging them in lovely floral patterns.

"Very good!" a woman's voice exclaimed from the far end of the room, and Wolfgang's head immediately turned to that direction. As recognition dawned, Wolfgang's jaw hung from his face, like that of a ventriloquist's dummy.

"Nirmala!" he mouthed, with the word barely making it out of his throat. "How come you're here?"

Nirmala too had seen him and had frozen in the middle of her yoga pose. "My my, if it isn't our gang leader!" she finally said, managing to find her voice. "What a pleasant surprise!"

As Wolfgang's eyes adjusted to the light, he noticed more familiar faces around him, Xianbin, Haresh, Ahmed—all of the Novo-Hekameses, in fact. "Are you hosting the Novo-Hekameses here instead of at my cottage in Germany, nowadays?" he asked with a chuckle. "Do you still think that place is haunted?"

"Ha! I never thought it was haunted." Nirmala dismissed the suggestion with a wave of her hand. "It's Alejandro's fault that I am here. He kicked me out. So, I had to move my operations underground. Literally," she added as an afterthought. They both laughed at this. When they stopped, they noticed that the others were laughing too. To Wolfgang, it felt like heaven to be able to laugh so freely again, for in the bygone months, he had surely forgotten how.

The students had abandoned their yoga poses and Seeing Crystals and gathered around in a circle around their teachers. In a corner, Kazhar too was grinning, enjoying their conversation. "I have to have a word with Alejandro, now that I'm back," Wolfgang said, when everyone had stopped laughing. "Did *you* teach them what they were doing before? The telekinetic stuff? Even all the Hekameses can't —"

"No," Nirmala said quickly. "It wasn't me. The Elder Mercuriva has mentored me. And them. Now, we just hone our skills through practice."

"Our Elders have some ability to pass on our gifts to the uninitiated, if they wish," Kazhar explained.

"Amazing! I would myself, be honoured to receive such training one day, if your Elders would be so kind, as to accept me as their student. But first, I need to know where I am. So that, I can plan our next move. When I asked Kazhar earlier, all he told me was that I would find out in good time."

Kazhar chuckled from his corner of the room. "And you did."

"We are in Amethyst," Nirmala explained. "It's a new Lumanian city under Canada."

"I see." Wolfgang turned to Kazhar. "And where is de other man? The one that was vith me? Did you expel him from your kingdom?" he asked, slipping briefly into his German accent, now that he was back among friends and no longer watching himself.

"He is evil, that one," Kazhar said. "He is being confined, until we are done with him."

"Done with him? What do you mean?" Wolfgang's eyebrows shot up.

"It's not what you think, Wolfgang," Nirmala cut in. "They're not going to kill him. They'll just wipe out parts of his memory, so that he can no longer remember the Aifra or his evil way of life."

"Yes, you are right." Kazhar nodded. "You are now a true Lumanian."

Wolfgang however, did not appear to have been set at ease by these words. In fact, it was quite the contrary. His face was flushed and his eyes seemed to be popping out of his head. "This is bad. Very bad," he whispered under his breath.

Noticing this Kazhar said, "Would you rather, we killed him?"

Wolfgang's head jerked up. "No, of course not! That would have been much worse. But this is still very bad and quite detrimental to my plan."

"Please explain," Kazhar insisted.

"You see, when I was captured by the Aifra, I was not alone. I had another man with me. A good man. A friend. Unfortunately, I could not bring him on my mission to Moscow University that day, because the Aifra General would not allow it. So, I had to bring Jeremy instead. Now, if I don't return and Jeremy too doesn't return, then they will surely assume that I had something to do with their mission falling apart. Knowing that Alex is my friend and still within their grasp, we can only imagine what kind of horrors they will bring upon him after that."

Kazhar's face was creasing with worry lines, as he spoke the next words. "I did not realize this. Why did you not tell me earlier?"

"I didn't think I needed to, right away. I assumed that once you looked inside Jeremy's head and realized that he was devious and violent, you would expel him from your kingdom immediately, so that he could return to the Aifra and report that we had been kidnapped. Is that not your custom?"

"It is. Except in cases where the crimes committed by the intruder are too horrendous for us to allow him to remember them," Kazhar explained, his eyes sad and apologetic.

"So, you will make him forget about the Aifra?" Wolfgang asked.

"We already have." Kazhar sighed.

Wolfgang rubbed his bearded chin and became silent, staring thoughtfully at a spot near his feet. After a moment, he said, "Where is the bomber? The plane we arrived on?"

"It's here, in Lumania. We sent some seniors to bring it down into our realm, later that night."

"Good. We must send Jeremy back in it."

Kazhar edged closer to Wolfgang, as if trying to restrain a blabbering lunatic. "We can't do that," he said in a warning tone. "He will never find his way. We erased all his memories of—"

"I know," Wolfgang interrupted with a dry smile. "But I can plant fresh ones in his brain. Cooked up memories that should be sufficient to guide him back to the Aifra camp. I may not be as powerful as you, but I do have my uses."

CHAPTER TWENTY-TWO

As Nikolai had promised, he arrived with his four-wheel drive to Chris and Amon's hotel, later that afternoon. Being early spring, it was already dark outside, and the road leading up to the log-cabin treacherous. So, Nikolai advised them to leave early the next morning. Although Nikolai was worried about his friend, he was also feeling optimistic, because in his mind, this seemed like a romantic getaway more than anything else.

Chris however, knew better. Zoya would not come here all the way from California just to go hiking in the mountains with a romantic interest. She was no ordinary girl of nineteen, but a Hekameses, the chosen one and hunted constantly by the Aifra. She was aware of the risks and consequences of travelling deep into the Siberian mountains, where there could possibly be a hidden Aifra base somewhere. Why was it that she travelled, then? She was hunting for something; this Chris was sure of. Now the question was, what?

Chris rose early the next morning, while Amon was still asleep and made sure, he packed everything for their journey. "Tent, check. Flashlight, check. Gun, check," he muttered to himself, as he inspected the contents of his backpack.

"Ughh, you with your check, check, check," Amon chuckled sleepily. "What time is it?" He rubbed his eyes and sat up.

"Four thirty. Rise and shine, love," Chris teased.

Amon stretched before getting out of bed. In another ten minutes, he was ready for the trip. He too checked his luggage one more time, before giving Chris a thumbs-up. Nikolai's four-wheel drive was in the underground parking and started up with a roar, when Chris turned the key. Maps at the ready, they took off from their hotel before five in the morning, when the sun was yet to slide above the misty grey horizon.

Their drive from Irkutsk was brutally scenic. Eerily similar as this was, to their previous trip to Siberia, it was also starkly different. The route they had followed last year had been much more remote, and travelling by foot had been their only option. This time however, the roads were still unpaved and treacherous, but at least somewhat drivable. But there was no telling what would happen, when they reached the log-cabin Nikolai had identified. Chris had a nagging hunch, that they would find it abandoned. They did not have a plan for what they would do, if that happened.

Shortly after mid-day, Chris pulled their jeep over to a scenic lookout point for lunch. Amon had made salted Omul sandwiches, like he used to, on their earlier trip.

Amon took a bite off his sandwich and stared into the horizon, his gaze heavy and reflective.

Chris nudged him gently with his elbow. "Whatchya thinkin', big guy?"

"Did I tell you about Sebastian?"

"Yeah, the archaeologist dude, right? You found him at your doorstep, injured. He was attacked by the Aifra. You told me."

"Yeah, that's the one. Do you know what he said to me after I found him?"

"No, what did he say?" Chris furrowed his eyebrows.

"I thought it was silly at the time, but now I don't know …" Amon paused, before continuing. "He told me about this monster."

"Ha!" Chris started laughing. "Since when did you start believing in monsters?"

"I don't, but I do believe in Egyptian legends. And this monster, he is from our legends."

"So, what about this monster? Did someone slay it already, or no?" Chris joked.

"That's the part I found silly," Amon said with a straight face. "According to legend, he should be thousands of years old, but Sebastian believes he's still alive."

"He must be watching too many fantasy movies." Chris chuckled.

"No, he has a point. Here me out. You remember the Script of Horus, that we found in Hawara?"

"Of course, how can I forget!"

"Okay, so it has an evil twin. And it's called the Script of Ra, Ra being the Egyptian Sun God. When we first found the Script of Horus, Wanda thought it was in fact, the one belonging to Ra."

"But it wasn't. So, where's the Script of Ra?"

"Exactly. Wanda and I have been wondering this for some time now, and based on some circumstantial evidence, Wanda believes that it has been stolen and that the leader of Aifra has it. If that is the case, then he could very well be the monster, Sebastian was talking about."

"How?"

"Because Sebastian did his own archaeological investigation on the Monster of Egypt and his conclusion is that it is an all-powerful being, that is still alive today. He seems to believe that it's because it had discovered the Script of Ra and had activated it somehow."

"I see. That would also explain the extraordinarily long life …"

"Correct." Amon nodded. "Wanda's theory and Sebastian's match up."

"And together they point to the leader of the Aifra," Chris whispered, his face as white as a sheet. "Have you told anyone about this yet?"

"No. I didn't get the chance. I wanted to speak to Wanda about it in person when I got to London, but I had to come here right away. And since then, we've been on Zoya's trail."

"Well, if this is true, we need to be extra cautious. I hope we find Zoya as soon as possible. Let's go, we still have a bit of a drive ahead." Chris stood up hastily and dusted the seat of his jeans. Amon followed him to the car. In half a minute, they were off again.

Neither of them, spoke much for the remainder of the drive, with Chris concentrating on the hazardous drive to their destination, and Amon ruminating on his latest realization. The sun was about to set beyond the cliffs, by the time they arrived at the lonely izba, standing like a watchtower above the desolation.

Chris parked the car right at the gate and walked up to the front door. He was half-expecting a padlock affixed to the knocker. But no such lock hung from the door. Feeling optimistic, he knocked tentatively. Although there were no lights inside, it did not mean that it was unoccupied. The occupants could be asleep or listening to music in the dark. Amon came to stand beside him.

"Why are we knocking?" he asked.

"I don't want to scare them in case, they are—"

Amon pushed the door open without waiting for him to complete the sentence. "Then, it would be locked from the inside, no?" He turned to say, as he walked in.

The pitch-black interior of the cabin looked empty, but not unkempt. Chris pulled out his flashlight and lit it. The room looked comfy and lived-in. The furniture did not have layers of dust coating them. The floor too appeared to have been recently swept. There was a fireplace at the end of the room and walking up to it, Chris noticed the half-burned pieces of wood, that could not have been there for more than a week.

"Someone was here recently," he said. Amon was at the other end of the room lighting a lantern. There was a light switch by the door, that had not worked. Perhaps, it was a power cut. But in all likelihood, this place was not connected to a grid at all. The wiring was probably there, just in case that situation changed in the future.

Amon brought the lantern to the coffee table and collapsed into a sofa. "I didn't think they'd still be here." He sighed.

"Me neither," Chris confessed.

"Should we rest here tonight?"

"I think that's best. Let's figure out a strategy and get some rest. I'm going to start a fire, and maybe you can bring out the food."

"Okay," Amon said, rising from his seat.

Chris leaned over the hearth and started rearranging the wood inside, with his hands. As he was doing this, something caught his eye. It was a folded piece of paper, burned unevenly along the edges. He grabbed it immediately and walked over to the coffee table. There, he flattened it out with his palms and brought the lantern closer.

Amon had seen him from his corner of the room. "What is it? What are you looking at?" he asked.

"It's a map." Amon, who was standing over him, squinted at the page. It looked like a map of the area, with two locations circled with a red pen. The lower one had no writing next to it. But right over the other one, it said, Frozen Saint's cave. "This is where we are." Chris pointed at the lower circle.

"And that," Amon said, tapping his finger on the second circle, "must be where the previous residents of this cabin wanted to go."

"Looks like it," Chris agreed.

"Do you recognize the handwriting? Is it Zoya's?"

"Nope. I dunno … should we just head their tomorrow, maybe?"

Amon shook his head. "We have no idea who this map belonged to. It would be stupid to waste our time following their trail, until we know who they were."

"You're right, but it does seem likely—"

"Let me see that," Amon interrupted, snatching the paper from the table. He kneeled on the floor beside the lamp and scrutinized it closely. He flipped it over to study the other side. As he did this, his lips widened into a grin. "I think it's safe to follow this trail," he said.

"What made you change your mind?"

Amon handed the page over to Chris. "This." There, sketched at the bottom right-hand corner of the page was a little heart, pierced with a Cupid's arrow, and inside, the words: "Yuri and Zoya."

* * *

Nancy was sitting guard outside their cave that night, when Zoya came to sit next to her. "What's up, chica? Can't sleep?" Nancy asked.

Zoya nodded. "You know, I've been wondering … when you ran from the Aifra, how many days did it take you to get here?"

"Three, four, five. I'm not really sure. I was running, like I was possessed or something." Nancy shrugged.

Zoya slung her arm over Nancy's shoulder. "I dunno how you did that."

"When you know that your life is at stake, you'll do anything, girl."

"Hmm. I suppose. So, if you got here on foot in a few days, then the Aifra camp's not that far, isn't it?"

"Yeah, I never thought about it like that. But I guess, it isn't. There are no roads though. So, they're not gonna get to us quickly."

Zoya nodded. "Besides, I think our cave is well hidden."
"It is."

"So where is it then, the Aifra camp?" Zoya asked, after a brief silence.

"It's in the north. In the mountains along the lake."

"Ummm … these are mountains along a lake. Is it in *this* mountain range?"

"Look chica, I was never as smart as you, and I have no idea about ranges and stuff. All I know is that, it's quite far.

After this hilly area ends way up north over there," Nancy pointed in the corresponding direction, "there are thick forests. For miles. If you pass through those forests, staying along the shore of the lake, then you can get to it. It's a huge camp site in a valley between hills. Once, you get there, you won't miss it."

"So, they were right!" Zoya whispered.

"Who was right?"

"My friends. They came to this region to look for an Aifra camp and never found it." She didn't mention that she had been here too, but in all honesty, she was not here to look for the Aifra, so this detail was currently irrelevant.

"Are they like you too? The Hekamissus or whatever?"

Zoya chuckled at the mispronunciation. "Yep."

"Then they're lucky they didn't find it. They'd have their asses skewered, if the Aifra had their way."

"Hmmm. But I don't think that would stop them. In fact, I have a feeling that they might be back here right now. Looking for me. I've been away for too long." Zoya yawned and stretched onto the grass next to Nancy. Before her friend could respond, Zoya had already dozed off into a quiet, blissful sleep.

CHAPTER TWENTY-THREE

It was an unusually warm morning, even by Aleppo's standards, when Alex stood in formation for their daily military drill. Their commander was an Aifra veteran with a face shaped like the crescent moon. Above his hooked nose were beady, jet-black eyes, that seemed to suck away your soul like a black hole.

"Atten … tion!" he croaked in his guttural voice, and the entire unit obeyed at once. "Repeat after me," he continued, "We must fight for our freedom!"

"We must fight for our freedom," the unit roared.

"We must die for our peace!" the commander said.

"We must die for our peace," came the echo. The slogans continued for a few more minutes, ending as usual with a tribute to the Sun God, Ra.

Alex was feeling dizzy. He was not used to such oppressive heat, and all the shouting was making it much worse. He wondered, if he was going to have a heat-stroke. What a pathetic ending that would be to his illustrious military career. He marched with his unit to the end of the courtyard and back five times. His clothes were sticking to his body, like an additional layer of skin. He wanted nothing more than this session to be over, so that he could hit the communal showers.

The thought of the showers relaxed him, as he raised his gun and aimed at a cardboard cut-out for their target practice. He wondered, where Wolfgang might be right now. His disappearance had not come as a surprise to Alex, but what made the situation worse, was that Jeremy had vanished as well. General Sapieha's suspicion had immediately fallen on Alex, which was strange, because if Alex had had any hand in Wolfgang's escape, then why would he still be here? Perhaps the General thought, he stayed behind as a spy. In any case, he had been grilled every day since their disappearance, and assigned a punitive shift of dishwashing in the kitchens.

Alex knew that the search for Wolfgang was on, and until his friend was definitively marked as missing or dead, they would continue to keep him alive. By the time the shooting practice ended, Alex's ears were ringing, and all he wanted to do was sit down. So, he found himself a boulder in the corner and was making his way towards it, when the deep, droning hum of a bomber-engine sounded overhead.

Acting on instinct, he ducked for cover, only to realize that the others were staring at him, like he was insane. He looked up and saw that the bomber was a friendly craft. A Russian Su-34, similar to the one he had repaired for Wolfgang's voyage. A pang of emptiness hit him like a hammer. In all these months, he had grown so accustomed to Wolfgang's companionship, that even the days of their captivity had not seemed as dire. But now, he was all alone, trapped in a situation, from which there was no easy way out, barring death.

Alex sat himself down on the boulder and stretched his aching legs. Soon, it would be time for lunch and after that another interrogation session with the General in Hama. Thankfully, they had not yet resorted to torture, but today might turn out different. He did not sit in the sun for too long, just enough to relax his muscles. Once this was accomplished, he got up and headed in the direction of the showers.

"Colonel!" someone hollered to him from nearby, "Colonel Costas!"

Alex froze in his tracks. No one called him Colonel over here. The man came up to him and rapped on his shoulder making Alex jump. It was Jeremy. Alex's mouth fell open and for a while, he stood there gasping under the bright mid-morning sun. "Sir, you need to come with me," Jeremy said, handing him a letter inside a sealed envelope.

Alex's hand trembled as he accepted the letter—surely his death sentence—and ripped it from its envelope. The handwriting inside was familiar. But in his anxious state of mind, he had to read it in its entirety to realize that it was Wolfgang's. He had instructed Alex to follow Jeremy to wherever he led him, without exhibiting any external emotion. He did not explain what the plan was after that. Nor did he sign or date the letter.

Alex folded the letter and stuffed it into his pocket. Whatever Wolfgang was planning, was certainly dangerous, since there was a search in progress for Jeremy. But this was Aleppo not Hama, so the General would not be here. Of the others in the camp, only a few were aware that Jeremy was missing and among them, even fewer knew the reason why.

"Okay, let's go," Alex said to Jeremy, who immediately

turned to walk towards the airfield. The courtyard was mostly empty now, their morning drill being over. The timing of Jeremy's arrival was perfect and knowing Wolfgang, Alex did not think this was an accident.

Crossing the courtyard, they turned left onto the path that led up to the airfield. Alex looked nervously around him, to make sure they were not being followed. His companion however, seemed unconcerned. In fact, he marched through the camp in broad daylight, without the slightest hint of fear across his features. As if nothing could touch him, as if he was strolling through a meadow in full bloom.

"Jeremy, what's going on?" Alex asked tentatively, once they were far enough away from the troops.

"Nothing. We're heading to my plane. It's over there," he said, pointing west.

"Umm ... do the others know?" Alex asked, lowering his voice considerably.

Jeremy stopped and scrunched his face up, like a child trying to understand the meaning of words he has never heard before. "What others?" he finally said, before continuing to walk.

Alex shook his head from side to side. He wanted to ask so many questions, but did not think it would be wise. Jeremy had either gone insane or was being deliberately evasive. Either way, he did not want to do anything, to attract unwanted attention to themselves. So, he followed his companion silently, walking at a brisk pace towards the military aircraft.

The bomber was standing in the middle of the tarmac that was otherwise deserted. Alex nearly ran up to it, but Jeremy followed at a leisurely pace, like they were about to embark on a joyride. In Alex's mind, none of this was making any sense. But then again, he knew that Wolfgang was a special kind of person, with unusual and otherworldly powers. Who was he, Alex, an ordinary human, to question his strategy?

The aircraft took off shortly after Jeremy had boarded, but instead of heading toward Hama or Damascus, as Alex had expected, it sped towards the northeast. For the next couple of hours, it continued flying in that direction, quickly departing Syria and crossing over what appeared to be the Caspian Sea. Alex sat stiffly in his seat for at least an hour before venturing a sidelong glance at the pilot. Jeremy seemed a lot calmer than usual and was navigating the skies with a sense of childlike enthusiasm, very different from the warlike posture he would assume before.

Noticing Alex stare at him, Jeremy turned his head towards him. "Chips?" he said, with a deadpan expression, while extending a bag of chips.

Alex hesitated, but finally decided to grab a couple of chips from the bag. "Thanks Jeremy," he said, and then, "You *are* Jeremy, aren't you?"

"Of course. Why?"

"Nothing."

Jeremy raised his eyebrow inquiringly.

"It's just …" Alex began, "you seem … different."

Jeremy nodded. "I had an accident, I think," Jeremy explained.

"What kind of accident?"

"I don't know. Don't remember exactly. I forgot some things." And after a pause, "Because of the accident." As soon as Jeremy said these words, Alex began to feel slightly at ease.

If it's a memory issue he's having, then Wolfgang probably had a hand in it, he thought. Out loud, he said. "I see. Where are you taking us now?"

"Back home," Jeremy replied, without any sense of irony.

Alex did not know whether to laugh or to cry. Jeremy's home was in Syria. Had been for years, since he had been adopted by the Aifra as a boy. But, by now, Alex understood what was going on here. Wolfgang must have messed with his mind somehow, that he no longer knew which were his real memories and which were implanted. In a way, this was cruel. In another twisted interpretation, it was poetic justice. A sort of retribution for all the cruelty he had been inflicting upon innocents over the years. But Alex did not know Wolfgang to be a cruel man. So, he realized that his friend might not have had any other option, but to do what he had done.

Before Alex could ask Jeremy where home is, the GPS in the cockpit gave him an answer. They were heading towards Irkutsk and were almost there. This was worrisome. Wolfgang had obviously gone to Russia, but western Russia. But now, he was somehow in Siberia? How? And more importantly, why? He wondered whether in his current state of mind, Jeremy was capable of answering any of these questions, but he asked anyway. "Is Wolfgang in Siberia?"

"Yes."

"What is he doing there?"

Jeremy shrugged. "Watch out for some turbulence as I fly over the mountains," he said.

Alex closed his eyes and wished that he had asked the Oracle of Delphi to look into his future, after all. If Wolfgang was camping out somewhere in the Siberian mountains, then it did not bode well for either of them. He decided to refrain from asking his befuddled pilot any more questions, before landing. He was attempting an extremely precarious landing through misty skies, and distracting him during it would be suicidal.

The strong Siberian gusts tossed the plane about, like a pebble on a beach, as Jeremy cut between the sharp peaks and valleys of the Sayan Mountains. Then, they cleared the turbulence and made for a clearing between the ridges. It was an extremely difficult landing, but Jeremy managed it and finally they were on land again. There was no one around them, neither bird nor beast nor human, and for a second Alex feared that he had stepped into a trap. He was about to open the door to step out when Jeremy stopped him. "Don't," he warned.

"Why not?" The plane began to tremble slightly, the ground falling away below it. "What's happening?" Alex shouted in a panic.

"We're going to Lumania," Jeremy said, and as if on cue, the plane bearing its passengers descended slowly into the earth.

CHAPTER TWENTY-FOUR

For a while, Alex did not know what was happening. Darkness encapsulated them from all directions, and a stifling, claustrophobia engulfed him. Jeremy, sitting by his side did not seem to be at all fazed by any of this. Although the earth was falling away below them, Alex did not feel any weightlessness, like he had expected to. Nor did there seem to be an earthquake happening, that could split the ground apart this way. Surely, there had to be an explanation.

In a couple of minutes, the darkness was dispelled by a soft, unearthly glow emanating from the walls around them. The plane was descending vertically like an elevator, through a wide shaft carved out of stone. The walls of the shaft seemed to have been doused with a photoluminescent material, that lit up the tunnel with its dreamy light.

Soon, the tunnel was cleared and the craft hung in mid-air above a gigantic underground cave. Below, at ground level, Alex could see three bald figures in flowing white robes, standing with arms raised above their heads and between them, a familiar smiling face. The plane landed on the cave floor with a thud. Immediately, two of the robed individuals walked up to the pilot and encapsulated him in a strange invisible cage. Then, they walked off with Jeremy's body suspended between them.

As Alex was watching all of this with awe, Wolfgang walked up to the passenger-side door and waited for him outside. Alex disembarked cautiously. "Where are we?" he asked, looking around.

"This is Lumania, a hidden underground kingdom with inhabitants more powerful than myself. Speaking of which, meet my friend Kazhar, a Lumanian native, who will escort us to our living quarters."

Alex noticed the third bald figure, smiling at him from Wolfgang's left. "Oh! Err … nice to meet you … Kazhar." He extended his hand for a handshake, but retracted it quickly when Kazhar merely nodded in response.

"Shall we?" Wolfgang said, extending his hand in the direction where they needed to go.

"Sure," Alex replied, still kind of giddy from the happenings of the last few minutes. They walked to the far end of the cave, where a beautifully carved tunnel led to the kingdom's interior. Kazhar led the way through nested tunnels and carved passageways, winding between picturesque town squares.

For a while, Alex remained silent, appreciating the amazing civilization, with its hanging gardens, trickling waterfalls and twinkling phosphorescent lights, that was unfolding before his eyes. He had many questions, but for the time being, he suspended his disbelief in order to simply enjoy the company of his friend in his newfound freedom.

After several minutes, he turned his head and smiled at Wolfgang. "So, you came for me?"

"Of course! Didn't I tell you, I would?"

"You did. It was silly of me to doubt you. After everything …"

Wolfgang slapped his friend's shoulder cordially. "It's alright. We are all human."

"Are we?" Alex asked with genuine curiosity. "What about them?" he whispered, pointing at Kazhar who was several feet ahead.

"They are human too. Difficult as it may be for you to believe. I will tell you all about them. We'll have plenty of time while you're in quarantine."

"Quarantine?" Alex sounded shocked. "Why, what's wrong with me?" He touched his forehead to check his temperature. They had begun to climb up a set of winding stone steps to a hanging corridor along the cave wall.

Wolfgang burst into laughter. "Nothing's wrong with you. It's just a custom over here. All strangers need to be quarantined for a few days. For security screening purposes." And then noticing Alex's confusion, he added. "Don't worry, you won't need your passport."

Before them, Kazhar had stopped in front of an open doorway along the hanging corridor. "We're here," he said, gesturing with his hands for them to enter. It was a small, austere room with a stone table at its centre, surrounded by colourful sitting cushions. Along the walls, were a couple of bare mattresses on the floor, with a blanket and pillow each.

As Alex was examining this arrangement, Kazhar stood at the doorway with his arms raised and face scrunched up in concentration. Moments later, a whirlpool of wind emerged from nothing and populated the area between the entrance to the room and the corridor.

"Whoa, what's that?" Alex yelped.

"I don't know exactly," Wolfgang explained. "But it'll keep us from leaving the room."

"So, we're prisoners?" Alex stared incredulously between Wolfgang's face and Kazhar's.

Wolfgang, who was sitting cross-legged on one of the cushions, looked up and smiled. "Not me. Just you." Then, he roared with laughter.

"That's not funny!"

Wolfgang stopped laughing. "Don't worry, I've volunteered to stay with you the whole time. Besides, Kazhar will visit."

Kazhar nodded. "It's only two days. Since you're Wolfgang's friend." He walked up to sit beside Wolfgang at the stone table.

"What about Jeremy? I hope you tossed him behind bars!" Alex said.

"Something like that," Wolfgang replied. "But we have more important things to worry about. Such as the safety of my other teammates. And your wife, Irene."

"Irene! What's happened to Irene?"

"She's safe for now, in the protection of my organization. But we have raised the stakes. With your escape and mine, General Sapieha will feel cheated. He'll most certainly redouble his efforts to hunt us all." He turned to Kazhar. "Tell me, my friend, is there a way to access Lumania from London, England?"

"There is not, my friend. Why do you ask?"

Wolfgang rubbed his beard. "Because that's where they are, my friends. And with me hiding in Lumania, I don't believe I'll be able to get them all the correct paperwork and visas to arrive in Russia any time soon."

"Visas? What are they?" Kazhar asked, puzzled.

"They are kind of entrance permits into each of our above-world realms. They're complicated and time-consuming to obtain."

Kazhar became thoughtful. At least, that is what it looked like from the tiny creases appearing across his forehead. Other than that, he did not seem to be generally able to show any real emotion. "Lumania used to be a vaster kingdom in the past," he reflected. "But much of the tunnels in heavily populated areas have been abandoned. Nevertheless, I have heard that they still exist …"

"Okay … and?" Alex, who was now sitting across from the other two, leaned over the table to inquire.

Kazhar turned to Alex. "Our realm extended to Western Europe in the good times, but our trains no longer travel there. However, we do have small carriages that do. And perhaps a few of us could travel using them …"

"Are they as fast as your trains?" Wolfgang asked.

"Oh, they are faster! But there is one problem."

"Which is what?" Wolfgang asked.

"The tunnels do not cross the English Channel. They stop in France."

"Oh, dear. That complicates things." Wolfgang furrowed his eyebrows and leaned back on his elbows. "Since this is France, not Russia, they could potentially fly to Paris or take the train. But I'd rather not have them use commercial transport, where official documents will be required for long distance travel. Given what we now know about high-profile US Generals being compromised by the

Aifra, anyone could be tracking them. Crossing the Channel would have been easier, but …"

"Nothing much crosses the Channel anymore these days," Alex cut in. "Except refugee boats, of course."

At the mention of refugee boats, Wolfgang jolted upright. "That's brilliant, Alex! Refugee boats. Why didn't *I* think of that?"

"Wait, what? How's that gonna help? The refugees travel from France to England and not the other way around. Besides, I'm quite sure they're not going to offer a bunch of strangers a ride. These are illegally trafficked humans—"

Wolfgang raised his palm to interrupt this exposition. "The refugees travel both ways. The ones seeking refuge, travel *towards* England and the ones turned away by immigration, travel *away* from it."

"Okay, you got me there," Alex said. "But even if that's true, how are your friends going to sneak into a refugee boat?"

Wolfgang sighed. "You're forgetting who you're dealing with here. My compatriots are all endowed with gifts similar to mine. They will find a way, trust me. Especially, since my friend Alejandro is going to be with them."

"I believe you," Kazhar said.

"Good. Now tell me Kazhar, where can they go to meet your people?"

"You need to ask them to cross over at the Strait of Dover, boarding from near Dover and arriving at Calais on the other side. Once there, I will make sure to meet them at the docks. We will be in disguise. So, it's better that I travel personally and perhaps, have Ishin and Larvo with me, if they agree. That way, Alejandro and the others will recognize us."

"Wonderful," Wolfgang said. "Thank you so much, my friend. You truly are, an unusual Lumanian."

"I would not say unusual. Our race is pacifistic, but we are also kind. We have always been known to take risks for people who truly deserve our protection. That is how, we had brought your kind to our realm, in the first place."

"Quite true. I forgot. My kind will always be grateful for your hospitality." Wolfgang bowed his head in a display of homage.

Kazhar smiled a half-smile. "Let us go then and have our dinner. After that, you can inform your friends of our plan. I hope to be able to meet them in Calais, France by tomorrow night.

Wolfgang turned to Alex. "I'll be right back. Your dinner will be served to you here by our hosts. And I assure you, it's going to be nothing like the garbage we were eating at the camp. I'll explain in detail the plan to bring Irene here, when I return."

CHAPTER TWENTY-FIVE

When Chris woke up in the log-cabin on their first morning in the mountains, Amon was already awake and munching an apple by the window. He had a piece of paper spread out over his lap, that he was studying closely. A beam of mellow, lemony light fell across the page, making it appear almost translucent.

"Good morning," Chris said, as he walked up. "How long have you been up?"

"Not long." Amon bit off a large chunk off apple as he spoke. "I was looking at the map."

"I see," Chris said, as he searched for his toothbrush. "And?"

"It doesn't look like we can drive all the way."

"Hang on, I'll be right back." Chris disappeared into the bathroom to wash up. He brushed his teeth and splashed his face with ice-cold water from the sink, to drive away the early morning sleepiness. Feeling more alert, he grabbed himself a muffin and returned to sit across from Amon. "If there are no roads up there then what do we do with the car?" he asked abruptly.

"Nikolai warned me this might happen. He suggested we leave it here, if we were planning to travel by foot later. The ranger will be back in a couple of days. He'll let Nikolai know."

"Fair enough. What about the keys?"

"We can drop it in the kitchen drawer."

"It'll be a long hike. Do we have enough supplies?"

Amon scratched his chin. "We do, but we can't possibly carry it all."

Chris got up and started pacing. "Hmmm. I don't know …"

"Don't know what?"

"What If we go all the way up there and don't find them?"

Amon nodded. "That's a distinct possibility. To know if they're still there, first we have to figure out why they were going, to begin with."

"You're right. And like I said before, it must have been Zoya's idea all along. I had guessed this before, but now I'm more certain than ever."

"How?"

"Because, look at where they're going." Chris pulled the map out of Amon's hand and pointed at the upper red circle. "Yuri marked it as the Frozen Saint's cave. I've heard Zoya speak about the Frozen Saint before. She was interested in finding out about him last year. At that time, I'd wondered why she wanted to know, but I never asked. Maybe I should've …"

"Okay, so Zoya went looking for this Frozen Saint person and dragged Yuri with her. But how do we know, if they found him?"

"We don't. We can't. Not in this desolate place at the back of beyond. But they certainly haven't returned to Irkutsk." Chris looked at Amon meaningfully.

"Which means ... they're still out there somewhere. In the mountains."

"Exactly. But probably, still not at the Frozen Saint's cave. Because, either they found him or they didn't and if they did, they would've probably returned. If they didn't, they could still be searching. Elsewhere in the neighbourhood."

"I agree. These are all the optimistic guesses. The pessimistic ones ... I don't even want to go there."

"Don't!" Chris cautioned. "No need to think negative, until we have a solid reason to do so. I learned this from the time *you* went missing." he added with a sad sort of smile.

"Good idea. Okay, so we just go there and search the area, until we find either or both of them?"

"More or less. But I brought something that'll help us to be slightly more precise." Chris walked over to his backpack and pulled out a wire mesh helmet with antennas sticking out of it.

Amon's eyes widened. "The puma-hunting helmet?"

"Well, it's human-hunting now. Basically, I just removed the snow leopard brain patterns from it and all it does at the moment, is stimulate my brain the way the RF towers do. That way, I will be able to pick up human brain activity within a certain range and determine how many individuals are nearby."

"Makes sense. Let's go, if you're ready. We have a long journey ahead."

Chris and Amon left the izba with about half the supplies they had brought with them, mostly deciding to discard their stores of food. Chris was fairly confident, that they could survive for a few days in the jungle, by foraging and perhaps even fishing. Additional supplies were just dead weight. So, they carried only the items they could not replace along the way. These included, weapons, equipment, climbing gear, tent, sleeping bags, water bottles and first aid kits. Not having any knowledge of the other log-cabins along the route Yuri and Zoya had taken, they travelled via a more direct and hazardous path.

The advantage Chris' party had, that Zoya's did not however, was Chris' rock-climbing expertise. He had secured Amon to himself with climbing ropes and carabiners as before, which helped them navigate the slopes better. Amon too seemed to have learned much from Chris during their previous expedition and was no longer a weak link. With spring in full swing by now, the weather was also starting to favour hikers.

Nevertheless, it took them three days and a half of rigorous hiking with brief nightly stops in between, to reach the shrine of the Frozen Saint. Amon was the first to crawl inside through the opening, Zoya and Yuri had dug up. Chris followed close behind, stopping to inspect Zoya's handiwork around the door.

"The snow here was kicked in," Chris began in full detective mode. "Must've been Zoya. There are boot marks in the dirt and …" He knelt close to an indentation in the ground. "And … sleeping bags. These are the outlines of sleeping bags. Two of them." He turned his head towards Amon, but his friend did not seem to be listening. He was standing close to the wall, flashlight in hand, staring at its surface in a semi-hypnotic state. "What's wrong, Amon? What did you find?"

"These writings, they are hieroglyphics," Amon

whispered.

Chris walked up to stand next to him. Presently, he reached his palm out to touch the markings.

"No!" Amon shouted. "Don't touch them. They could be dangerous. Hieroglyphics sometimes have mysterious powers."

Chris retracted his hand and turned to Amon. "Are you sure, that's what they are?"

"Fairly sure, yes."

"Strange." Chris furrowed his brows in confusion. "What is an Egyptian script doing, etched across a cave in Siberia?"

"I don't know and that's why I'm worried." Amon took out his phone and switched it on. He had kept it switched off, hoping to preserve the battery until they found a tower again. The plan had worked, because the phone turned on without any difficulty. He quickly clicked some pictures of the script and turned the phone off again. "Whoever has written this script is definitely no longer here. So, where are Zoya and Yuri?"

"They were surely here. I saw marks from two sleeping bags on the floor," Chris mumbled. "And two sets of footprints." He sat himself down on the floor as he spoke.

"At least that means they weren't captured."

"Correct. No additional footprints, no signs of a struggle," Chris sniffed the air and searched the floor with his flashlight. "No traces of blood."

"I didn't see any footprints outside. Other than ours, of course," Amon reflected.

Chris sighed. "There must have been some fresh powder since they were here, which wiped out their prints."

"The only way now is to use your head-set."

"Correct. We can try right away." Chris started removing his backpack to retrieve the device in question.

"Let's not. I don't like the feel of this cave. We should get out of here first."

When they stepped out of the cave, the sun was setting behind a cliff along the western horizon, covering everything around them in a pinkish blanket. "It's dusk already," Chris said softly. "We should pick a spot and set up camp for the night."

Amon nodded and pointed north. "That way looks better. There are trees."

Walking north for about a kilometre or so, they reached a clearing between trees in relatively flat land. Chris got busy pitching their tent, while Amon collected dried branches for a fire. It was rather late, so they decided not to use their headsets, to search for their friends right away. They would have no access to any electricity in the wilderness, so saving the battery on their equipment was essential. If they detected any activity tonight, it would not be wise to go wandering into the forest at this hour. So, they made a meal out of some dry chunks of bread and a few slivers of cheese, they had salvaged from their initial stock and went to bed early.

In the morning, Chris was awakened by the sound of birds chirping in the trees. As he sat up and rubbed his sleepy eyes, he heard a different distinct noise from the distance—that of twigs crunching under booted feet. His heart leapt violently inside his chest. He nudged his sleeping friend to wake him.

"What?" Amon said, a little too loudly.

"Shhh! Listen. Can you hear it?"

Amon squinted. "Birds?"

"No, not birds. There it is again."

Amon cocked his head to one side and listened.

"Crunching sound."

"Yep. Could it be …"

"Maybe." Amon leapt up. "Grab your gun," he said, as he pocketed his own.

The sound was coming from deep within the forest to their left, but the source of it was hidden from view, because of their sheltered location behind some thick bushes. "I'll go that way." Chris pointed to an opening between the bushes. "You go there." Amon immediately disappeared through the brambles; his gun raised. Chris stood there a second longer, to train his ears on the sound. It was intermittent, muffled and seemed to be coming from more than one direction. Chris picked one of those directions and pushed forward through the foliage.

The touch of spring seemed to have worked wonders for these woods. New leaves sprouted from every bough in sight and hung like a canopy over his head. As he progressed farther, the thickness of the foliage nearly blotted out the sun. Chris advanced cautiously through the semi-darkness, always on the alert for wild animals. The sound of crunching feet grew closer. He wondered if he should call out Zoya's name to alert her, but decided against it, in case It was someone else entirely.

In front of him, a couple of metres away, he could see a glade between trees, he made his way towards it. In the open, at least he would have a larger field of view. He regretted not having checked the area for signs of human activity, using his head-set, last night. That way, they could have at least been prepared. One more step and Chris was out of the woods and standing in broad daylight, inside a small clearing. He was not alone.

In front of him, a tall, muscular man was plodding

across the clearing, with his back turned towards Chris. The man's head was turning rapidly from side to side, as if he was searching for something.

"Stop, don't move! I have a gun," Chris hollered. The tall man raised his hands, dropping a weapon, and pivoted quickly on his heels. He had a wild and rugged face and an even wilder gaze that he now fixed upon Chris, with such intensity that it felt like he would burn holes into his assailant's skull. "Who are you?" Chris continued. "What are you doing here?"

"I could ask you the same question," the feral man all but roared.

"You could. But I'm the one holding the gun," Chris retorted, trying to exude more confidence than he felt.

In the blink of an eye, the tall man kicked his own fallen gun up with his boot and caught it in mid-air with practiced ease. "How 'bout now?"

Chris swallowed heavily and took a step back. The stranger was too far away for Chris to access any of his thoughts. The only other option would be to jump. As Chris was weighing his options, someone called out from his right. "What the hell are you doing?" asked a familiar voice. "Is that you, Chris?"

Chris turned slowly to his right; his gun-hand still raised before him. "Yuri!" He smiled. "Who's that guy?"

"He ... he's a fiend," Yuri said. "Please drop your guns," he added, turning to nod at the other man.

Chris lowered his hand and walked up to Yuri. He noticed that the wild-looking man was also advancing cautiously in this direction. Up close, he noticed something strange across Yuri's features. Was it panic, worry, frustration? He could not tell. "What's wrong?" Chris asked, furrowing his face.

"Well … I … we were looking for something."

"Some *thing*, or some *one*?" the tall man asked Yuri.

Yuri looked visibly flustered by these words. Opening his mouth to speak, he closed it again quickly. His second attempt at speech was interrupted by Amon's recognizable voice. "There you are, Chris! And looks like you found them. Where's Zoya?" Amon said in his booming voice.

Chris looked up to see Amon approaching from the other end of the forest. "Yeah, exactly. Where *is* Zoya, Yuri?" Chris asked pointedly.

There was a loud bang behind Chris, like the report of a gun. Everyone turned in that direction. Before anyone could stop him, the tall man rushed across the clearing and straight into the forest, in the direction from which the noise had come. A couple of minutes later, he emerged with a scrawny young lady in tow. Seeing them, Yuri hurried towards that direction. Chris and Amon followed, reluctantly.

Yuri was speaking now, in a rushed sort of way. "Did you fire that gun? Why? What happened?"

The girl was sobbing. "I … I didn't fire … I tripped and fell. And the gun went off."

"Oh, I see," Yuri said comfortingly. "Sit down, you're alright now. Why were you in the forest?"

The girl sat down on the grass hugging her knees. Then, hiding her head between her arms, succumbed to an onslaught of fresh tears. She raised her head after a few seconds and started mumbling through her sobs. "She left. Right before dawn. So, I followed her. But … I couldn't …. couldn't …"

"Couldn't what, Nancy?" Yuri urged. He was now kneeling next to the weeping girl with his hand over her shoulder.

Nancy said nothing for a while, her slight frame quivering with every new bout of tears. "Couldn't find her," she finally said.

"Can someone please explain what's going on here?" Amon asked at last, turning to Yuri and then Chris.

Chris shrugged. Yuri sighed deeply and stood up. Then, stammering slightly he said, "Zoya … she's … missing."

CHAPTER TWENTY-SIX

By the time Chris and Amon arrived at the cave, where everyone else had been hiding, a piercing, icy drizzle had begun to fall. Nancy, who Chris had learned, was Zoya's childhood friend, was shivering slightly when they went inside. The tall, savage man had introduced himself as Peter Cobb, Dr. Cobb's lost son. But beyond that, he had not said much more.

They had walked the distance between their tent and the cave, in a somber sort of silence, like a funeral procession. Now, they huddled around the cave floor, as Peter quietly worked at building a fire. Once the fire was lit, Chris removed his boots and brought his feet closer to the crackling warmth of the flames.

Yuri was sitting on the edge of a straw mattress, his head bowed, while Nancy sat crouched in a corner, still weeping softly. Amon crawled over to sit beside Chris on the floor, and Peter was still stoking the fire.

"Does anyone want tea?" Amon suddenly said, breaking the silence. "I've got some."

"Sure," Chris replied and a few other muted agreements were heard across the room.

As Amon dug into his backpack for the tea, Peter had already poured some water from a five-litre plastic bottle into the only saucepan they had in the cave. When the tea was ready, everyone extended a receptacle for the warm beverage, either a flask cover or a crude mug and Peter poured the contents of his saucepan into them.

Taking a sip of his tea, Chris said. "Nancy, when did you find out that Zoya was gone?"

Nancy wiped her eyes and nose on her shirt-sleeve and looked up, "It was when I woke up for my guard duty at the cave door. Around four, I think. Her bed was empty and there was this note on it, look." She reached into her pocket and took out a crumpled piece of paper.

Chris leaned forward and accepted the note from her hand. "Dear Nancy, I've realized that I'm the reason, everyone is in danger. So, I'm going to fix this. I am the only one who can. It's my fate. It's my destiny. Please be safe. I love you and tell my parents, I love them too," Chris read. "What the heck does *this* mean?"

"I don't know," Nancy replied in a teary voice. "But It doesn't sound good."

"No, it doesn't," Amon agreed.

"So, what happened when you got this letter? You went after her?" Chris asked.

Nancy nodded.

"And how did you know which way she went?"

"I didn't. But I could guess. She probably went north."

"What makes you think that?"

"Because of something I told her before. I mean, she wanted to know …"

"Wanted to know what?" Chris coaxed. Nancy seemed to be drifting in and out of a dream. Her eyes weren't completely focussed, and the words she managed to squeeze out of her mouth just trailed off abruptly.

"Where the camp was."

"What camp?"

Again, Nancy fell silent. As if, she had fallen asleep with her eyes open.

Peter cleared his throat. "The Aifra camp," he explained. Adding, "I think Zoya's gone to the Aifra camp, the one which Nancy fled from. And the very memory of that nasty place is having this kind of effect on Nancy. Especially, now that her best friend is probably on her way to face some of the same horrors, that she had once encountered."

Chris' eyebrows shot up. Partly because, he had not expected this kind of eloquence from Peter to begin with. *Appearances can be deceiving*, he thought to himself.

Out loud, he said, "But why? Why on earth would she go to the Aifra camp all by herself?" Peter shrugged. Chris looked at Nancy who shook her head from side to side. "Gosh, this is terrible, if it's true. Do you know the way to the camp?" Chris asked Peter.

"I don't remember much. My memory has many gaps in it. Like parts of it have been erased. Zoya mentioned something about some ancient magic that caused this."

Chris sighed. "Yeah, she was mostly right about that. What about you, Nancy? You must know where this camp is."

"I do. It's in the mountains to the northeast of here," Nancy said.

"Can you point it out for us on a map?"

"Even better, I can take you there. We can leave as soon as—"

"No!" Amon cautioned. "You're not going anywhere. Going straight to the lair of the Aifra is an extremely dangerous thing. We have to work out a solid plan first and get backup if we can."

"Backup? Where are we going to find backup?" Yuri, who had been listening the whole time, now spoke up.

"I can think of a place where we can go to get some help, but more on that later. First tell me this, Nancy, how large is this camp you speak of?" Chris asked.

"Oh, I can't say exactly. But there were dozens of tents. And thousands of soldiers. It's huge. We can't hang around here and chat about it all day. Not while Zoya has gone there to get herself killed. Why can't we go right now? All of us? We are five! Peter and I can fight. And you two can do magic like Zoya. Plus, we have Yuri," she added almost as an afterthought.

"Five of us is not enough, if, like you say, there are thousands of soldiers in that camp. Besides, we have every reason to believe, that they aren't going to kill Zoya. At least, not until they try to use her as a bait, to get to the rest of us. The ones with the magic, according to you," Chris explained. "So, if we go right now, unprepared as we are, we'd be walking straight into their trap. And that means, we are all going to be dead. And swiftly."

"You see," Amon joined in, "last year, we had a hunch that the Aifra headquarters are here in Siberia somewhere, and we had come here to search for it—"

"Yes, Zoya told me. But you didn't find it," Nancy interrupted.

"Correct. But if we had, then we could have done a reconnaissance of their position and arrived here more prepared. Now, we are at a disadvantage. Our enemy has the upper-hand. By the time we find them, they will have a valuable hostage, so we will lose all leverage over them."

"Okay, you lost me. I'm no military general. Please, just tell me how we can save Zoya." Nancy begged; anxiety written all over her face.

"Like my friend Amon just said, we'll need backup. But we also can't wait for that backup to arrive. We need to send a scout out there, as soon as we can, to scope out the situation ..." Chris turned to look at Amon, who nodded with understanding. "Okay, here's what we're gonna do," Chris began and everyone gathered around to listen. "One of us will go up to the Aifra camp as a scout. It has to be either myself or Amon, because we have some special abilities. I suggest it be me, since we're going to need stealth and that's something I'm good at."

"I'm okay with that," Amon said. "It might require some climbing too, since the camp is in the mountains."

"Correct," Chris agreed. "The second part of the plan will be to find back up, and that will be Amon's job. Amon will lead everyone else—"

"No! Not everyone else!" Nancy objected. "I'm coming with you to the camp."

Chris chuckled inadvertently. "I can see why Zoya is friends with you. She would've said the exact same thing. Anyway ... you joining me is not going to help our cause. In fact, you're just going to be a liability. A wanted Aifra defector, who will only attract too much attention to herself. So, no, you're not coming." He ended authoritatively.

Nancy mumbled something inaudibly under her breath.

"What was that? Chris asked.

"I said, I'm not happy about this," she clarified.

"That's too bad." He paused for a second and then, "So as I was saying, Amon will lead the rest of you to safety."

"Safety? I though he was going to get backup!" Nancy exclaimed.

"That too," Chris said, before turning to Amon. "Do you think you can make it all the way to the Sayan Mountains with everyone?"

Understanding his meaning, Amon said, "I don't have to, there's a Lumanian entrance near Irkutsk, remember? I'll retrace our path back to the car and drive back to Irkutsk. Kazhar will let us in."

"Lumanian ... why does that name sound familiar?" Peter murmured almost to himself.

"Because, they are the ones who wiped your memory," Chris explained in a matter-of-fact kind of way.

Peter jolted slightly. "And we are going back to them why, exactly?"

"They are a powerful, pacifistic race, who are sure to give us shelter. And some among them have helped us fight our enemies in the past. So, there's a good chance, we can ask for their assistance again this time."

"Pacifistic, eh?" Peter spat. "I beg to differ. There's no way I'm going back there again!"

"Well ... I do understand how you must feel. But they could have done so much worse to you, couldn't they? They didn't kill you or torture you. They just—"

"Are you even listening to what you're saying?" Peter growled. "How is wiping someone's memories right out of their heads, not torture?"

Chris fell silent. He really did not have any appropriate comeback for this. Peter definitely had a point. But before Peter could claim victory over the situation, Amon decided to step in. "There are certain memories that are better forgotten, don't you think?"

"No, I don't," Peter said, viciously. "I think memories are a part of a person's identity and nobody has the right to wipe them out without that person's consent." Now, Amon too had nothing more to say. For the next several minutes, everyone sat quietly in their corners without speaking a word.

Finally, Chris stood up and shook his cramped legs. "In that case Peter, would you rather stay in this cave? We can come and get you—"

"No! I'm coming with you. To the Aifra camp. I didn't actually defect, so they're not going to kill me right away. Besides, I want to help. This is important to Nancy. And therefore, to me." He looked at Nancy, whose eyes seemed to be welling up again.

"I …" Chris began.

"Take him with you," Amon said. "It might even help him remember some of his past. He has years of training with the Aifra. Some of that must be ingrained inside him, like a muscle memory. He will be a good asset to have in a fight against them."

"But we aren't fighting; just scouting," Chris objected.

"Still." Amon persisted.

"Okay, you do have a point. Fine. Myself and Peter are going after Zoya. The rest of you will head to Lumania—"

"Is it worth mentioning that *I* want to go to the Aifra camp too?" Yuri cut in.

"No!" All the others said at once.

"I do know these mountains better than all of you combined," Yuri insisted.

"I know," Chris said, "But like I explained before, we want to be surreptitious, not conspicuous. One person was best for this mission, two is still a bit much and three would be a big no no. Please. I hope you'll understand." Chris placed his hand on Yuri's shoulder in a placating kind of way.

Yuri sighed. "Alright then. But I can come back with the reinforcements, right?"

"Hopefully, yes," Chris said.

"Very good. When shall we start?" Amon asked.

"Let's cook some lunch first. And after the meal we can take off. We have heavy hiking ahead of all of us. So, we can't leave on an empty stomach," Peter declared decisively, and muted murmurs of agreement were heard from around the room.

CHAPTER TWENTY-SEVEN

Zoya had been plodding tediously through the jungle in the pre-dawn darkness, when she had heard footsteps behind her. Rapid footsteps approaching closer with every step she took. Realizing that someone must have come after her, probably Nancy, she had sprinted at once. She had jostled hanging branches out of her way, scraped her arms and legs against brambles and protruding rocks, fallen on her face a few times, but she had kept going. Gotten up and kept going, until there was no energy left in her. Until her feet were leaden and her arms hung limply by her side.

By around mid-day, Zoya had collapsed in a heap, behind a copse of trees. She had a tent in her backpack, but was too tired to set it up. Other than a vague notion, that she had to travel northeast, she had no particular sense of direction. Nancy had mentioned having run for an indeterminate amount of time, anywhere between three to five days. This did not help Zoya much at all.

Lying in the tall grass under the shade of a tree, she

217

wondered if she had made a mistake. Whether she should have planned this better, before leaving. There would have been no point involving the others, because she was certain that knowing her purpose, they would not have let her come at all. Right now, her brain was too tired to operate with full efficiency. So, she decided to take a nap.

When she woke up, maybe an hour had passed, maybe several; her body could not tell. The sky, however, was inviting upon itself, a foreboding sort of darkness. Digging into her backpack Zoya pulled out a flashlight. Her stomach growled. She felt a pit of emptiness inside her belly that was not merely a crushing hunger. The hunger she could quell, however.

She reached into her bag and found a solitary granola bar lying at its very bottom, like a crumbling reminder from a happier time. She wolfed it down within minutes. Last night, Nancy had made wild rice and rabbit stew. Zoya had saved some in a small plastic bag, but now was not the time to eat it. She still had a very long way to go.

Once she was done eating, she pointed her flashlight bravely into the darkness and matched forward. Although, inside the forest, it had seemed like night had already fallen, outside, the lingering last rays of the sun were just fading into twilight. Zoya looked around her. To her left was a sheer cliff, dropping hundreds of feet into a rocky bottom by the lake. To her right, a forked path winded down into a wooded area.

Standing at a fork in a path is always a moment of deep conflict for humankind. And for Zoya it was no different, both literally and metaphorically. She stood there, full of indecision, as well as a deep sense of longing. A longing for everything and everyone she was erasing from her life, her childhood, her school, her friends new and old, her parents, Yuri. The thought of Yuri had not crossed her mind until now. Why did it matter that she was leaving him? After all, their recent chemistry had been a mere flash in the pan. Or had it?

Over the many sleepless nights at the cave, ever since they had found the Frozen Saint's shrine, she had figured out the connection between herself and the so-called saint. She had been determined from that day onwards, to make it right for herself and for everyone else, suffering because of it. It had been a visceral sort of feeling, that had buoyed her feet forward up until this moment. But right now, standing at this physical crossroad, her fierce resolve seemed to waver.

Zoya knew that the clock was ticking. Soon, she would run out of food and water and perhaps even the motivation to continue. Yet, her feet refused to move forward, her mind refused to make a choice and her heart refused to leave it all behind.

Only if there was a sign, she thought wistfully.

Just then, something fluttered overhead. *A bat,* she thought, ducking instinctively. The animal flew over her and landed on a tree along the left arm of the forked road. Zoya squinted at it. It was no bat, but a beautiful bird, white as first snow.

"A dove!" Zoya exclaimed, not expecting such a bird in this part of the world. Inquisitively, she walked towards it. The bird did not flinch or try to fly way, but sat there on a hanging branch with its head bent and staring at Zoya through intelligent glassy eyes. "Hey you, little bird. How are you?" Zoya said softly to it, and as if on cue it fluttered to her shoulder. She petted it gently, ruffling its soft feathers with the palm of her hand. It seemed to understand her in a peculiar sort of way and cooed its understanding with a rhythmic bobbing of its throat.

As soon as she stopped petting it, the bird flew away again and landed on a tree further down along the path. Then, it turned its head and watched her, as if waiting for her to follow. Her intuition told her to follow it and so she did. Thus, her path was decided. They trotted forward into the woods, bird and girl, the one cooing and the other humming softly, as they made their way to their grim destination.

* * *

A few miles away in Irkutsk, deep under the surface of the earth, in ancient and magical Lumania, Kazhar had gathered Ishin and Larvo and the three of them were ready to embark upon a journey of their own. The plan was to travel to the western most city of their kingdom, a region under modern-day Turkey, and from there, to uncover the ancient tunnels, that had once extended all the way to Calais. Just before their departure, Wolfgang joined them in a meeting room, after having spoken to his friends in London.

"Were you able to contact them?" Kazhar asked, as soon as Wolfgang arrived.

"Yes, I went to Irkutsk and made a call. I've explained everything."

"Good. You told them the plan?"

"I did. They are prepared to travel as refugees. They will disguise themselves accordingly and travel to the Strait of Dover tonight."

"Will they be able to gain passage on the returning boats?"

"I hope so. Some subterfuge will have to be used. And

memory tampering perhaps. But Wanda and Albert can handle that and Alejandro will be there too."

"Very well. There will be no way for us to communicate with them henceforth. They are aware of this, yes?"

"Yes, of course. It's a risk we are all going to have to take. However, there is another issue that is worrying me."

"And what might that be?"

"It is concerning my friends Chris and Amon."

"Oh! What has happened to Chris and Amon? Are they in any kind of trouble?" Kazhar asked agitatedly.

"They are …" Wolfgang hesitated. "Currently untraceable."

"Why?"

"You see, some time ago, they had left on a mission to Irkutsk that required them to travel into the mountains. At first, they kept in touch with our friends in London. But after that, the communications stopped. We have every reason to believe that it is because they are in the mountains, where our mobile communication devices do not work. But we can't really be sure."

"In that case, would you like us to go look for them, instead?"

"No, I think you should go to Calais, because without you there, we cannot get the others to safety, quickly enough. If it is necessary, I will go after Amon and Chris. In the meantime, who watches the Lumanian portals in the Irkutsk area in your absence?"

"Why do you ask?"

"Because, my belief is that, if they run into any trouble, Chris and Amon might try to seek shelter here, hoping that you will be around to let them in."

"I see." Kazhar turned to Ishin. "Do you know who will be watching the gates here?"

"I do not know. But I could ask Pala, if you wish?" Ishin said. "She is very dependable."

"I agree. However, she has never met Chris or Amon, and I fear that she will not recognize them." Kazhar replied. Then, turning to Wolfgang, "would you mind accompanying her, perhaps?"

"No, not at all," Wolfgang said.

"It is settled then," Ishin concluded. "What about the other shift? We need at least two shifts per day, to cover a whole day's worth of surveillance."

Kazhar became thoughtful and for a while no one spoke. Then, suddenly Larvo stepped up. "I've heard that Nirmala's Seeing abilities are improving every day, perhaps we might ask her?"

"That is an excellent idea!" Kazhar replied. "Please wait for me at the station, while I make these arrangements before our departure. I will be back as soon as I am done." They left the room and parted at the doorway, with Ishin and Larvo going off to plan their journey and Wolfgang and Kazhar making their way to Amethyst.

CHAPTER TWENTY-EIGHT

"*A*lejandro, wake up," *someone was saying to him. It was a lulling female voice. Nirmala, Alejandro thought. His heart leapt up with joy. He rubbed his eyes and sat up. It was a foggy morning and a dreary drizzle was pattering onto the windowpane next to his bed. For a moment he could not recognize where he was. It felt like his childhood home in Mexico with his mother making tamales in the kitchen. He could almost smell those tamales. He looked at the smiling face of Nirmala. Except, it was not Nirmala at all, but another beautiful face. It was Maria, his wife. Now long dead.*

"Alejandro, wake up," the voice came again. He jolted up. It was neither Nirmala nor Maria, but Wanda Faraday. He was no longer in his childhood home, but in a tiny flat in London, sleeping on a couch in the living room. But the rain was still gently pattering onto the window pane, staining it with tear tracks, like it always does in London, nine months out of twelve.

"What time is it?" He said yawning.

"Time to get up," Wanda replied.

"But the refugee boats arrive in the night," Alejandro protested.

"Before that, we will have much work to do. Make-up, costumes and other gear, need to be taken care of. And then, we would have to travel separately. Albert has all the routes planned. One of us will have to travel by bus, which will take the longest. The others will need to take the train or use ride share. We'll decide who travels by what, later. But for now, breakfast is in the kitchen. Chop chop!" Wanda said in a peppy tone before taking off to her kitchen.

"Jeez," Alejandro grumbled, as he rolled out of bed. He took a few minutes to clean up, before heading to the kitchen. He wasn't allowed to shave because that would make him stand out like a sore thumb among the refugees. So, he satisfied himself with simply brushing his teeth and washing his face.

Irene was already in the kitchen with Wanda, when he arrived. Albert was in his own apartment and would be joining them later. The air was heavy with the savoury smell of fried eggs and crackling bacon.

"Mmmm, I'm starving," Alejandro said, as he sat at the table.

Irene swerved around, frying pan in hand and smiled. "Sunny side up?" she asked.

"Yes, please." Alejandro rubbed his belly as Irene whisked over and slid the eggs expertly onto Alejandro's plate before returning to make some for herself.

Wanda, who was cooking herself some oatmeal, came to sit across from him. "Irene will be in charge of our make-up department," she said, after swallowing a mouthful of gelatinous porridge.

"How's that?" Alejandro eyed Irene across the room.

"I used to be in a theatre group in high school," Irene remarked over her shoulder. "They always put me in charge of costumes, because I was so good at it." She walked over to sit at the table, carrying her plate of eggs.

Alejandro reached over and grabbed some bacon from a tray in the middle. "I see. You are a woman of many talents. So, what's the plan?"

"The plan is—" Wanda began, but was immediately interrupted as the doorbell rang. "Ah, that must be Albert." She went to open the door, returning only a moment later, with Albert puffing and panting behind her.

"What happened Dr. Cobb, you look exhausted?"

"Oh, nothing … it's just." He plonked down on a chair. "Been collecting all the costumes and make-up on my way here. It's all in the bag. In the foyer." Albert pointed in that direction with his thumb.

"Excellent," Wanda said, munching on an apple. "We should start getting dressed after lunch and then we can leave separately. Albert, I suggest you take a cab. You will likely be the most conspicuous of us all, so I don't want you taking public transit, lest a student of yours recognizes you on the way."

"Aye," said Albert.

"I will take the train. Which is a bit slower, so I will have to leave before you. But you two, will have to be the first to leave because you're getting there by bus." Wanda pointed first at Alejandro, then at Irene.

"Oh, we're going together?" Alejandro asked, with a slight pang in his heart from the memory it resurrected, that of him and Nirmala in disguise, travelling to Dwarka at night, many long months ago.

"Why, is that a problem?" Irene retorted.

"No, not particularly," Alejandro mumbled weakly.

Taking the hint, Wanda jumped in. "It makes sense strategically for you two to travel together. You see, Irene should ideally travel with one of the Hekameses for her protection. And who is better suited for it than you. Because you could easily pose as a couple."

"And that would raise less suspicion," Albert added.

"Fair enough. But how will we disguise ourselves? Me, I can probably blend in with the refugees. My skin is dark enough. What about you three?" Alejandro asked.

"See, I have a plan for that," Irene said. "A majority of the refugees will be from the Middle East and Northern Africa. So, to blend in, Wanda and I will wear hijabs. You, like you said, will blend in just fine with a bit of light make up. I'll take care of that before we leave. Dr. Cobb however, will be the biggest problem. I don't want to use too much make-up on him, because someone will surely catch that. I'm going to go with a long beard and bushy eyebrows instead. I hope that's okay with you, Dr. Cobb?" Irene turned to Dr. Cobb for approval.

"Yes, perfectly fine as long as they don't see my bloody face. Beard and eyebrows are in the bag, as per your request."

"Perfect. We'll also have pandemic masks handy to cover our faces. I'll go and sort out the costumes right after I clean up." Irene got up to wash her plate.

Wanda leaned over the table and said to Alejandro. "Don't wait for us when you get there. Albert brought in some sensors from the lab. Use them if you have to. Use your other skills and get to the French side. We will meet you there."

"And what if you can't make it?"

"We will," Wanda assured.

"What happens when we make it across? Kazhar will be there?"

"And Ishin and Larvo. We have to look for them as soon as we land, do you understand? If we linger there for too long—"

Alejandro raised his hand to stop her. "Yes, I know exactly what'll happen if we linger too long."

"Good. I'm going to my room to make some more arrangements. In the meantime, please help Irene with the dishes," she said with a smile, before getting up to leave.

* * *

That afternoon, after lunch, Alejandro stood in the foyer of Wanda Faraday's small flat in London, dressed like a Kurdish refugee. Irene had done an excellent job with the costumes and make-up, just as she had promised. She had spent all morning, adding the final touches with incredible detail. She had messed up Alejandro's hair and dusted it with talcum powder to make it appear unkempt. She had also drawn dark circles under his eyes, grimed up his hands and gotten him into weatherworn clothes from Value Village.

Irene herself had covered her entire head with a hijab to hide the reddish-brown locks underneath. Since full burqas are forbidden in France, she had covered her face with a pandemic mask instead. Thus dressed, she appeared in the foyer at around two in the afternoon, shortly before it was time for them to take off.

Wanda and Albert, completely unrecognizable in their costumes, walked them to the door and wished them luck. "Remember what we discussed?" Wanda quietly said to

Alejandro at the last minute. "Don't wait for us, once you find them."

Alejandro nodded and took off. They did not speak much to each other along the way, to avoid drawing any attention to themselves. There was no direct bus to their destination. So, they took a roundabout path involving multiple buses along a preplanned route, and finally arrived at Dover Harbour, before dusk.

The harbour was far from empty at this hour, with a couple of cruise ships ready to take off with their passengers and sail to beautiful holiday lands. A cool, salty breeze brushed their faces and the smell of faraway cuisines wafted from the kitchens of the luxurious foreign vessels, docked along the harbour. In the distance, the sun had already been swallowed up by the sea, leaving behind a horizon streaked with bright orange brush strokes. Soon, absolute darkness would descend upon the earth and then, their actual journey would begin.

"What do we do now?" Irene asked softly, when they arrived.

"Well, we can wait here and keep an eye out for the boats. Although, I doubt that any would turn up before it's dark, or ..." Alejandro trailed off. An elderly couple was approaching them, probably returning to their cruise ship. The woman smiled as she passed, but the gentleman grunted his disapproval.

"Or what?" Irene insisted, once they were out of earshot.

"We could walk north along the coast towards the lighthouse of South Foreland."

"Why? What's over there?"

"The White Cliffs of Dover. They are very scenic and a famous tourist attraction. So, might as well, right?" Alejandro teased.

"How can you do it?" Irene asked incredulously.

"Do what?"

"Joke at a time like this?"

Alejandro shrugged. "I told you. I'm immature."

Irene punched his arm playfully. "No, seriously, why should we walk north?"

"Because ... the Channel is narrowest around that area, so a refugee boat might just sneak up that way to avoid detection."

"Oh! That's a great idea! Let's go then."

They turned towards the Eastern Docks and located the footpath leading to the White Cliffs. As it was starting to get dark, the foot-traffic along this path had become staggered. Nevertheless, it was still extremely scenic with the path curving gently upwards along the glistening coast and a blood-tinged sky hanging above it all, like a circus tent. Alejandro pulled out a pair of binoculars from his raggedy backpack and looked through it at the Channel.

"I don't see anything yet," he said. "But this path runs for a few kilometres, so I'll continue to keep an eye out."

"I don't think we should go too far, though," Irene cautioned. "This path is rising steadily upwards and when it goes all the way up to the cliffs, I imagine it'd be too steep for any refugee boat to unload its passengers."

"Good observation."

They continued to walk silently and Alejandro scanned the waters intermittently with his binoculars. But, after about fifteen minutes of continuing thus, they were yet to spot a refugee boat.

Alejandro sighed and turned to Irene. "Looks like a quiet day today."

"Damn! That can't be good. Perhaps we should've stayed at the docks and waited for the others."

"No. It's best if we keep our distance from the other two. If they find another boat before us, then they can get there earlier and let the Lumanians know we're coming. If we travel separately, we won't risk everyone at once, in case one of the boats gets into trouble." Alejandro turned away from the coast and moved towards a boulder, along the opposite end of the path. "I think I need a cigarette," he said.

He found a flat piece of rock against the edge of the path and sat down for a smoke. Irene came to sit beside him. "My husband smokes too, you know," she said fondly. "It's a terrible habit. So, I'm gonna tell you what I always tell him. You should stop. If not for yourself, then for those you love."

"There's no one I love."

"Oh, c'mon! I can tell that you're lying—" A disturbance further down the path cut her off in mid-sentence. "What was that?" she whispered.

Alejandro tossed his half-burnt cigarette and crushed it under his boot. Then getting up, he said, "C'mon, let's find out!"

They didn't have to walk far, before the source of the commotion became clear. In front of them, a large crowd had gathered around a cordoned-off area. Behind the picket line, two motorcycles stood at a thirty-degree angle to each other, each carrying several life jackets. Beyond those, several people in coast guard uniforms stood peering down the edge of the cliff and shouting instructions over a megaphone.

"DO NOT DISEMBARK THE BOATS! I REPEAT, DO NOT—" a fat man was yelling over the edge.

Alejandro didn't wait to hear the rest of it. Instead, he grabbed Irene's arm and pushed his way towards the motorcycles. "C'mon," he whispered into her ear.

"What are you going to do, point your gun at them?" Irene asked; her eyes wide.

"No, I don't have my gun. Guns are not allowed where we're going. I have something much better." They were very close to the motorcycles now. The crowd had dispersed from this area and were gathering around the coast in a huddle. Alejandro boarded the motorcycle closest to them and indicated with a wave of his hand for Irene to join him.

"But you don't have a key—" Irene began, while mounting behind him on the bike.

"Shh! I don't need a key. Don't talk." Alejandro stared intently at the dashboard and in a second, the engine roared to life. He turned the vehicle sharply around and made their way down the sloping path to where the edge of the road was closer to the sea. Then, he stopped the bike and dismounted. Untying a life jacket from the vehicle, he tossed it to Irene. "Put it on," he said brusquely, as he began removing a second life jacket for himself. With his vest securely fastened, he walked over to the edge and scanned the coast below. Just as he had suspected, there was a refugee boat down there. Actually, not one, but two refugee boats. Both packed to the brim with passengers. He pointed at a path in front of him.

"This will take us down to the coast. It's a little steep. Can you manage?"

"Don't underestimate me, Garcia," Irene said cockily. She scampered down the path with great skill and

Alejandro followed close behind. Soon, they were at the bottom and near enough to the boats to run to them, if they wanted.

As Irene was about to do just that, Alejandro pulled her back. "We can't be conspicuous. We should wade in through the water. If someone asks, I'll tell them we fell over. You don't open your mouth, got it? Your accent is too American."

Irene nodded. They stepped into the icy-cold water that cut through their clothes like dozens of knives. Then, stepping as quietly as possible through the gently lapping waves, they arrived at the second boat, the one farther away from the coast. There was a lot of chaos around it when they arrived. A few of the passengers had stepped off the vessel and were negotiating with the coast guards standing above their heads. Others had merely waded into the water and were watching the events unfold with anxious curiosity. Children clinging to their mothers' arms were crying bloody murder from both boats, and no one was noticing what the other was doing in this utter confusion.

Taking advantage of this situation, Alejandro and Irene slipped into the second boat and sat down right at the back, with their heads bowed. People were speaking around them in rushed, unfamiliar languages. There was a lot of shouting back and forth, instructions barked through megaphones, pebbles hurled, curses exchanged and guns waved from above. In the end, after what felt like an endless night of futile negotiations, the boats began to turn back. Alejandro sighed a breath of relief.

The boats sputtered their way back to Calais amid an air of heavy uncertainty hanging over its passengers, like an ominous cloud. People sat packed tightly together, like potatoes in a sack; their knees and shoulders bumping against one another with every rise and fall of the waves. No one spoke anymore. The children, hoarse from crying, were beginning to dose off, lulled by the waves. The mothers sat sullen-faced, wiping tears from their eyes. The fathers and brothers and uncles grumbled unspeakable curses in their respective mother tongues. Among them, Alejandro sat as invisible as the eclipsed moon. Beside him, he could hear Irene's soft and rhythmic breathing, but he did not turn his head to look.

After what seemed like forever, Calais became visible in the distance. The first boat docked before them and the passengers disembarked in a disorganized jumble. Then, their boat reached the shore. Alejandro jumped off and looked around him. It was crowded and chaotic everywhere. Satisfied with this view, he extended his hand to help Irene out. She hopped off lightly, into roughly a foot of water. Alejandro could see that she was shivering slightly. "We're almost there," he whispered comfortingly. Now we just need to—"

A flashlight in his face blinded him momentarily. "You two! Where are you from?" A husky female voice barked at them from the darkness. She had a heavy French accent. Beside him, he could hear Irene give out a tiny squeak.

"Iraq, madam," Alejandro said, in his best attempt at an Iraqi accent.

"Mademoiselle," the woman corrected.

"Sorry," Alejandro mumbled.

"Take off your mask!" the woman said, pointing at Irene.

"She has fever, Mademoiselle," Alejandro intervened.

"Ah, okay. You have passpo'?"

Alejandro had his Mexican passport. He was pretty sure Irene was carrying her passport as well. But producing them would be disastrous. The visas would not be the problem. The fact that they were trying to sneak into the country, disguised as Iraqi refugees, would beg all kinds of questions.

"No," Alejandro said promptly. "No passport."

"Okay, come with me," she said, pointing the flashlight in the direction, she intended them to go.

Alejandro's hands felt clammy, as he shoved them into his pockets. Unconsciously, he felt for his trusty revolver inside them, but all he found, were his wallet and a half-empty pack of cigarettes. Disappointed, he followed the lady along the muddy path leading away from the coast. Irene was breathing heavily by his side. But thankfully, she did not resist or open her mouth to speak.

They walked up the gravelly path and onto a paved quay where a motley group of individuals were crowding around in confusion. Floodlights lit up the area where they stood, and in their illumination, Alejandro could see several uniformed guards herding people into small groups and escorting them away.

Their captor turned to them. Alejandro noticed that she was wearing a similar uniform. "Go stand there," she said, pointing to a group of about twenty refugees, waiting less than three metres away.

Alejandro and Irene obeyed dutifully. The lady followed close behind. Before leaving them with the rest of the party, she whispered something into the ear of a colleague, who was nearly seven feet tall and wore a dark, menacing expression. Irene gasped ever so quietly at the sight. Alejandro covertly extended his arm and gave her shoulder a soft, comforting squeeze before turning to face the officer.

"This way," the menacing man said to the group. Murmurs were heard from around them. Then, some signs of lack of comprehension. "You speak English? Parlez-vous français?"

"Yes, English speak." Alejandro raised his hand, wearing a naïve sort of expression.

"Good. And Arabic? You speak Arabic?"

"Yes Arabic," Alejandro lied. He could see Irene turning a shocked face in his direction.

"C'est bon. Tell them to follow me," the tall man instructed.

Alejandro breathed in deeply. Streams of sweat were trickling down his forehead and clouding up his vision. He wiped them off with the sleeve of his shirt. Then, he turned to the group and started speaking gibberish, while gesticulating heavily with his arms. At first, the crowd stared at him in bewilderment. One of the younger men in the party pushed forward to accost him. For a split second, Alejandro felt the urge to turn on his heels and run. But that would be unthinkable. So, steeling himself, he grabbed the young man by his shoulders and stared into his eyes, his lips still moving rapidly, churning out a string of unintelligible words.

Memory tampering was never Alejandro's thing. He had very limited success with it on his best days and failed miserably on his worst. But today was an exceptional day. The lives of many innocents hung in the balance. He could not fail them. He reached out with all the tentacles of his mind and searched for an opening, his face scrunched up, his heart thumping violently in his chest.

Several breathless seconds passed before anything noticeable happened. Then, through his flattened palms, Alejandro felt a surge of heat rise up from the young man's body into his own, like a transference of energy, a signal of understanding. Alejandro relaxed his arms and stopped blabbering. The young man flashed him a crooked smile before turning to the others and explaining Alejandro's message in fluent Arabic. There was some more murmuring. At last, the company started walking towards the tall security officer.

"Bon! This way," the man said, before leading them away from the harbour.

They walked together in a huddle for about a hundred metres or so. Then, the guard led everyone into an abandoned shipyard, that seemed to be operating as a temporary immigration booth. It was extremely crowded inside, with the stuffy air reeking of sweat and vomit. Babies were crying from all directions. Toddlers were ripping their parents' documents to shreds. The floor was grimy from spilled, sticky beverages of many colours. Some figures were shouting and others sleeping, bunched up on the sweat-slicked floor.

Their escort zigzagged between the scruffy throngs without stopping to even glance at them, as he led his captives all the way to the back of the room. He stopped in front of a set of closed doors, lined up along the rear wall. Opening one of these doors, he led his party inside. It was a small office with a desk at the back, overflowing with paperwork. There were rickety wooden benches against the other three walls. "Wait here," their guard said, as he left them inside.

"What do we do now?" Irene whispered into Alejandro's ear, once the officer had left.

Alejandro had no idea. They had backed themselves into a corner from which he did not see how they could escape. He nervously picked at the collar of his shirt while his eyes roved around the room. "I don't know," he murmured. Suddenly, just as he had said this, he spotted something on the ceiling. It was a small round object with a twinkling red light at its center. Alejandro immediately knew what it was and grinned to himself at the recognition. But this was only half of his solution. Now, he needed to find the other half.

Getting up, he casually strolled towards the door through which they had come in, without venturing to step outside. It was partly open and through the opening, he could see security guards posted at regular intervals around the premises, with a couple of them stationed very close to their room. As they spotted him, he immediately turned away and pretended to be pacing around the room. He walked all the way to the other end and retuned, once again reaching the half-open door. He stared out briefly from this angle and finally saw what he had been looking for. Now, the last and crucial part of the plan needed to be executed. He eyed the man who he had communicated with mentally, while they were still out in the docks. He was leaning over his knees and scrutinizing some documents. Alejandro sauntered over in that direction and accidentally bumped into his knees. The pieces of paper fell from the young man's hands and scattered all over the floor.

"So sorry," Alejandro said, ducking to gather up the fallen pages. Collecting them all, he handed them to the man, who looked up gratefully. There was a momentary eye contact, and that was all Alejandro needed. His previous success at mind-bending had emboldened him beyond belief. But this time, he had a smaller window of opportunity. Quickly, he shot his mental waves out towards the man. A flash of understanding passed between them, like electricity between live wires.

Alejandro nodded and returned to his seat next to Irene. Bending his head towards her, he whispered, "Soon, a fire alarm is going to go off. And when it does—"

"Wait, how do you know that?"

"Shh! Don't ask questions. There's no time," Alejandro admonished. "When the alarm rings, we're going to run, okay? Straight to the fire exit at the back. We have to get there before anyone else does, got it?"

"O ... kay ..."

"Okay. At the count of three." Alejandro focussed on the flat round object affixed to the ceiling that he had noticed earlier. "One. Two. Three." The alarm started ringing deafeningly through the room. But before any of the security guards could react, Alejandro and Irene had shot out the door like a pair of bullets, pushing and shoving through the crowd. Behind them, the young man Alejandro had just groomed was leading the rest of the party in the same direction, straight for the fire exits at the back.

In no time, they were at the exit which Alejandro pushed open, leading them all outside into the cool night breeze. But they did not stop running. Alejandro's plan was to run all the way to the end of the pier, where they were supposed to meet Kazhar.

"Why are they following us?" Irene asked, pointing to the remainder of their party as they ran.

"Because, I asked them to. Can't leave them here. Keep running," Alejandro replied, panting.

A couple of security guards had seen them and were sprinting towards them from their left. "Stop!" one of them yelled. "Stop!" she repeated. But the escapees did not heed this warning. They only doubled their pace instead. Alejandro kept scanning the area as they ran. They had left the shipyard far behind them and no other security guard had given chase. However, the two who had decided to follow, were gaining on them quickly.

The second security guard removed a gun from his holster. "Stop, or I'll shoot," he warned viciously. Alejandro was a fast runner, but never did he think himself capable of outrunning a bullet. Yet, with inexplicable instinct he turned sharply left and shot towards the man with the gun.

Irene's shriek tore through the night. "Noooo!"

The group had come to a halt and was watching this grim theatre play out before their eyes. But just as the guard was about to point his gun straight at Alejandro's heart, he stopped short. His arm dropped to his side as he sank slowly down to his knees. Then, he smoothly slid to the floor and seemed to be falling asleep. Next to him, his partner was exhibiting similar symptoms. As the two guards dropped to the floor, the reason behind their somnolence became apparent. A portly old man stood there with his arms raised and grinning wildly.

Alejandro laughed out loud. "Albert!" he greeted.

Albert lowered his hands. "C'mon you fools!" he said. "Kazhar and Ishin are waiting."

CHAPTER TWENTY-NINE

Amon, Yuri and Nancy arrived at the Lumanian portal near Irkutsk, close to midnight, nearly three days after they had set out from their hideout in the mountains. Being close to a city, this portal was different from the others. The approach was through the crypts below an abandoned church.

Amon guided his companions down a winding metal staircase to the very core of the building, several meters below the surface of the earth. The crypts here were empty, but the spacious chamber remained, serving as an entrance hall to the Lumanian realm.

Amon walked up to the rear wall of the room and placed his palm on a specially demarcated slab of stone, in a typically Lumanian gesture. He knew that Kazhar manned the Seeing Crystals here. At least, on some of the shifts. He knew most of the others, who watched these gates as well. He waited for any of them to respond.

"What are we doing?" Nancy asked, confused.

"Requesting entry."

Nancy crossed her arms across her chest. "But there's no—" she stopped short of completing the sentence as the wall Amon was touching, began to move aside. Amon removed his hand and waited.

Lumanian magic was efficient but oftentimes painstakingly slow. It took several minutes for the hefty stone slab to slide away, revealing the passage to Lumania beyond. In the semi-darkness of the interior, Amon could see a blurry figure beckoning them inside. It was definitely not Kazhar, but someone much shorter, perhaps even female. What was most unusual however, is that this person was not bald like most Lumanians, neither was she dressed in traditional Lumanian garb. Instead, she was wearing, what looked like a faded pair of jeans and a polo shirt. Her long, jet-black hair was pulled up in a messy bun.

For a heartbeat, Amon began to back away, but Nancy had already rushed forth. He followed her inside, almost in order to caution her. But, as soon as he stepped into the dimly glowing Lumanian hallway, he recognized the emissary who stood before them.

"Nirmala! What are you still—" he started, but was immediately cut off by the hurried and jumbled volley of words that leapt from Nancy's rapidly moving lips.

"She is missing. She left. My friend … gotta come with us … please … back up. Need back up," she pleaded with Nirmala.

"Please, calm down. What's going on? Who's missing?" Nirmala asked anxiously. Then, turning to Amon, "Who is she?"

"She's Nancy. Zoya's friend. And this is Yuri … er … another friend of ours. And Zoya, is sort of … missing."

"Oh, dear! Not again!" Nirmala gasped, raising her palms to her cheeks in an involuntary gesture. "Where is

Chris? Wasn't he supposed to be with you?"

"He was. He went after Zoya. To scout the area before we return with reinforcements," Amon replied.

"We need to take these two to quarantine," a sweet, youthful voice said from behind her. Amon turned towards the voice and noticed for the first time that Nirmala was not the only one who had come up to receive them. Another, youngish bald woman, in a flowing blue robe, stood behind her with a face as inscrutable as the Sphinx's.

"No, Pala, I don't think that would be necessary. They're friends of ours. Perhaps they can stay with the Novo-Hekameses. I'll ask Mercuriva. Could you find out if she would be willing to see us now?"

"I will go at once," Pala said and departed in a hurry.

Nirmala turned to the others. "Now, what is it that you were saying about Zoya?"

"She left. We were hiding in a cave and one morning before sunrise, she just went to the Aifra camp!" Nancy blurted breathlessly, her cheeks turning a shade of ripe strawberry. "It's all my fault, really. My fault—"

"Now, now, don't blame yourself. And you really do need to calm down, young lady," Nirmala said, assuming the tone of a compassionate school teacher.

At that moment, Pala jogged into the room, panting audibly. She held an elegant glow-worm torch in her right hand and clutched her belly with her left, in an effort to calm herself. "Mercuriva is not available until the morning," she said after catching her breath. "But in the meantime, she said that the strangers could spend the night with Nirmala and Amon. Does this suit you, Nirmala?"

"Sure. Nancy can stay with me and ..." Nirmala squinted at Yuri. "Yuri, is it?"

"Yes, Ma'am."

"Oh, call me Nirmala! Yuri, you can stay with Amon, if you don't mind."

"Not at all," Yuri said.

"Very well. Let's go then." Nirmala nudged Pala forward, who led the way through the winding tunnels ahead of them.

As they travelled deep into the subterranean heart of the district they were in, Nancy told Nirmala how she and Zoya had been friends since childhood. She told her about the unfortunate events that had subsequently led to Nancy's joining of the Aifra. Finally, she filled her in, on how she had fled from the Aifra and hidden inside a cave with Peter, before suddenly running into Zoya and Yuri one day.

By the time this story had been narrated, they had already arrived at Nirmala's room.

"Perhaps, I could prepare the adjacent room for Amon?" Pala asked.

"That'd be fantastic. But why don't we do that later? Our guests must be hungry, and I was hoping we could all eat in my room, while these guys tell me more about what's going on with Zoya. I know you have your Seeing Shift right now, Pala, in which case perhaps we can—"

"No, I no longer have my Seeing Shift. I passed it on to Hota, when Mercuriva asked me to prepare the rooms for our guests," Pala explained.

"That's perfect. Would you join us then, Pala?" Nirmala asked.

"Certainly. Please make yourselves comfortable, while I arrange for some food." With these words, Pala turned around and left.

"Shall we?" Nirmala gestured with her hands, inviting the others to join her in her room.

They walked in and sat cross-legged around the circular centre-table with Yuri leaning back on his elbows to relax.

"Now, let's start at the very beginning," Nirmala said to the others, once they had settled down on the floor. She turned to Amon, "I knew that Zoya had come to Irkutsk and that you and Chris had followed her, but none of us know what she was doing here, to begin with. Yuri, Nancy do you know?"

Nancy did not respond, but Yuri sat up straight. "I know what she told me, but if she had a hidden agenda, then I haven't figured it out."

"Fair enough. Tell us what she told you," Nirmala said.

"Okay. Last year, when she was in Irkutsk with Chris, she had asked me about the Frozen Saint of Baikal. I didn't think much of it at that time and told her that it was a myth I had heard about as a kid. She wanted to know, if there was a shrine of this saint in the mountains, and if I could take her there. I told her that I could take her to the place where I think the shrine might be. But then, a few weeks ago, she called me from America and said that she wanted to find this shrine as soon as possible. When I asked her why, she told me a very strange story …"

"Go on … what was her story?" Nirmala urged.

"According to her, she wanted to go there to 'balance the scales' or something like that."

"I don't get it," Nirmala confessed.

"Well, there's a legend that the Frozen Saint of Baikal can bring people back from the dead. No one I ever met, has any direct proof of this, of course. But apparently, Zoya thinks that she herself is the proof."

"Why is that?"

"Because, her parents told her so. They told her, that she was a stillborn child, but her mother refused to accept her death. So, as per the advice of her father's friend, they had taken her to this saint …"

"And he had revived her?" Nirmala asked, appearing shocked.

"Not exactly, no."

"Okay, you lost me," Amon intervened. "We know that our Zoya is very much alive. So, if the saint didn't bring her back, then what happened?"

"Her parents seem to think that it was the saint who brought her back. But that sounds absurd to me, since when they had gone to see the saint, his shrine had been empty. There was no one there at all. So, my theory is that, maybe she had not died after all. Maybe, she was in a coma or something."

"If that is what you believe, then why did you bring her to the shrine?" Nirmala quizzed.

"Because … I wanted her to see for herself that there's no such person as the Frozen Saint. That he is a legend. And therefore, she owes him nothing." Yuri sighed.

"And is that what you found? When you went there?"

"I … we …"

"No. That's not what they found," Amon replied in his thunderous voice.

"Oh?" Nirmala raised her eyebrows and turned to face Amon. At that moment, Pala returned with a couple of companions carrying several trays of food.

"We have brought you some food," she said, laying the plates across the stone table. Fresh aromas of exotic herbs and spices drifted from them in gentle waves. The Lumanians bowed and left as soon as the meal was served, leaving the others to dig ravenously into the items.

"Mmm … I'm starving," Amon said, helping himself to a large bowl of root vegetable stew.

Yuri grabbed hungrily at a plate of wild rice pilaff, while Nancy slathered her slice of homemade bread with a gooey and delicious helping of jam. "Wow, what *is* this stuff?" she asked, taking a bite out of her bread.

"Ground-cherry jam," Nirmala explained.

Amon noticed that she wasn't eating anything. "What about you, aren't you joining us?"

"No, I'm alright, thank you. I've had dinner. So, Amon, you were saying something about the Frozen Saint, before we got interrupted …"

"Oh yeah … right." He swallowed down the rest of his soup and reached for the bread and jam. You see, Zoya and Yuri weren't the only ones who visited that cave. Chris and I found it too. When we went looking for them."

"I see. And what did you see? Was anybody there?"

"Not at the time. But the possibility of the Frozen Saint having lived in that cave, in the not-too-distant past, is not as remote as Yuri might think."

"What makes you say that?"

Amon reached into his pocket and pulled out his phone. Turning it on, he opened his photo album and showed it to Nirmala. "This. We saw this etched on the wall of the cave, where the shrine of the Frozen Saint was supposed to be. Does the writing look familiar?"

"Oh my God! It looks a lot like …" Nirmala glanced at Amon with horror in her eyes.

"Hieroglyphics," Amon completed. "See, there's something else you need to know," he continued. "Based on some new information I've received from an archaeologist friend in Egypt, I have reason to believe that the leader of Aifra—"

"Commander in Chief," Nancy, who everyone had ignored up until this point, suddenly interrupted.

"Okay, whatever ... I think that he is in fact, the Monster of Egypt—a legendary being, who was granted an extraordinary boon by the Sun God Ra himself."

"I can believe that," Nancy cut in. "Ra worship and sacrifices to Ra are a very important part of the Aifra rituals."

"Thanks for sharing," Amon said. "Wanda has believed for a long time, that the Aifra is in possession of the Script of Ra, and now I am convinced that this gift that was bestowed was in fact, The Script of Ra itself."

"I see," Nirmala said gravely. "So, it follows ... that the writings on the Frozen Saint's cave—"

"Are probably excerpts from the Script of Ra. We need Wanda to confirm it but for now, this is my hunch," Amon explained.

"Could this mean that the Frozen Saint is actually, the *leader* of the Aifra?" Yuri asked, his face chalk-white.

"Yes, I—" Amon was cut off by a shrill shriek from his left. It was Nancy. She had her head bowed and seemed to be intently scrutinizing a crumbled scrap of paper.

"No, no, it's insane!" she stammered.

Amon turned to her. "What? What is it, Nancy?"

"Look! Look, what Zoya said here ... she handed the page to Nirmala."

Nirmala read it silently. *Dear Nancy, I've realized that I'm the reason, everyone is in danger. So, I'm going to fix this. I am the only one who can. It's my fate. It's my destiny. Please be safe. I love you and tell my parents, I love them too.* Then, looking up, Nirmala said, "And?"

"But don't you see? She said that she'll *fix* it."

"Okay ..." Nirmala looked perplexed.

"I mean, if it's true what Yuri is saying ... that ... that ... Zoya was brought back from the dead by this Frozen

Saint and she wanted to meet him to balance the accounts ... what is she balancing?"

"I ..." Nirmala glanced around the room helplessly, to see if anyone other than herself was able to make any sense of what Nancy was saying. Receiving no such indication from the others, she said, "We still don't get it."

"The equation of life and death," Nancy said definitively.

"What?"

"You know, life for a life, death for a death. She is trying to restore that balance. Since she was given life when she had already received death, she wants to return that life to preserve the balance. And somehow ... she too must've figured out that the Frozen Saint is our Commander in Chief—"

"So, she has gone in search of him to return the life she was given," Nirmala's jaws dropped to the floor. "Oh, dear me! I think you might be right." She turned to Amon, "What should we do?"

"We need to go there as soon as possible to rescue her. For that to happen, we need to mount a full-scale invasion against their base. But first, we need to have everyone on board. Including the Lumanians. According to Nancy, there are thousands of soldiers in that base. We need to assemble as many fighters on our side as we can, before we can even think about wresting our hostage, free from their grip. Do you think, we could ask the Lumanians for their help at our meeting tomorrow?"

"I could ask Mercuriva, the Elder, but you know how they operate. She cannot command the others to go. Each Lumanian acts of his or her own free will."

"True. But perhaps, if she sympathizes with our cause, she could spread the word."

"I'm pretty sure that's what Wolfgang is going to say as well."

"Wolfgang! That's right!" Amon exclaimed. "I can't believe I never asked. Where is he?"

"Don't worry, he's fine. He made it here. And the others will be joining soon. In fact, Wolfgang has gone to receive them, as we speak." Nirmala stood up and dusted her pants. "I'll get Pala and the others. We'll clear the plates and take Amon and Yuri to their room. You stay here." She indicated towards Nancy. "Tomorrow morning, we'll tell Mercuriva everything."

* * *

The next morning, Pala arrived bright and early to lead them to their destination. They had a hasty breakfast in the dining hall, before heading to the train station.

"Are we going to Amethyst to see Mercuriva?" Nirmala asked Pala.

"No, we are going to Zircon," Pala explained.

"Oh! Why?"

"To meet with all the Elders, of course."

Nirmala cursed under her breath and turned to Amon. "Mercuriva knows."

"Knows what?"

"That we're going to ask for their help again. That's why she's not going to see us alone."

"Isn't that a good thing?" Amon asked, as they stepped onto the train.

"Nope. The thing is, Mercuriva is very different from Solaris." Nirmala found herself a seat at the back of the compartment and waved Amon over. "I've gotten to know her quite well, in my time under her tutelage. And ..." she trailed off as someone walked past them.

"And?" Amon asked when the coast was clear.

"And she might've been more open to our request. You know what Solaris is like. I doubt that we'll have any luck with him."

"Hmm, there's nothing we can do now, but wait and see."

The journey to Zircon was a couple of hours long, and neither of them spoke for the rest of the ride. The complimentary tour of Zircon for the guests was avoided this time, because the new arrivals were still under their quarantine period. So, they made their way straight for the Room of the Elders at the heart of the city.

Upon entering the room, Nirmala and Amon prostrated themselves on the floor in the traditional Lumanian bow of greeting. The Elders reciprocated warmly. But this time, instead of Solaris, it was Mercuriva who spoke first.

"Welcome, newcomers. We are happy to receive you in Lumania."

Nancy bent her head towards Nirmala and whispered. "Should we thank her?"

"Yeah sure." Nirmala nodded. "But you should call her, Wise One."

"Thank you, Wise One," Nancy said, subserviently.

"Bow your head," Nirmala muttered, nudging her with an elbow. Nancy did as she was told.

Mercuriva's lips curved up elegantly. She turned to Nirmala, "Dear One, would you like to speak on their behalf?"

"Sure, Wise One. Would it bother you too much if we allowed Yuri and Nancy, our new guests, to stay with the Novo-Hekameses, instead of in quarantine? I promise that my team will watch over them the whole time."

Mercuriva shot a sidelong glance at the other two Elders. And then, "No, it would not bother us. They may stay with your team, starting immediately. But that is not merely what you wish to ask, is it?"

"No, Wise One. But how did you know?"

"You are probably aware that we can read your open thoughts. And your companions' thoughts were not particularly difficult to read. Especially those of the young lady, Nancy, over there." Mercuriva paused to smile at Nancy. "Pala read those thoughts. And when she approached me, I in turn, read hers."

"I should've known. Nothing is hidden from you, Wise Ones. You must then be well aware of our predicament."

"We are," said Solaris, his voice reverberating around the room. "However, you do know our credo."

"Yes, Wise One, 'those who can, may not', we are aware. However, I also recall you saying to us once, that the Frozen Saint of Baikal is a very vile sort of being. And this time, we have reasons to believe that it is he, who has our friend Zoya within his thrall. We must find a way to save her from his hands. Do you not agree?" Nirmala's tone was beseeching.

"As much as I do agree with this," Solaris began, his voice slow and deliberate, "it is however, not within our power to defy the forces, that prevent us from rising up and assisting you."

"Perhaps not you yourselves, Wise Ones. But what if, some of the others might be able? Would it be too brazen of us to ask you to spread the word among the populace?"

"Dear One, you already know our credo regarding this, as well. We do not, in any way, try to influence the freewill of our citizenry. Therefore, any nation-wide message of that nature from us, would sound like a deliberate attempt to bend their wills, which is in contravention of our credo."

Nirmala had an inexplicable urge to roll her eyes, but she checked herself. Instead, she lowered her head to avoid eye contact. An eerie kind of silence descended upon the room, as no one came forward to either endorse or contradict this argument. But just as Nirmala was beginning to wonder, whether this was their cue to take their leave, Mercuriva began to speak. Surprisingly, she seemed to be addressing Solaris instead of Nirmala in her response.

"The times are changing; do you not think so? I can feel it in my bones."

"Perhaps they are, perhaps they are not. It is not for us to judge," Solaris said mysteriously. "But until the sand starts flowing, we will remain condemned to our fates."

"Sand? What sand?" Yuri asked bewildered, but before Solaris could respond, Nirmala spoke again.

"How will you know?"

"There will be a sign. A redemption. A sacrifice. A shift in loyalties. Only then, shall the headwinds start clearing. And we shall move forward."

"Do we need just one of the above or all three," Nancy whispered into Nirmala's ear.

"Shh!" Nirmala said. Then, turning to Solaris, "What do you suggest we do then, Wise One?"

"I suggest … you follow your heart," he said cryptically. After that, he spoke no more.

When a minute had passed in silence, Nirmala bowed her head to take their leave and the Elders reciprocated. Quietly the party walked out the door to the passage, where Pala was waiting to escort them.

"Well, that was disappointing," Nancy murmured, once

they were outside.

"It wasn't anything we hadn't expected," Amon clarified. "I do believe that at least Kazhar, Ishin and Larvo would still join us though. Maybe that'd be enough?" he asked Nirmala.

"Maybe …" Nirmala's thoughts seemed to be drifting away.

"We have to host a meeting with the others. When do they get here?" Amon asked.

"I don't know … should be soon …" Nirmala kept trailing off, like someone talking in her sleep. Suddenly, she turned to Pala, her eyes regaining focus. "Pala, could you please escort these three to their chambers? I need to meet with the Novo-Hekameses, who are going to be in Zircon shortly."

"Sure, no problem," Pala said.

"Amon, please ask Pala to come and get me when the meeting is confirmed. She can also let you know when Kazhar and Wolfgang return with the others."

"What's going on Nirmala? Why do you suddenly look so agitated?" Amon asked.

Nirmala smiled, but the smile felt like a front, a façade to hide what she was really thinking. "It's nothing, Amon. If we're going to raid the Aifra mothership soon, then I need to train my forces." With that she turned around and rapidly strode away.

CHAPTER THIRTY

Zoya had walked from the beginning of time to the end of time, and if there was a destination beyond time itself, then she had walked all the way up to that very timeless place. Now, she finally understood why Nancy did not seem to remember how many days she had run, to get to Peter's cave from the Aifra camp in the north.

She was lying on the new spring grass, slightly damp from a nightly drizzle. It was probably close to dawn, but the sun's first rays had yet to emerge through the thick foliage. Her body was as stiff and unwieldy as a corpse. She could barely raise it enough to turn on her side.

The dove was still with her, dozing on a low-hanging branch over her head. So far, she had followed wherever it had led. But now she questioned her judgment. Perhaps, she should have brought a compass when she had left home from Los Angeles. Even a printed relief map of the Baikal region would have helped. At that time, she did not think she needed any of these. She had relied solely on Yuri's knowledge of the region.

254

It was too late now. Too late to regret the decision, but also too late to turn back. The only way out was forward. Forward, forward, forward until she reached the dreaded camp or an Aifra soldier found her in their territory and dragged her to their leader. She had seen a rough map of the region before she came here. So, at least she knew that the coast of Lake Baikal bends towards the northeast, as it moves away from the Irkutsk region. So far, she had stuck close to the shore of the lake, which was the correct direction. That meant, there was still hope of finding the camp.

A few birds chirped overhead. Zoya looked up. The trees ahead of her were filling up with birdsong. Morning must be near. She stretched clumsily, her arms aching from the mere effort of raising them above her head. Slowly, she sat up.

Last night, she had been too tired to pitch the tent or pull out her sleeping bag. She had simply collapsed at the foot of a tree without bothering even to eat. Now, her stomach twisted with the pangs of hunger. She searched her backpack for any remnant of food. All she had left, was a tiny chunk of hard, crumbling bread. She pounced on it with feverish zeal.

Just as Zoya was about to dig into the last morsel, the dove awoke and fluttered to her shoulder. She looked into its glistening eyes and lowered the hand, that was ready to shove the final piece of bread into her mouth. She crumbled the piece between her fingers and scattered them on the forest floor. The dove glided instantly off her shoulder and onto the grass below. Then, it began pecking merrily at the dry crumbs. Once it was done eating, it flew to a branch in front of Zoya, beckoning her forward.

Zoya staggered to her feet with difficulty. Her backpack felt like an unnecessary burden that she was ready to chuck at the first moment of weakness. Nevertheless, she hoisted it up and slung it over her back.

BANG! Something exploded or erupted right in front of her, and a flutter of terrified bird wings ripped the air. It took Zoya a minute to figure out what had happened. A gun had gone off in the distance. A human, perhaps a hunter, had fired into the trees overflowing with seasonal birds. For a fleeting second, Zoya hoped against hope that it was Nancy or Yuri or Peter even, having followed her from the cave. Tentatively, she maneuvered through the bushes and made her way to the grove beyond her clearing. The forest abruptly ended further ahead, and in the distance, Zoya could see steep peaks raising their stark heads into the pre-dawn sky.

She shot past the remaining trees and moved into the valley bellow the hills. The sky overhead was lightening fast and from here, Zoya could make out the finer details of the terrain in front of her. There were some structures, nestled amid the crags and crevices of the mountain. At first, Zoya thought they were natural structures, but as she moved closer, she recognized them for what they truly were—encampments. Dozens, even scores of them, large and small, dotted the rugged hills and valleys of this range.

There was no further doubt in Zoya's mind as to what she was looking at. It was undoubtedly the Aifra camp she had been looking for and despite Nancy's earlier descriptions, it was much larger than Zoya could have ever expected. There were probably Aifra soldiers around in these woods, and it must have been one of them who had shot at those birds. But Zoya did not try to find them and hand herself over, as she had once imagined she would.

Neither did she feel the joy or relief that a mountaineer feels at the end of their long and arduous journey to a coveted destination.

All she felt right now, was utter dread and a deep sense of foreboding. She stood there like a statue, staring at the encampment, as if she could wish it away with her mind. She knew fully well however, that even the most powerful Hekameses or Lumanian could do no such thing. As she was thinking this, the dove appeared from nowhere and flew out in the open, to land gracefully a couple of feet in front of her. Then, it cocked its delicate little head to one side, inviting Zoya to step forward.

"All right little bird. I trusted you the whole way, so I'm gonna have to trust you again this time." Zoya sighed and extended her arm for the bird to perch on it. The dove obeyed, and with it by her side, Zoya marched forward.

It did not take Zoya much longer to get to the base of the hills. The flatness of the valley, coupled with her determination to barge forward undaunted, made the minutes fly by effortlessly. Soon, Zoya and dove were at a dirt path that curved up to the first set of camps. Zoya winded her way along it, making sure to frequently swing her head in both directions and survey her surroundings. No one was following her. Nor was anyone ahead of her along the dirt track.

She kept going for another couple of minutes, before she heard something that stayed her advance. It was a low sort of growl, almost like a purr, but fiercer. It was coming from multiple points at once. Her stomach liquified into a bowl of mush. She knew exactly what that sound meant. She cleared a bend and stopped dead in her tracks. They were right in front of her—a leap of snow leopards, just like the ones they had seen last year. She could count four

257

right in front of her and another seemed to nag at her peripheral vision, but she dared not turn her head. Motion would induce them to pounce.

She was done for. Her life would be sacrificed in vain. If she was torn to shreds right here, right now, would that count as a rejection of her artificially bestowed life? Will this restore the balance or would her death have to come at the hands of the Frozen Saint, in order for the reversal to be complete?

She did not have time to come up with an answer, because the dove flew from her arm and dashed at the leopard that was closest to them. Reflexively, Zoya closed her eyes. She did not have the nerve to watch her travel-companion lay down its life for her. Thankfully, she did not have to, because a shot rang through the air and the sounds of scurrying padded feet, filled her ears. Cautiously, she opened her eyes. Three Aifra soldiers were standing there, heavily armed and menacing. One of them had fired the gun. It was a rugged-faced woman of about fifty. Another, short chubby man, separated himself from the group and walked towards Zoya. He raised a Kalashnikov and aimed directly for Zoya's heart. Zoya raised her hands above her head without thinking.

"Who are you and what do you want?" the short man, hollered.

Zoya inhaled deeply and let out a slow rasping breath. "I am Zoya Carter," she said slowly and deliberately, "And I am here to surrender to the Frozen Saint." A look of awe flashed across the man's face. He glanced over his shoulder at the others, who nodded their heads at him.

"Okay, come with me," the short man finally said. He led Zoya up the path and followed close behind with his gun pointed at the centre of her spine.

CHAPTER THIRTY-ONE

Alejandro arrived at a meeting room with Dr. Cobb in tow, the morning after his arrival in Lumania, to attend the emergency meeting that Wolfgang had convened. Irene was still in quarantine, where she had finally been reunited with her husband, and Wanda and Wolfgang were already seated around the central table when Alejandro walked in.

"Any news of Chris and Amon?" Alejandro asked agitatedly, as he entered.

"Chris ... is not here, but Amon will be along shortly. He has gone to fetch Nirmala."

"Nirmala?" Alejandro's heart skipped a beat. "What is she doing here?" His breath was coming in sharp gasps now, as if he was at the top of a mountain.

"That's what I should be asking *you*." Wolfgang smirked.

Alejandro blushed and fidgeted with the collar of his green polo shirt. There was the sound of footsteps at the door. He held his breath in anticipation, turning slowly on his heels. But it was not the one his eyes had longed to see. Instead, two Lumanians walked through the door with a man and woman in their midst. The Lumanians were Ishin and Larvo, the woman was Irene, but the man Alejandro had never seen before.

"Ah, there you are," Wolfgang hollered to the newcomers. Then, turning to Alejandro, "I asked Ishin to allow Irene out of her quarantine to join us this morning. And oh yes, let me introduce you to my good friend, Lieutenant Colonel, Alexander Costas—Irene's husband." He walked over to Alex and placed his hand warmly over his shoulder.

"Hello everyone," Alex said in greeting. He sauntered over to the cushions on the floor and sat down next to Wanda Faraday. More footsteps were heard from the passage outside and once again, Alejandro's heart skipped a beat. He braced himself for the moment, he had been dreaming about for months, and turned to face the door. Even this time, it was not who he had expected.

Amon had entered with a couple of unfamiliar faces and among them, a familiar one. "Haresh!" Alejandro exclaimed, realizing who it was. "You're here? Where's Nirmala?"

Haresh looked like a deer in the headlights, his eyes flitting from person to person, searching for a supportive face in the audience. Finally, he cleared his throat and began, "I … went to her room—"

"My dear Haresh, please sit down before you tell us what happened. No one is punishing you." Wanda's smiling face assured.

Haresh walked nervously over to sit next to Wolfgang, who looked up at the other three standing at the door.

"Amon, Yuri, Nancy, please join us." He indicated the scattered cushions on the floor with a flourish of his hands.

With everyone seated, Haresh said in a meek voice, "We were supposed to go to Zircon yesterday, our whole team. There were meditation classes in the Central Meditation Room. But I had discovered something that morning and was trying to piece it all together, so I missed the class. When I went to find Nirmala in the evening, she had not returned. So, I went to dinner, but she wasn't there either. Neither were any of our other teammates. Still, I thought that they probably got delayed in Zircon and would return to our room at night." Haresh sighed and hung his head.

"And they did not?" Wolfgang asked.

"Nope."

"*What?*" Alejandro jumped from his seat. His face was sweaty, his eyes bloodshot. "We must go immediately—" someone tugged on his arm. It was a gentle gesture, but it arrested Alejandro's speech.

"There, there," Irene's musical voice cut in. "I thought you said you loved no one." There was a mischievous look in her eyes.

"I don't … it's not …" Alejandro stuttered.

"Perhaps Pala would know where she is—" Wolfgang began, but was quickly interrupted by a voice that floated in from the doorway.

"Pala is gone!" said the voice, sounding breathless. It was Kazhar.

"Oh my! Where could they have gone?" Wanda wondered out loud.

"I think I have a fairly good idea," Amon offered with a sigh. "They have gone to the Aifra camp to save Zoya."

"Save Zoya? Aifra camp?" Could someone please explain what the hell is going on here?" Alejandro shouted, throwing his hands up in the air in an exasperated gesture.

"Calm down Alejandro," Wolfgang admonished. "I will most certainly explain everything. And that is precisely why I convened this meeting, to begin with. But first, tell me Amon, how does Nirmala expect to even find the Aifra camp? Have any of you told her where it is?" He looked from Amon to Yuri to Nancy and all of them shook their heads from side to side in denial.

"We haven't told her, but I have a feeling that Pala probably knows. Because she screened Nancy's ... and Yuri's thoughts, before admitting them into Lumania," Amon clarified.

"I see," Wolfgang said. "And that would explain why they took Pala with them."

"*Now* can someone explain what's going on, please?" Alejandro asked, still unable to calm down.

Wolfgang had opened his mouth to speak, but Amon raised his hand to stop him. "I'll have a go at it, if you don't mind. I'll try to keep it short, because we don't have much time. So, when Zoya went to Irkutsk all by herself, it was because she wanted to find the shrine of the Frozen Saint of Baikal—"

"The Frozen Saint ... the Frozen Saint ... where have I heard this name before?" Alejandro mumbled to himself, as he clicked his fingers in mid-air. "Ah, I remember! The Babaji at Badrinath told us about him. What did she want with this saint?"

"Apparently, she had learned from her parents that her life was a boon bestowed upon them by the Frozen Saint. Or in other words, the so-called saint had brought Zoya back to life, after she had been pronounced dead at birth."

"Oh my God!" Alejandro exclaimed. "What happened when she tried to find the shrine?"

"So … Zoya had convinced Yuri to take her to that shrine," Amon continued. "Or at least where he thought the shrine might be. When they got there however, it was empty, and as they were leaving, they were kidnapped by Nancy," he pointed at Nancy, "Zoya's childhood friend and Peter, who were deserters from the Aifra."

"Peter? Which Peter?" Dr. Cobb, who had been silent this whole time, suddenly spoke up, shock oozing from every pore in his body.

Amon nodded sadly. "Yes, *that* Peter. Your son, Albert."

"Well, I'll be damned—" Dr. Cobb began.

"He's fine, Albert. No need to get hyper," Wolfgang assured.

"Is *that* right? If he's fine, then where the hell is he?"

"He didn't want to ever come to Lumania, so he volunteered to go with Chris to save Zoya instead," Amon explained.

"I still don't get how Zoya ended up going to the Aifra camp," Alejandro said, impatiently tapping his fist against the wall of the room.

"That's because I haven't quite finished my story yet," Amon said irritably. "After Zoya and Yuri were captured by Nancy and Peter, somehow Zoya figured out, that the Frozen Saint of Baikal is the leader of the Aifra and that she owes him a life debt. I think, she also believes that the source of the Frozen Saint's power is his skill in necromancy. She's probably under the impression that the very fact, he has brought some people back from the dead, is what ultimately binds him to his power. So, in order to ruin him, everyone who received a life they did not deserve, would have to—"

"Return it. To balance the equation between life and death," Alejandro completed, a gasp escaping from his lips as he did so.

"Exactly," Amon agreed. Horrified murmurs were heard across the room.

"But where did she get the idea that the Frozen Saint is the leader of the Aifra?" Alejandro asked.

"From the markings in the cave where this saint's shrine had once been. There were hieroglyphics on those walls, and I have a hunch that they are passages from the Script of Ra. I can show them to Wanda later, for corroboration," Amon explained.

Haresh cleared his throat. "May I say a few words, if it's okay with you?"

"Why, of course, Haresh, please go on," Wanda said indulgently.

"Zoya, as we have established earlier, is a re-incarnation of Meerabai, is she not?"

"Depends on how you look at it, but sure," Wolfgang replied.

"Okay, in that case," Haresh continued. "She is a devotee of Vishnu and a beloved of the Lord. As per legend."

"Perhaps. But what is your point?" Wolfgang asked cynically.

"My point is," Haresh paused to retrieve a small, yellowing notebook from a tote bag he was carrying. "Dr. Sinha's diary."

"And what about this diary?" Wolfgang asked.

"I was studying it yesterday, when it felt like I had made a discovery. That's why I went looking for Nirmala. To tell her all about it ... it says in this diary ..." he flipped through the pages as he spoke, "It says here that 'the Aifra are looking for the weapon of Vishnu, but perhaps they do not seek this weapon to wield against an enemy at all, but to destroy it. Because otherwise, it would destroy *them*. Furthermore, this weapon may not be a thing at all, but a *person*.'"

Alejandro's mind was suddenly lucid. "Does this mean Zoya—"

"Being the incarnation of Meera, she could in fact, be this weapon. The weapon that will destroy the Frozen Saint and consequently the Aifra," Haresh completed.

"Brilliant!" Alejandro exclaimed. "Now, the question is, how do we harness her power?"

"We use the Script of Horus," Amon said decisively.

CHAPTER THIRTY-TWO

Zoya was walking between somber looking tents, up a path, down a path, and then sharply around corners. The sun had risen, but it was still fairly cold. Zoya felt tremors crawl up her skin like creepy crawly insects. Her forehead moistened with bouts of cold sweat. She realized that it was not simply the cold she felt, but a primal sort of fear.

Death is not something one usually thinks about, until it raises its ugly head and looks us in the eye. Zoya refused to let its piercing stare stab through her skin and burn into her bones. Yet, the shivering would not stop, no matter how hard she tried to resist it.

They walked up and down rugged winding paths, skirting around stark-looking tents and their grim occupants, and finally arrived at the mouth of a cave, set at a descent elevation from the base of the hills. The mouth of the cave was guarded by two monstrous sentries with chained snow leopards at their sides.

As Zoya and her captors passed by, the leopards growled in a low menacing tone, much like their close feline relatives, yet so unlike them in all the ways that matter. The inside of the cavernous cave, was lit by flaming torches, mounted on the walls that gave it the appearance of a movie set. In this light, Zoya noticed that the walls were inscribed with familiar hieroglyphics, similar to those, she had seen at the Frozen Saint's shrine.

On the other hand, in the dark crevices of the room beyond the reach of the torches, Zoya saw odd rectangular structures shrouded in shadow. When they approached closer, she balked at the sight of what she was witnessing.

In the cavities of the wall where no light ever fell, were human-sized cages lined up in rows. Emaciated, disheveled wrecks of humans crouched inside these cells, some barely conscious, others gazing wild-eyed into oblivion. Zoya let out a little shriek. The Aifra soldier in front of her turned at the sound.

"Welcome to the Cave of the Condemned," she said, in an oddly welcoming tone, as if it was a privilege to have been admitted here.

Zoya's voice faltered as she tried to respond. "I … you're not … taking me to the Frozen Saint?"

"Not yet," the woman replied with a smirk. She turned again and led Zoya to the cell that was farthest from the entrance. With a click, she unlocked it. The man behind Zoya snatched the backpack from her shoulder and pushed her roughly into the cage, locking it immediately. Then, the soldiers made for the exit.

Zoya felt a dryness in her throat, but fighting against it, she spoke up. "Wait!"

The men did not pay any attention, but the woman turned around. "What?" She sounded irritated, as one often is, with an annoying little bug.

"Wh ... en?"

"When what?"

Zoya gulped down the bile that was rising in her throat. "When will I see the Saint?"

"The Commander in Chief," the woman corrected. "You will go when he's ready." And with that, she turned around and left.

Zoya had expected a silence to descend upon the cave as she departed. But no such silence came. With the soldiers gone, the surroundings filled with low and ghastly sounds—that of rasping breaths being drawn from one corner, blood curdling whimpers from another and perhaps, the most annoying of them all, a dull buzzing sound inside her own head. If her thoughts could actually speak, then this must be how they sounded.

Zoya moved to the very end of her cage and dropped down to the floor with her back against the rear bars. During her days in Peter's hideout, Nancy had told her, how the blood sacrifices used to occur at this Aifra camp. Usually, many were summoned at once. At first, they were bathed and clothed and prepared for the ritual, then they were made to drink a holy drink, spiked with an inebriating substance. Finally, they were brought before the Saint. Here, passages were chanted that harnessed the life forces of the sacrificial humans and attached them to the being of the Frozen Saint, thereby making him the receptacle into which all life flows. Herein lies the secret to the Saint's true power, and perhaps also his immortality.

Zoya wanted to be the antidote to this power—a fitting rebuke to his monstrosity. Since her life was a gift from the

Saint, she was all but certain, that her death at his hands would revert his wrongs and destroy his supernatural abilities. She did not understand why she knew this, but she did. It was her impeccable intuition at work again.

However, there still remained one fallacy for her to resolve. If the votive offerings were made before her life was taken, then the Saint would be able to usurp the energy of her soul and thereby gain in strength. Thus, her plan to destroy him would fail. So, her life had to end before the sacred passages were chanted, and it also had to happen at the Frozen Saint's hands. The only solution to this paradox was in the inebriating liquid that would be fed to her before the ritual. Nancy had confirmed that it was hand-brewed by the Saint himself.

Nervously, Zoya shoved her right hand inside her jacket pocket. There, under a dry crust of bread, was the magical thing that would solve her problem when the time comes. She fingered the smooth surface of the poisoned mushroom and sighed deeply into the darkness. The cave walls echoed her breath back to her. She felt drowsy and soon dozed off to sleep.

* * *

Nirmala stood at the mouth of a dark passage and squinted into its depths. There was a musty smell rising from the earth, which gave it the sense of an abandoned place, free from human footfall.

"Where are we?" she asked Pala, who was standing beside her bearing a glow-worm torch.

"This is the place, I mentioned before. The passage that will lead us under the mountains. We have not used it in hundreds of years."

"Are you sure, it's not blocked up further ahead?"

"Perhaps, it is. But there is no faster route to take us there, that I am aware of."

"So ... do we walk?" Nirmala asked, her eyes darting around the tunnel surreptitiously.

Pala chuckled, betraying a rare instance of her youthful frivolity. "Of course not." She lifted her arms up in front of her and contorted her face in concentration. A minute later, a vehicle whooshed into existence, floating in mid-air. "We'll take this. It's faster than our trains."

The vehicle was slim and elongated but large enough for their entire party, with five rows of two seats each. "It's just like an amusement park ride! Neat!" Xianbin said, as he hopped in.

Nirmala and Pala boarded at the head of their ride and the Novo-Hekameses took their seats behind the pair. Once everyone had boarded, Pala raised her forearm in front of her face and whistled like a bird. Before Nirmala could wonder what was going on, a tiny sparrowhawk landed on the offered perch. "Our *lodebird*, we call it. He will show the way," Pala said softly. Hearing this, the bird instantly sprang from her arm and flew ahead into the darkness.

Their vehicle lurched forward behind the bird at an incredible velocity, with the hawk struggling to match its pace. Then, it came to perch again on Pala's extended arm, as they glided effortlessly through the abandoned tunnel.

The path, as Nirmala had predicted, was far from clear. And if it had not been for the bird flying forward from time to time to check the passage, a fatal collision would have been inevitable. However, the lodebird was precise and exact every single time, as it returned to Pala's arm to wordlessly report the status of the road ahead. Whenever they were warned of a roadblock, they slowed down and Pala telekinetically whisked the boulders away to the side, clearing a passage for their vehicle.

Thus, they continued for several hours, going up a steep incline and down another, making a sharp turn to their left and then, to their right in rapid succession, their stomachs lurching with each unexpected manoeuvre, until they reached a dead-end. The vehicle slowed down and came to a halt, about five feet from the rocky wall that barred their way. Pala turned her head towards Nirmala and smiled.

"We are here," she said.

"What? How? It's a dead-end."

"Hold on." Pala disembarked the vehicle and approached the wall. Up close, she shone her torch onto its surface, as if in an attempt to scan the smooth stone slab for something specific. Then, finding it, she placed her palm flat on the stone and waited. A little later, the slab of stone began to slide away. She hung her glow-worm torch from a rusty-looking bracket on the wall and stepped outside. "This way," she said.

Nirmala followed Pala out into the pitch-black surroundings with trepidation. There was no moon in the sky, nor any visible stars. A frigid, cutting wind tore through her layers of clothing, and her teeth chattered as she tried to speak. "Shouldn't we have brought the torch?"

"No, it's too dangerous. We don't want to be seen," Pala whispered.

Silently, the other members of Nirmala's team emerged from the dimly lit tunnel and walked over to stand at her side. Once her eyes had adjusted to the darkness, Nirmala realized that they were standing on a narrow ledge, from which a gravelly path led up to several layers of encampments above their heads.

"I don't believe any of the sensors we brought will work well on the Aifra. They tend to be very technology averse," she said to them. "We need to use the techniques that we learned in Lumania instead."

"Got it," Xianbin replied.

"Now, stay close and follow me," Nirmala instructed, as she turned towards the path.

They walked in a single file, treading as quietly as possible, with Pala and Nirmala in the lead. It was hard to tell what time it was, but it must have been late in the night, because the sturdy looking metallic structures that served as the camps, did not have any light emanating from within them. A pervasive kind of silence encompassed them from all directions, punctuated only rarely, by the indistinct sounds of nocturnal animals and birds among the vegetation.

They cleared a bend and arrived at a plateau between hills. Not ten feet away, was a camp and in front of it, an armed Aifra soldier was patrolling the grounds. His head jerked up and his eyes immediately fell on the intruders. He turned and strode forward with deliberate steps, his AK-47 locked and loaded. Nirmala raised her arms over her head without thinking, but then, as the soldier advanced further, she recognized who it was.

"Dr. Sinha! Oh my God! What have they done to you? Are you—" she began, as she ran towards him in a panic.

But before she could respond, someone pounced on her and toppled her to the ground, face first. Almost simultaneously, a volley of bullets rushed over her head, ringing through the air like claps of thunder. She dragged herself out from under her attacker and sat up. It was Xianbin who had thrown himself at her and was trying to restrain her with both his hands around her waist. "No,

Nirmala don't!" he yelled, as she struggled to extricate herself from his grip.

In front of her, Pala was standing with her arms raised. Lifting Dr. Sinha's writhing form off the ground, as his machine gun floated in between them. With a sudden jerk, Nirmala freed herself and rushed forward. "What are you doing, Pala? Stop! I know this man. It's Professor Sinha."

"No," Pala said, tossing her captive to the ground, where he dropped unconscious. "He's not your friend. I have looked into his mind. He has been resurrected by the Frozen Saint. Now, he's a new man with no memory of his past and instilled with a violent urge to kill everything that moves."

Nirmala gasped. "No way! That can't be true. Can it?" She turned her horrified face towards Pala.

Pala nodded remorsefully. "I'm sorry Nirmala. But I speak the truth."

"Did you ... did you ..." Nirmala swallowed through a dry throat.

Pala shook her head from side to side. "I didn't kill him. We don't kill people. Even undead ones. I put him to sleep. Now, let's go, before he wakes up."

"Which way do you think we should go?"

Pala pointed north. "You see those tiny dots assembling over there? Those are people gathering for some event. We should go that way. I think that is where they will take Zoya."

Nirmala turned to take one last look at her now unconscious, fallen professor and sniffled. Then wiping her eyes, she marched forward into the darkness.

* * *

Chris sat in front of a blazing flame, roasting an Arctic grayling, when Peter came barging through the bushes. He had gone looking for some wild turnips and thyme to complement their mid-day meal. They had walked since sunrise, yet they had no idea, how much further they needed to go to find the Aifra camp. Peter dropped his sack in front of the fire with a thump.

"Did you find anything?" Chris raised his head to ask.

"Plenty. Somehow, I knew exactly where to look," Peter mumbled, the crackling fire almost chewing up his last few words.

"What was that?"

Peter plonked down on his haunches. "I can remember this place."

"Oh really?" Chris exclaimed, nearly dropping the fish into the fire as he tried to turn it.

"Yeah. I've been here before. Hunting."

"Is that so? What else do you remember?" Chris deposited the freshly cooked fish on a bed of leaves and turned to face his companion.

Peter looked up from chopping the turnips with his hunting knife. "There was this guy … a very scary guy. He was a General or something. His name was …" he scrunched his face up, in an effort to remember. "I can't remember exactly."

"Was it … Józef Sapieha?"

"That's it! That was his name. But how did you know?"

"He captured one of our friends. So, what about this General Sapieha?"

"He used to bring me here. To these woods. He was … strange."

"Oh? Strange how?"

"I don't know, but I have a feeling in my gut that he was …"

"He was what, Peter?" Chris sat up straight, his heart throbbing with anticipation. Any new piece of information about Wolfgang's captor and undoubtedly a high-ranking official of the Aifra would be useful at this point.

"Unnatural. He was unnatural. I don't remember anything else, sadly."

"I see." Chris sighed. "Would it help, if you saw him again? Maybe the visual cue would jog your memory?"

Peter shrugged. "It's possible. But for that, we have to find him first."

"Not necessarily." Chris smiled. "I can show you. If you will allow me."

"Okay … are you gonna mess with my memory again?" Peter's forehead crinkled with worry-lines.

"Not at all. I'm just going to show you one of *my* memories. You are my professor's son. I have no reason to hurt you," he added placatingly.

For a moment, Peter did not stir and just sat there studying Chris from head to toe. Then, he nodded. "Sure. Go ahead."

"Look at me," Chris instructed, as he proceeded to transfer the memory of Józef Sapieha's twisted form into Peter's brain.

Peter gasped. "Oh my God!"

"What? What is it?"

"It worked! I remember him now. And I remember why we feared him. He was a Sybriak. A Polish noble, who was exiled to Siberia for rising up against the Russians."

"No, but that can't be!" Chris exclaimed. "The Józef Sapieha who was exiled in Russia, died in a gulag in the mid-twentieth century. If he is still alive today, then that would make him—"

"Undead," Peter completed. "Sapieha was resurrected by the Frozen Saint. As were many other high-ranking officials of the Aifra. A large part of their core army is an undead army. I remember this now, as clearly as I did back then." He paused for a breath, before continuing, "Thank you Chris, for restoring some parts of my memory." A hint of a smile played on his lips for the first time since Chris had met him.

"Sure, no worries, man. But this is really disturbing, if true. Even for someone like me, who is ever so familiar with the occult. The idea of an undead army is …" Chris trailed off.

"I agree. It *is* quite disturbing. Although, I must not have thought so when I was serving them. But I still can't remember, why I didn't feel revolted by this at that time. A part of me wants to have that section of my memory back as well. So that, I can understand my motivations. Yet, another part of me …" Peter shook his head like a wet dog shakes its body in order to dry itself. "Anyway, the good news is that, I think I know where we are now," he added.

Chris' head shot up. "You do?"

"Yeah, c'mon. Let me show you." Peter got up and hurried towards the north.

They scrambled through the bushes and pines to reach a dirt road that was lined with boulders on the far side. Beyond the boulders, was a precipice that fell sharply down to the lake below. Peter clambered up one of these boulders and gestured with his hand for Chris to follow. Chris climbed up next to him and turned his sight in the direction of Peter's extended arm.

A mountain range lay in that direction, and in-between its valleys and troughs, was a sprawling complex of man-made structures, shaped like tents, but made of more durable material, perhaps even a metal.

"That must be it!" Chris breathed, as he stared at the formation.

"It is. I recognize it. Now, the question is, has Zoya found it?"

"She probably has. Given that Nancy gave her directions and she had a head-start on us. But hang on—" Chris hopped off the boulder and hurried into the forest. He returned a couple of minutes later, carrying his human-tracking helmet. He fastened the helmet on his head and climbed back up to stand beside Peter. With his face twisted and eyes focussed in concentration, he scanned the signals around him for a minute or so, before speaking. "I can't catch her brainwaves. It's too far, and I don't have the range. What I *can* catch however, is a large group of humans heading towards a central point in that area, like being drawn to that point by a magnet or something."

"It's the ritual. The blood-sacrifice. It only happens during new moons. Which means, they must have one tonight. Because there will be a new moon. The whole encampment gathers for it throughout the day," Peter explained.

"Impressive that you remember so much."

Peter nodded. "It's been coming back slowly. Since you did that thing to me earlier."

"No, it's very good. I'm not complaining. Unless of course, all of it comes back and you suddenly change your mind about helping us." Chris chuckled.

"That's not likely to happen. Not anymore, anyway." Peter brushed the suggestion off with a wave of his hand.

"But what do we do now? Do we go ahead or wait for backup?"

"You think that Zoya might be sacrificed tonight? If this ritual is happening?" A shudder went through Chris as he uttered these words.

"I think Zoya is the reason they are having it, to begin with. These rituals are usually scheduled when high profile enemies are captured. So, having caught Zoya, seems like a great reason to host one. If, what Nancy said about Zoya being on the most wanted list, is true."

"Oh God! In that case, my choice would be to go on ahead without the others. But I do have an obligation to let them know first. I'll try to reach Amon through my headset and see what he says. If they can come soon, we'll wait. If not, we'll go in. Yeah?"

"Yup."

Just then, Chris felt a tingling inside one of his pockets, like a surge of static. Absentmindedly, he reached inside it and pulled out the offending object. It was the Lumanian hourglass. As he gazed into it, his eyes grew wide and his heart thumped violently inside his chest.

"Oh my God, the *sand*! It's flowing!"

CHAPTER THIRTY-THREE

Alejandro was sitting across from Nancy in a meeting room, in the Lumanian city of Zircon. "You are sure that they chanted during these rituals?"

"Yes, absolutely sure," Nancy confirmed.

"Like I said, Alejandro, they need to chant passages from the Script of Ra, to harness the damned souls," Wanda said from Alejandro's left.

"And to counter it, we need the Script of Horus. Yes, you mentioned this. I guess you were right. Lucky you brought it with you then."

Wanda smiled. "The Lumanian scribes are making copies as we speak. But the real question is, do we even know when—"

"Ugh!" someone groaned from behind Alejandro. Turning quickly, he saw Amon crouched on the floor clutching his forehead. He rushed to his side.

"What's wrong buddy?"

"It's … it's a message … from Chris … ugh … it hurts!"

"What? How is he doing this?" Alejandro asked, looking baffled. "Is he in Lumania?"

"No," Wolfgang explained. "He's using his headset, I think. It has never been used to send long distance telepathic messages before. I guess, now we know that the process is painful."

"Phew! It's over." Amon wiped the sweat from his face and leaned back on his elbows. "I told him to use the headset, because his phone wouldn't work."

"I see. And? What did he say?" Alejandro asked anxiously.

"They've found it. The camp. And the ritual to sacrifice Zoya is tonight!"

"What? Shit!" Alejandro shot up from his seat. "There's no way we'll get there in time if we use the abandoned tunnels. Is there, Kazhar?"

Kazhar, who was leaning against the wall beside the door, shook his head. "I'm afraid not."

"Then? What do we do?" Alejandro asked the room at large.

"The only way would be to fly there," Wolfgang said sullenly.

"Wait!" Amon interrupted. "There's more!"

"More of what?" Alejandro asked.

"Chris' message. He says … the sand is flowing or something like that."

"Oh!" Kazhar exclaimed. "Is that right? That would be a message for the Elders. Ishin!" he called to his friend, who was standing near the door, "Could you let Solaris know about this?"

"Most certainly," Ishin said, before bowing to take his leave.

With Ishin gone, Kazhar turned to face the others. "Now, about flying to our destination, I can assure you that even the most powerful amongst our kind have not yet mastered that art. However, over the years, we have intercepted some flying machines from your world that could possibly be used, if they continue to be operable."

"Fantastic! Please take us to them. Also, can someone get Alexander Costas?" Alejandro asked.

"We also need to let Chris know that we are coming to get them, and they should stay where they are. But none of the Hekameses have the ability to send a telepathic message that far … er … could you help?"

Kazhar smiled. "Very well. I will send Chris a message and Larvo can bring Colonel Costas to the Contraband Room."

"*Contraband* Room?" Alejandro did a spit take on the water he was drinking. "What else do you have in that room? Drugs?"

"Alejandro!" Wanda cautioned. "They are anti-war, pacifists. So, any equipment related to warfare would be contraband to them."

"That is correct," Kazhar confirmed. "However, we are not anti-humour. We will provide the drugs for our kind guests, if needed," he added with a rare smirk playing across his lips. "Now, please follow me."

Zircon, being the capital of Lumania was a colossal city, housing everything of importance to the populace. But Kazhar was a consummate guide, who led them expertly through its labyrinthine streets and alleyways in such a way, that they were at the Contraband Room in no time. "We are here," he said, as he glided a stone slab away with his raised arms, thereby clearing the doorway.

The party entered the gigantic room with a vaulted ceiling and walls so distant, that you could barely see them in the bioluminescent lighting of Lumania. A solitary aircraft stood there, a few feet from the entrance. It was the Su-34 bomber that had brought Wolfgang and Alex to Lumania.

Alejandro's face fell. "*This*?" he said, with a poorly concealed incredulity in his tone. "It's only a two-seater. How will it—"

"You above-worlders are always so quick to draw conclusions," Kazhar cut in, clicking his tongue disapprovingly. "We have just entered the room, not reached our destination. Please, follow me. The machine I wish to show you is at the back." Kazhar plucked a glow-worm torch from a bracket on the wall and made his way around the bomber, towards the dark interior of the chamber.

Once they had cleared the Su-34 entirely and emerged directly behind it, another aircraft became visible in the distance—a massive military transport helicopter, capable of carrying dozens of passengers.

"Whoa! Where didjya get *that* baby?" someone exclaimed from behind them. Alejandro turned to find Colonel Costas standing a couple of feet away.

"It was parked near one of our portals, about to transport many soldiers and weapons into a civilian area. We made a conscious call to hide it in our realm."

"So, you sabotaged them?" Alejandro asked.

"Perhaps." Kazhar flashed him an uncharacteristic wicked grin.

"You do that? I thought you were all non-interventionists to your very cores."

"There are certain exceptions," Kazhar replied cryptically.

"Anyway," Wolfgang began, turning to Alex Costas. "Are you comfortable with flying us there in this helicopter?"

"Sure … but …"

"Yes?" Wolfgang urged.

"Well, I won't be able to fly over the camp in this thing. It's too large and easily detectable. It would've been handy to kinda patrol the area after dropping you off, just in case …"

"I see what you mean." Alejandro nodded. "It would certainly be useful to have a bomber circle the skies; in case our ambush goes awry. What do you think, Wolfgang?"

"I agree. And for that we should use the Su-34. My suggestion is, we take both."

"But who's gonna fly the other one?" Alex asked.

Wolfgang smiled his usual wry, half-smile. "Jeremy, of course."

"You're going to have *him* do rounds with the bomber? How can you trust—" Alex began.

"No Alex," Wolfgang interrupted. "I'm not stupid. *You're* going to fly the bomber and also pick up Chris and Peter. *Jeremy,* will take the rest of us to the camp in the helicopter. That way, we can be with him the whole time and make sure he does everything according to plan."

CHAPTER THIRTY-FOUR

"Chris! Chris! Look! Up there!" Peter was screaming. Chris heard it before he saw it—a speck in the sky, growing larger by the minute, its roar splitting the heavens asunder.

"What do you think it is?" he asked nervously. They were sitting inside a clearing around a large bonfire, to make themselves visible, just as Kazhar had suggested.

"What else? Backup." Peter grinned like the Cheshire Cat.

"No way, that plane is too sma—"

"WATCH OUT!" Peter lunged at Chris, knocking him to the ground, as the bomber rapidly lost elevation and darted towards them.

Chris rolled out from under Peter's massive frame and dusted himself. "Jeez! Did you think it was going to bomb us?"

"You never know. We're too close to the Aifra base. Anything could happen." Peter shrugged.

The bomber had landed less than a hundred feet away. Throwing all caution to the wind, Chris stood up and ran towards it at full speed. The pilot was emerging from the cockpit as Chris arrived. He removed his helmet and smiled.

Chris' arms immediately sprang above his head. "Woah! Who are you?" His expression was one of cautious skepticism. "Sorry, scratch that. What's the password?" Chris added as an afterthought.

"The password is 'The Frozen Saint'. And I'm Lieuten … er … Alexander Costas, Wolfgang's friend. A pleasure to meet you." Alex extended his hand in greeting.

As soon as they shook hands, Chris remembered the pilot's face from Wolfgang's memories. "Oh, right. My bad. Sorry I reacted that way. It's a pleasure to meet you too, Alexander. I'm Chris, by the way, and my friend over there—"

"Friend?" Peter interrupted from over his shoulder, his face more mischievous than a toddler's.

"No? Enemy then?" Chris teased.

Peter chuckled. "Never! Nice to meet you, Alexander. I'm Chris' friend, Peter," he said with a wink and mock salute.

"Pleasure," Alex said, grabbing Peter's wild bear-paw with both his hands.

"Where are the others?" Chris asked looking up at the sky through cupped hands. "Are they coming?"

"They're already there. We are going separately."

"Gotcha! So, what's the plan?"

"The bomber's got two seats, so we need to squeeze in. Once we're close, but just outside the encampment, you two will parachute down, and I'm gonna circle the perimeter, keeping an eye out for trouble."

"No," Chris objected. "Peter's not going in there. He may be on their wanted list for having absconded. We can't risk—"

"I didn't abscond," Peter objected. "At least, they don't know that I did. I can fight. Believe me, you'll need me where you're going."

Chris turned to smile at his companion. "My friend," he said, laying a hand over his shoulder. "You may not have willingly deserted the Aifra, but we can't stop them from assuming that you *did* and wanting to kill you anyway. Besides, we *do* need you. We need you to help Lieutenant Costas find his way around the strategic points over the camps, so that you can open fire, if at all it becomes necessary."

"We should go," Alex checked the time. "If Nancy was right, the ritual will start in less than an hour. We need to get there before that."

Chris and Peter nodded before boarding the plane. The flight time was under ten minutes, and with Peter's guidance, they maneuvered over to an area of the settlement, where they were less likely to be detected at this hour—the community kitchens.

Chris had never parachuted before, but being an avid rock climber, he did not have any fear of heights. As the aircraft hovered low over a saddle between hills, Chris got ready to dive. The area was deserted, just as Peter had expected. Chris landed gracefully on his feet like a bird alighting on a hanging branch.

He looked up. Alex was still hovering overhead. He pointed his hand skyward and gave his companions a thumbs up. The bomber engine growled like a hungry stomach, as the aircraft zoomed out of sight. According to his tracking head-set, which he had worn on the plane to hone in on the centre of activities, the sacrificial rite was possibly being held somewhere to his northeast. He headed in that direction with surefooted, silent steps.

He had made it less than 50 meters, when the sound of heavy booted feet stalled him. Looking up, he saw an Aifra contingent of at least a dozen heavily armed soldiers approaching in mechanical unison. He dived to take cover behind a jutting rock, but it was too late. One individual from the party had seen him.

"Who walks there? Come out with your hands up!" a hoarse voice yelled.

Chris debated his options for a second. His body was half-hidden behind a rock, with his feet sticking awkwardly out. Behind him, were some thick pines. He could slide into the forest and disappear, no one would find him in there. But the forest stretched towards the south and he needed to go north. The clock was ticking, with Zoya's life on the balance. He made a judgment call and stood with his hands over his head.

"I was hiking. I'm lost," he said through chattering teeth, feigning fear.

The man who had hollered at him, glanced sideways at a companion, who nodded once. "Come with us," he then said, waving his Kalashnikov at Chris.

Chris cleared the boulder he was hiding behind and tottered forward, arms still raised. The other soldiers came around to encircle him, as the first man prodded the middle of his back with the muzzle of his gun, egging him to move forward.

Chris walked without looking back, the rest of the party surrounding him like a pack of wolves. They winded up the mountainous path, heading northeast, just as Chris had expected. At once, he knew that he had made the right call.

They would lead him where he wanted to go. After several minutes of climbing, the leader of their party came to a halt. Before anyone could wonder what was going on, she turned a horrified face towards the others. "What is *he* doing here?" She was pointing to a cliff above her head, her face as white as mother-of-pearl.

Chris' eyes shot up to the cliff. A crouched milky shape was lurking there in the shadows. A feral growl escaped from its throat, floating through the procession and sending a shiver down their spines. Just as some of the soldiers began readying their guns to fire shots into the air, the creature lunged. Quicker than lighting, it was upon them, a milky white snow leopard, as graceful as a ballerina.

It was not alone.

Right behind it were several others. They were pouncing furiously on the puny humans below with surprising alacrity, landing only inches from their unsuspecting victims. There were sounds of screaming and screeching all around, as the soldiers began to disperse in all directions, running for their lives, their weapons abandoned, the leopards close on their heels.

For one terrified moment, Chris contemplated running as fast as his legs would carry, away from this pummelling onslaught. But then, his better judgement prevailed. He knew, he could not outrun a leopard. Nor would climbing help. Fire. It was his only hope. It had saved him once before. Just as Chris was about to pull his lighter from his pocket and set his jacket ablaze. A familiar voice hollered at him.

"Chris, don't!" the voice shouted. "Don't light a fire. They won't attack you. They're following my instructions." Chris turned in the direction of the voice and saw Amon stooping over the cliff as he lowered a climbing rope. "Now c'mon! Climb up here! We have work to do."

Chris flashed his friend a wolfish grin. He had forgotten that Amon could speak with animals. "Just a minute," he hollered back, before running towards the bushes, where two loaded Kalashnikovs lay abandoned on the rocky ground. He picked them up and made his way towards the climbing rope Amon had dropped.

CHAPTER THIRTY-FIVE

Zoya was awakened by the same woman who had spoken to her earlier. "It is time," she said. At once, Zoya knew what time it was and her heart sank into a dark fathomless place. She fingered the mushroom in her pocket and swallowed in a dry throat.

The woman tossed a blood-red gown of handwoven cotton into her cell. "Put this on," she instructed. "Leave your other clothes in here. I'll be right back." She did not open Zoya's cell door as she turned around to leave.

Zoya glanced surreptitiously around her. It was very dark inside the cave with only the areas under the torches visible. No one would see her undress in this darkness. Realizing this, she began to strip out of her grimy jeans and T-shirt. As she did so, she chuckled sardonically. There would be no pain or shame in the place where she was heading. Yet, till the very end, she would feel all of these things, as does all of mankind in their last, desperate attempts to cling on to this material existence.

The mushroom poked out from the pocket of her jacket, when she shrugged it off. Catching it in mid-air, she tucked it into her ponytail, securing it tightly with the hairband. Nancy had told her what would happen next. They would wash her limbs and face and cover them with markings in a charcoal-coloured paint. But they would leave the hair intact. This practice was mostly a relic of the past, when the sacrifice used to be a beheading, where later, they would lift the severed head up by the hair and offer it to their Gods.

Now however, they hung all their victims. It was cleaner and more pleasing to the eye. That way, they could avoid accidentally turning one of their own against them. Unnecessary brutality often makes even the staunchest believer question their beliefs. The Frozen Saint did not want to risk such an eventuality.

Zoya put on the red gown. It was full length, but tied at the back with ribbons, like a hospital gown. It smelled of death and unshed tears. Her stomach growled. Her bodily processes prodding her one last time, before she slipped permanently beyond their grasp. She took the rock-solid crumb of bread from her jacket pocket and softening it with her saliva, forced pieces of it down her throat. Footsteps near the cave mouth jolted her back to the present.

Five soldiers had entered, including the woman from earlier. They unlocked the cage and led her out of the cave into an all-consuming sort of darkness. Nothing stirred. Nothing lit their way, as they marched sombrely forward across the river Styx and into the realm of Hades. Zoya shivered involuntarily in her light cotton dress. But the days of physical exertion, coupled with her near-starvation had brought on a much-welcomed numbness. So, in her conscious mind, Zoya barely felt its sting.

They continued to walk for time unending, until they reached the top of a hill. A huge pillared structure stood at its centre. For a fleeting second, Zoya wondered how such an elaborate construction came to be, in such an inaccessible place. But she let that thought slide. It no longer mattered. Nothing mattered anymore, but the inexorable march towards her desired ending.

They entered the building, where a group of women were waiting for her. They were dressed not in Aifra fighting gear but in flowing long robes, similar to hers, except for their colour. Hers was red but theirs, black. They made Zoya sit on a low stool, as they proceeded to wash her arms and legs. One of the women, a small girl actually, dipped a fine brush inside a sticky kind of ink and bent over Zoya's forehead. It felt like being at a very morbid kind of nail-spa. With expert strokes, several women marked Zoya with creepy crawly symbols.

Zoya recalled the carvings on the wall of the Frozen Saint's shrine and how they had seared her skin. She recoiled at the thought. Just then, a similar sensation prickled her left-forearm where the little girl was intently drawing something. Zoya jolted. "Ouch!"

The girl looked startled. She brought Zoya's arm closer to a lamp on the floor to inspect the marking. It had vanished. In its place was a reddish welt. She dipped her brush into some more ink and tried again. But the same thing happened. Zoya jerked her arm free from the girl's grip this time. The girl made a pitiful face, as if she was about to cry. She turned her eyes up towards her companions and scanned their expressions beseechingly. No one seemed to pay her any heed, each working on a different pattern on Zoya's limbs. The girl dipped her brush again. But before she could raise it, Zoya spoke up.

"No!" she said authoritatively.

The girl flinched a little. "This ... is another one. I swear," she whispered in an assuring voice.

Somehow, Zoya believed her. There was honesty and gullibility in her eyes. Even in this grim moment, Zoya found it in her heart to feel sorry for the kid. She nodded, thereby giving her consent to proceed. Although she knew her consent was hardly necessary, but something told her, this particular girl would not go ahead without it, and perhaps endanger her life in the process.

The girl smiled nervously and painted a rune onto Zoya's arm—a very different one this time. One that did not burn. Satisfied with her handiwork, she stood up and was about to leave, but something stalled her. She turned back and bent her head close to Zoya's ear. Before Zoya could understand what was happening, she muttered a couple of words and left.

"Take the amulet," the girl said. Zoya did not understand the meaning, and nor did she care. The armed Aifra soldiers had already appeared to take her to her destination, and that was all she could focus on at this time.

They were inside a metallic building, built in layers, to accommodate for the mountainous topography of the area. Each layer was connected to the next by sets of metallic steps on either end. The set up was similar to that of a theatre or opera house with each higher layer hanging like a balcony above the lower ones.

The lowest level, where they now stood, had rows of uniformed soldiers standing along the walls, carrying their machine guns, all straight-faced and somber like museum exhibits. The upper layers were also starting to fill up.

Slowly, the Aifra soldiers were trickling up the narrow staircases and seating themselves in the balconies like spectators at the Colosseum.

A large circular area around the centre of the lowest floor, had been cleared to make room, for what appeared to be the stage. Except, there was no stage. Instead, a huge throne sat on a raised platform at the very heart of the room. In front of it, was what Zoya dreaded the most—the votive gallows. Two black-clad executioners stood on either side of it, their faces as blank as freshly-stretched canvas.

Zoya's head swam, and her guts twisted up inside her. Her breath came is shallow, rasping bursts. As she tried to move her feet forward, they felt as heavy as lead. But she knew she had to continue. She could not balk. Not now. Not anymore. If they shot her before she was fed the ritualistic drink, then her entire mission would fail and her life would be lost in vain. So, she steeled herself and stepped forward. One step at a time, her eye on the prize, her mind set firmly on her goal.

As Zoya approached the gallows, she noticed that it was set inside a circular marking on the floor. Within this marking and right in front of the noose, was a shimmering pool of liquid inside a shallow metallic receptacle, that was large enough to be a baby's bathtub. A steel rod protruded from its centre like the mast of a flag. The liquid inside was dark red with a strong metallic stench. Realizing what it was, Zoya bent double and retched on the floor in front of her. A sharp prod in her back forced her into an upright position. "Keep moving!" the guard behind her growled.

Zoya put one foot in front of the other, as cautiously as if she was walking on glass. Her captors led her to the edge of the pool and one of them pushed her forward. She stumbled as she stepped over the edge and into the puddle of blood that drenched her feet and seeped up the hem of her dress. She had another violent urge to retch, but caught herself in time. Instead, she held her breath and tried to imagine beautiful things to distract her mind, as her captors secured her to the metallic mast.

Zoya imagined lying on freshly cut spring grass after the rain, in her college campus, reading her favourite romance novel. She imagined, her mother's large doe eyes and bright effervescent smile that filled up any room. She remembered her dad crouched over the rose bushes, tending to their garden on a hot summer day. She imagined the adventures she had had with Chris. With Alejandro. With Nirmala. She imagined Yuri, his tattooed arms and sparkling, mischievous eyes. In the end, she imagined Kalki emerging from the desert, clad in saffron, riding like the wind on a stormy day, a dewy ethereal light bathing everything in her wake.

Zoya jolted out of her reverie as someone shoved a goblet into her hands. This was it. The potion that would lead to their emancipation. She drew in two deep, calming breaths, before reaching one hand up to the back of her head, as if to scratch it. The mushroom was still there. She removed it quickly from the tangles of her hair and plonked it into her drink when no one was looking.

A woman was walking towards her with slow, deliberate steps. She had the aura of a priestess. In her hand she carried a scroll. Her intricately embroidered crimson gown trailed along the ground behind her. Her hair was done up in a high bun and decked with colourful wildflowers. She could have been an angel, but of the fallen kind.

She came to a halt right in front of the pool of blood and stood face-to-face with Zoya. "I am a priestess of Ra," she said in a husky voice. "I am here to guide you on your path." Just as she said this, a rhythmic beating of drums reverberated through the room.

Being tied securely to the post, Zoya did not have a view of the entire room, but through the corner of her eye she noticed Aifra soldiers bowing and murmuring all around her. Even the priestess in front of her, fell to her knees, lowering her head to gaze at the floor. The room suddenly became darker and chillier all at once. Then, a door opened directly across from Zoya and through it, a tall, slender, hooded figure garbed in a black flowing robe emerged. His face was completely hidden from view, and on either side, he was flanked by fierce-looking armed Aifra guards.

The Frozen Saint, Zoya thought, her pulse quickening. The Frozen Saint glided to the raised dais containing his throne, like a seal skidding over a frozen lake. Raising himself above everyone else in the room, he ascended to his throne and motioned with his arms for his followers to rise.

The priestess of Ra stood up and cleared her throat. "I will proceed with the ceremony," she said imperiously. "But first you must drink the holy water you hold in your hand."

Zoya's moment had arrived. Yet, as she raised the chalice to her lips, her hands trembled violently. She pulled it away from her lips and steadied herself. Then, she tried again. But just as she was about to raise the goblet a second time, it automatically rose from her hand and slipped out of her grip, soaring towards the ceiling like a hawk taking flight.

Then, it corrected course and began plummeting downwards until it nosedived to the floor with a resounding clang.

"Oh no!" The words slipped involuntarily from Zoya's lips. The people around her were chattering and pointing wildly. Although Zoya could not make out any of the words, she turned her head in the direction of their pointed fingers.

There, about fifteen feet away, stood Nirmala, arms outstretched, with the Novo Hekameses standing around her, mimicking her gesture.

"Noooo!" Zoya screamed. But it was useless. Several Aifra soldiers had already surrounded her friends. A couple of them raised their guns. Zoya could no longer watch. She knew what was coming next. A volley of bullets would rip through them all, and it would be her fault. Her fault alone. She blinked against an onslaught of tears, as she pressed her eyes shut. In that moment, she wished she could cut off her brain as well.

But then, she heard a familiar voice. "Oh no you don't!" Zoya's heart leaped. She opened her eyes and turned in the direction of the voices. Alejandro was standing there with Haresh and Kazhar at his side, both of whom had their arms raised. The Kalashnikovs had floated out of the Aifra's hands and were making their way to Alejandro and Haresh who plucked them eagerly from thin air.

More Aifra soldiers were rushing towards the conflict area, blocking Zoya's view of the confrontation. There was a commotion to her right and turning her head that way, she saw some more familiar faces, Wanda, Wolfgang, Dr. Cobb and what looked like several Lumanians, Zoya had never seen before.

Soon, the entire background descended into chaos in such a way, that it became impossible to tell which side was winning. Large items were being raised and tossed around, guns being fired, people being tied up. Zoya's head spun.

For a minute, she forgot to pay attention to her immediate surroundings—the goblet that had been tossed and the priestess in front of her. A harsh, husky voice brought her back to reality.

"Here," said the priestess, bearing the same goblet, now filled to the brim with a fresh dose of the inebriating liquid. "Drink this."

Zoya accepted the glass with a sinking feeling. It was all over now. Her plan had failed. Only if there was a way to communicate to the others that she needed to die at the hands of the Frozen Saint before the ritual was complete—

"What are you waiting for?" the priestess growled, her face contorted into an unnatural shape.

Zoya lifted the cup to her lips. A sparkling globule of tear landed at its centre, creating a circle of tiny waves where it fell. Then they subsided, like the lull before a storm. A terrible calmness that is just the beginning of the end. Zoya took a sip of the liquid and immediately the chanting began. The drink sizzled down her throat like concentrated acid. Her head felt lighter, her eyelids heavy. She sucked in a deep breath before taking the next sip. But just as she was lowering the chalice, someone kicked it out of her hands.

Zoya had not realized that she had closed her eyes. She opened them now and saw Yuri standing in front of her. He was grinning like the devil. "How ..." Zoya managed to mutter.

"I swung in on that noose over there," Yuri pointed to the gallows. "C'mon, let's go!" As he spoke these words, someone untied Zoya from the post and came to stand beside Yuri.

"Nancy!" Zoya exclaimed.

"Let's go chica! We're getting you outta here."

Before Zoya could object, Yuri had whisked her into his arms and was running. Nancy, a few paces behind. From the corner of her eye, Zoya saw the priestess suspended in mid-air, held in place by a couple of Lumanians.

They ran through the crowded room, dodging and elbowing forces from both sides. Everything was a blurred mess wherever Zoya looked, little skirmishes breaking out randomly around them, like ripples on the surface of the sea. There seemed to be many Lumanians, far more than Zoya had ever expected to join them in a fight, but the fight still seemed to be evenly matched.

They were bolting at a breakneck speed towards the door. Zoya could finally see it now, not ten meters away, when suddenly, an earth-shattering roar ripped through the room. Everything stood still. As if, frozen in time. Fighters stood locked in their last poses of battle. Zoya was petrified mid-run, with one leg outstretched, Yuri beside her with a dumbfounded expression stuck permanently to his face.

Zoya tried to move her lips but could not. She tried to move her limbs, but they were as stiff as a statue's. Her heart thumped in her chest. A moment later, something else thumped—the marching boots of dozens. They were coming in through the doors like a swarm of bees. Dozens, perhaps scores of new Aifra soldiers. But these ones were different. Their uniforms were pitch-black. Their faces were twisted like a mummy's, their gazes extraterrestrial.

An undead army, Zoya thought trying unsuccessfully to gulp down the saliva that had accumulated in her mouth.

A battalion of the undead headed her way. One of them glanced behind her before making a fluid gesture with his arm, that unfroze Zoya instantly. Zoya flicked her head around to see what he was looking at. It was the Frozen

Saint. He stood behind them with his arms raised above his head, holding everything and everyone in his field of view, hostage to his otherworldly power.

The soldier who had unfrozen Zoya, bound her securely with a rope and tossed her over his shoulder like a sack of potatoes. Then, the battalion proceeded towards the sacrificial alter. As they were moving, more and more similar soldiers began to come of the woodwork and surround the room with their looming presence. This was it. The end of it all.

Zoya was lowered into the pool of blood and a cup brought to her mouth. She drank again. This time a numbness began to spread over her limbs, a soothing, anaesthetic feeling that momentarily washed away all concern. The chanting had resumed in many voices, a rhythmic ululation that chilled her to the bones.

Zoya took another sip. More drowsiness. Then, something different. A loud explosion. Like a bomb being dropped outside. The chanting stopped and some of the undead soldiers rushed outside. Another explosion. Some more soldiers left. After that, the pounding continued at intervals, punctuating the otherwise silent night with its ear-splitting booms. But the chanting had begun again. Slower this time. More cautious.

Several seconds went by like this, perhaps even minutes. But then, the rhythm of the chanting changed. It became more upbeat, more bright, like the promise of the new sun tearing through a moonless night. In fact, to Zoya's addled ears, it did not sound like the same words at all. A new verse was being chanted, completely different in purpose and meaning. Although the words of both were incomprehensible, their energies were markedly opposing. What was more surprising was that, the new voice was one,

Zoya had heard so many times before, in encouragement, in reprimand, even in university lectures. It was the unmistakable sound of Wanda Faraday's wise and prophetic voice.

Zoya blinked away her tears. The hand that was feeding her the liquid had moved away, clearing her line of sight. And through the opening that was created, Zoya glimpsed the objects that were transmitting this strange new rhythm. They were tiny crystals of many colours, much like the Lumanian Seeing Crystals, but smaller, each about the size of a tennis ball, rising from the ground and floating all around the room.

The Frozen Saint stood up abruptly, livid with rage. With another deafening roar, he snapped his fingers and the crystals shattered to a million pieces, crumbling to the ground like stardust. Now only the dark, ominous chanting remained, filling everything it touched with eternal gloom. A crackling wicked sort of laughter filled the room as the Frozen Saint's chest rose and fell with its swells.

Zoya sank into the pool of blood, all life draining out of her, her eyes retracting into their sockets like a hiding turtle. There was a soft rumble, as if the earth was shaking with agony. Zoya gave in to it in a final moment of surrender.

It would be a good time to pass out, she thought vaguely. But that blissful unconscious state did not automatically arrive, as she had hoped it would. The earthquake stopped and the floor before the Frozen Saint's throne slid away. From the ensuing cavity, three bald, robed figures slowly rose to the surface. This was certainly either a dream or hallucination. Yet, Zoya could not bear to tear her eyes away.

The figures were chanting, the same sweet wholesome script, the one that had soothed Zoya before. But this time the sound resonated through the hall, like from a megaphone. The Frozen Saint seemed to balk and take a step backwards. The chanting continued until it drowned out all the other notes, the darker more scathing ones. With every new note uttered, the Frozen Saint shrunk back, diminished a little, his light fading away.

But just like any cornered animal strikes its final blow, the leader of the Aifra leaped once more. His arms flung forward and a ghastly reddish beam erupted from it, flinging the robed figures to the floor, like dried leaves tossed by the wind. Zoya saw them then, the prone figures. They were the Elders. The Elders of Lumania.

At this sight, something feral woke up inside of Zoya. She fought against the onslaught of inebriation and yelled at the top of her lungs. "The amulet! Get the amulet!" she said.

The Elders turned to her startled, but before they could react, a white dove shot past them like a bullet. In the blink of an eye, it was upon the Frozen Saint clawing at the chain that secured a locket to his throat. In a moment, it was airborne again, clutching the amulet with its beak. It fluttered its wings and transformed, first into a horse. Then, a winged horse. And finally, a horse with a rider in a billowing cloak. The rider turned a radiant, smiling face towards Zoya, before transforming into pure light.

"*The Kalki*", Zoya whispered. The Elders had risen and surrounded the Frozen Saint. Their extended arms restrained his writhing form, bound him, controlled him. And then, vanished him from existence. This was the last thing Zoya saw, before she crawled out of the bloodied pool and passed into a state of blissful oblivion.

EPILOGUE

Zoya was in Wanda Faraday's rustic cottage in Hope Cove, Devon, sitting on the bed in a spare bedroom, looking out the window. It was a bright, sunny day outside. The room was small but primly decorated, true to Wanda's style. There was a twin bed by the window and a desk and chair across from it. A small dresser stood by the door on the carpeted floor. The colour scheme was fuchsia, interspersed with hints of purple and ivory black. Overall, it was a bright and peppy atmosphere.

Zoya had been up for about an hour, after being asleep for God-knows-how-long. She reckoned, it must have been at least two days, since they got out of the Lumanian tunnels in Calais and came to England via the English Channel. Legally this time. She had been in a stretcher during their journey, flitting between the realms of awareness and slumber.

Once they arrived at the cottage, she had been assigned to this room and given a hot meal and various herbal concoctions to drink. She had slept like a baby since then, not being able to tell the difference between night and day.

Now, the aroma of something savoury wafted into the room, making her stomach growl. Although the long hours of sleep had refreshened her somewhat, she still did not feel like getting out of bed and going downstairs to check on what was cooking. There was a knock on the door.

"Come in," Zoya said, feeling hopeful that someone had read her mind and brought her something to eat.

As if on cue, Wanda walked in with a loaded tray in her hand, grinning widely. "Good morning!" She greeted cheerily. "Nice to see that you're up so early, for a change."

"Ha! I've been sleeping forever."

"Don't worry about it. You needed the rest." Wanda set the tray down on the nightstand. It was loaded with goodies: orange juice, scrambled eggs, sausages, hash browns, a bowl of fruity yoghurt, and two slices of toast with Zoya's favourite peanut butter. "I got you some breakfast," Wanda said, gently.

"Mmm, yumm! Thank you." Zoya smiled as she snatched the tray and began digging ravenously into the meal. As she ate, her professor came over to sit at the foot of her bed.

"How are you feeling now?" Wanda asked.

"Better." Zoya took a swig of orange juice, to swallow down her food. "How long have I been out?"

"Two days."

"Ah, I thought so. Though I wasn't really sure." Zoya bit into her toast. "Mmmm, this tastes so good. I can't remember the last time I ate this well."

Wanda chuckled. "Of course not. You did a really reckless thing back there." She paused for a breath and became serious. "Bold. But reckless, nonetheless."

"But I *had* to!" Zoya protested.

"No, you did not." Wanda's voice was stern.

"You don't get it. The Frozen Saint ... his life was tied to *me*. If I didn't—"

"No Zoya, it wasn't. His life wasn't tied to yours. Because if it was, then how are you still alive?"

"Well ... I guess ... I figured ..." Zoya stammered.

"Yes?" Wanda urged.

"I mean, maybe it was like just one of us could survive and since he's dead—"

"He's not *dead*, Zoya."

"Oh!" Zoya stopped chewing and looked up, her eyes wide with astonishment. "He isn't?"

"No. But you need not worry. He's as good as dead."

"How?"

"The Lumanian Elders have dealt with him. They have bound him and sent him to a different dimension."

"They can *do* that?" Zoya's mouth fell open.

"Apparently. And that is partly why, they were cursed to remain within their tunnels until such a time came, when the world had atoned for its sins and was ready for a new, enlightened age."

"And that's why the sand in the hourglass had stopped flowing? Because the world had sinned?"

"Correct."

"Interesting. But what changed? What did we do, that fixed this and made the sand flow again?"

"It was a series of things actually. Peter and Nancy defecting and coming to our assistance. Colonel Costa's reluctance to wage war. Some Lumanians breaking their credo and helping us and other such events. There are many more examples that I won't go over right now. But the bottom line is that, the final nail in the coffin was *you*."

"*Me?* How?"

"Your willingness to make the ultimate sacrifice, that of your life, is what really turned the tides, I believe."

"Wow! Okay. So, my going there *was* a good idea after all." Zoya grinned cheekily.

"No, it wasn't," Wanda countered. "Not like that. Not alone. You should have told us what you were thinking and we could have worked out a plan. Together."

"Well, we didn't really have time for that …"

"We had plenty of time," Wanda scolded. "You were just afraid we wouldn't have let you go."

"Well … would you have?"

"Probably not." Wanda smiled.

"See what I mean?" They burst into laughter. "But I still feel like I owe the Frozen Saint a life debt. And … if he ever gets free, it isn't going to end well for me," Zoya said, once she had stopped laughing.

"About that, you are wrong again, my child. Do you know what happened to all those people he had resurrected from the dead?"

"No, what?"

"Once the Frozen Saint ceased to exist in this dimension, all those undead beings finally died. They just dropped dead."

"Oh my God!" Zoya's hands flew to her cheeks. "Does that mean I … will I …"

"Certainly not. You're not going to die. Those whom he had resurrected, fell immediately. But you were fine. Which could mean only one thing."

"That I was not a stillborn?" Zoya's eyes sparkled.

"Ummm … not exactly. Your father is a doctor. He didn't make such a misdiagnosis. It just means that you were not resurrected by the Frozen Saint, but by someone else entirely."

Zoya's pupils dilated, as if they were being doused with Atropine Sulphate. "The Kalki?"

Wanda nodded, a sly grin playing across her lips.

"Seriously? Have you always known?"

"On some level, perhaps. But I became certain when Haresh told us something in Lumania."

"What did he say?"

"He told us that Dr. Sinha had figured out, why the Aifra were looking for the weapon of Krishna. It was because, they wanted to destroy it. Dr. Sinha believed that this weapon may not even be an object but a *person*. Therefore, you being an incarnation of Meera could possibly be—"

"That person?" Zoya asked.

"Exactly. That's when I figured it out. I knew that you were a gift to us from Krishna and that you were brought back from the dead by His hands."

"I see. Can I ask you something?"

"Yes, anything."

"I heard a chanting in *your* voice, right before I passed out at the Aifra base. Was that a dream?"

Wanda shook her head. "Not a dream. It was the Script of Horus. We had recorded verses from it in my narration and stored it in Lumanian crystals. All of us were carrying these crystals in our pockets and were planning to play them when the Script of Ra began to be chanted. However, the Frozen Saint had stopped time and frozen us all in place, thereby foiling our plan. But everything changed when the Elders rose to join the fray. They levitated the crystals from our pockets and began to play them. This was right before the three of them appeared in person to duel with the Saint."

"Incredible! Thanks for explaining. I didn't know *what* I was hearing or seeing during that phase. It's all a big blur to me really." Zoya sighed and set aside her tray, which she had emptied of its last crumb by now. Leaning back against the pillows, she spoke again. "Where's everyone else?"

"Ah, of course! I was wondering when you'd ask that." Wanda smiled indulgently. "The Lumanians are back in Lumania, except for the few who are with Wolfgang. Amon went back to his family in Egypt. Nirmala, Alejandro and Haresh took Dr. Sinha's body back to India. Albert, Peter and Chris are at the university in London and Colonel Costas and Wolfgang are in Canada."

Zoya, who was nodding along this whole time, jerked upright at the mention of Canada. "*Canada?* What are they doing in Canada?"

"That's a long story."

"Oh c'mon! Tell me. I have all the time in the world."

Wanda chuckled. "Alright. I'll keep it short, because *I* don't have all the time in the world, unfortunately." She paused for breath. "Once the Frozen Saint was dealt with, we needed to come up with a plan, to explain this whole thing away to the rest of the world. So, we decided to tell them the truth."

"Whaaat?" Zoya was shocked.

"Partially," Wanda corrected. "At least we began with the truth. We told them that Colonel Costas and Wolfgang were captured by the Aifra and brought to their camp. This part is mostly true. The rest: well, you could call it a white lie. We asked Alex to explain to his superiors that once they were captured by the Aifra, they were able to motivate others and enlist defectors, such as Peter and Nancy."

"Interesting. Go on ..."

"With the help of these rebels, Alex organized a siege. He used a downed Russian bomber plane that was in the Aifra's possession, to weaken them militarily. Then, they did a strategic strike and went after their leader, who was demolished by one of their warheads. After their leader fell, the remaining Aifra soldiers surrendered and were rescued. The US Army was relieved to hear this and offered amnesty to the rescued Aifra members. They commended Alex and Wolfgang and promised to reward them handsomely. Meanwhile, it turned out, that several of the rescued Aifra soldiers were Canadians. So, the Canadian government expressed its own share of gratitude, by granting refugee status to everyone in that camp and offering them a piece of land in Nunavut, to build a colony. So, that's where Wolfgang and Alex are right now, inspecting the land and trying to make it habitable."

"*Nunavut*? Isn't that like in the middle of nowhere?"

"Well yes. But some of the Lumanians who had joined the fight, have also been declared as defectors from the Aifra and they can live in this colony, if they choose to. So, given how reclusive the Lumanians are and how many years it has been since any of them have actually lived outside of their tunnels, it is preferable that the colony be built in an isolated place."

"I suppose. By the way, where is Nancy? And ... Yuri?" Zoya added, after a bit of hesitation.

"*Nancy* is back with her family in California. You can see her, once you feel ready to go back. She has located Jake, by the way. He is alive and well, staying with his brother in Colorado." Here, Wanda paused for breath.

"And *Yuri,*" she continued, her lips curving into a sly grin, "is in the backyard. Gardening."

Zoya forgot all her weakness and exhaustion and leaped to her feet at these words. Grabbing her empty tray from the side table, she turned to Wanda, "I'll take this to the kitchen," she said, before disappearing beyond the door.

After taking care of her dishes, Zoya tiptoed out the back door. The sun assaulted her face like a sharp slap. She blinked against the brightness. Once her vision had steadied, she looked around her. She was standing in a small kitchen garden, bright with its first blossoms. Right at the back, behind some sunshine-yellow tulips, was a familiar face prodding in the dirt. Zoya's heart leaped as she made her way to the crouched figure.

"Hey!" She hollered, standing in front of the tulips.

"Oh, hey there! You're awake!" Yuri stood up and dusted his hands.

"Yep! How come you're here?"

"Ummm … I like gardening?" Yuri scratched his head in mock confusion.

"No! I meant *here*, in England." Zoya gestured with her hands.

"Ah! Didn't Dr. Faraday tell you? I'm training to be a Novo Hekameses. Come, let's go sit over there." He pointed to a bench beside the vegetable patch."

"Is that all?" Zoya asked, as they walked towards the bench. "The only reason you're here?"

"No, of course not! I had never been to England, so …" Zoya smacked Yuri on the arm. "Ouch! What did you do that for?"

"You're lying!" Zoya protested.

"No, I'm serious, I'd never been—"

"Cut it out!" Zoya crossed her arms over her chest, as she sat down on the bench.

Yuri came around to sit beside her. Then, turning to look her in the eye, he said, "So, what if I *was* lying?"

Zoya blushed. "You shouldn't," she mumbled. "Don't you have to go back to your Masters program?"

"I'm done, mostly. I was writing my thesis when you barged into my life again." Yuri chuckled. Seeing Zoya roll her eyes, he shook his head and continued. "Anyway, as I was saying, I just have to go back to defend my thesis. And then I'll be free to do whatever I want."

"I see. Good for you."

Yuri reached over and grabbed her hand. "When do *you* have to go back to school?"

"*About* that! Actually, I've been doing some thinking—"

"When? You were mostly sleeping," Yuri teased.

"Shut up!"

"Okay. Continue …"

"I've been thinking, that I don't want to go back to school. I want to dedicate my complete attention to becoming a Hekameses."

"What? That's crazy! I thought studying neuroscience was what you had wanted all your life."

"It was," Zoya admitted. "But that was before I knew what I really wanted. Before I knew what existed beyond the world that everyone can see and understand. Now … now, it's different. My destiny has brought me this far and I want to trust it to take me where I ultimately need to go. Like … like flotsam you know," Zoya added, remembering Alejandro's philosophy.

"I don't know what flotsam means." Yuri shrugged. "But I like everything else you said." He grinned wildly as Zoya bent to rest her head on his shoulder.

* * *

Chris walked up to Dr. Cobb's office and knocked lightly on the door. "Come in," his elderly professor croaked.

"I brought someone to see you," Chris said, emerging through the door.

"Well, what are you waiting for? Bring 'em in!"

Chris poked his head out the half-open door and waved the visitor inside. He was a rugged, broad-shouldered man, about a head taller than Chris. His salt and pepper beard had been neatly trimmed and washed. His wavy hair, now free from dreadlocks, hung loosely over his shoulders.

Dr. Cobb jumped from his seat. "Peter!" He placed a shaking palm on his desk and leaned forward. "I ... you ..." His lips were moving, but no further words came out.

"Father," Peter said. "Taking a step forward. He pulled up a chair across from the professor and made to sit down. "May I?"

"Yes. Of course." Dr. Cobb glanced up at Chris. "You too."

Chris pulled up the chair next to Peter and sat down. When everyone was seated, Peter began to speak again. "I know, I should have done this a long time ago. But believe me, I couldn't. There was something ..." he trailed off; his face contrite.

"He was in the Frozen Saint's thrall," Chris cut in helpfully.

"Alright, alright, come to the point. What do you want?"

"I want ... your forgiveness," Peter replied.

"Hmph!" Dr. Cobb grunted, crossing his arms over his rotund belly.

"What I'm trying to say is that, I am sorry that I never believed you, Father." Then, after a pause, "Sorry that I left. Sorry that I made the wrong choices at every turn," Peter continued, noticing his father's reticence.

"Hmph!" Dr. Cobb grunted again. "And what is that supposed to mean?"

"I was young and foolish and jealous of your powers and in my juvenile self-loathing, I sought strength somewhere else. In the wrong place. From the wrong sort of people. But ... you were right all along. I *do* have your powers. I had it the whole time."

"Eh?" Dr. Cobb sat up straight. "What's that now?"

Chris spoke up. "You see Dr. Cobb; I've been teaching Peter some things in the last couple of days. Some Hekameses stuff, and he's been picking it up real fast. Show him, Peter." Chris grabbed a paperweight from the middle of Dr. Cobb's desk and handed it to his newfound friend.

Peter took the paperweight and placed it delicately at the centre of his left palm. Then, he hovered his right palm over it. In the blink of an eye, the small glistening object rose above his hand and floated for about half a minute, before sinking back down.

"See that?" Chris said, enthusiastically. "He *is* a Hekameses. He has our abilities, after all!"

Dr. Cobb glanced first at Chris, then at Peter and sighed. "So that's what this is about? It's all about power?"

"Oh no, of course not," Chris objected. "All I'm saying is that, whatever the Frozen Saint did to him, cast a sort of veil over his true-self all along. But when the Lumanians found him and erased that part of his memory which had been corrupted by the Aifra, he was free to come into his own and discover his unsullied self, his purer nature. He is essentially good, Dr. Cobb. I'm sure, you must know it too?"

"I asked *him* not you," Dr. Cobb scolded.

Peter cleared his throat. "No. It's not about power. It's about seeing what I had failed to see. The light from the darkness."

"Don't you think that makes sense?" Chris asked, smiling up at his professor. "That the Lumanian magic has cleared his confusion, and underneath, he has discovered his Hekameses powers that he had failed to actualize for so long, because of his doubts?"

"Of course, it's possible! In fact, that's exactly how our power works. But what's your point now, my boy? What do you expect me to do?" Dr. Cobb asked.

"Can you forgive him?" Chris asked meekly.

"Let me teach you something about parenthood, my boy," Dr. Cobb began. "A parent can always forgive a child. It is not a question that needs to be asked. What you should ask instead, is whether the lot of you will ever forgive him."

"Well, I … obviously believe him. And that's why I'm here to plead his case. About the others, I spoke with Wanda and she wants to have him join us. I didn't get a chance—"

"If Wanda says he can join, he can join." Dr. Cobb interrupted. Then, turning to Peter, "But I'll be keeping an eye on you, myself. And if you set one foot out of line—" Dr. Cobb's voice was rising.

Peter rose abruptly from his seat. "I won't, Father. I'll do you proud. I promise." And then, without warning, he leaned over the desk and encapsulated his old man in a giant bear-hug.

Dr. Cobb gently patted his son's back before extricating himself. A single tear had slid down his right cheek and was pooling around the crook of his nose. He sniffed and wiped his face with the back of his hand. "Go on now! Get busy getting trained," he said with a dismissive wave of his hand.

* * *

It was midday in Rajkot when Alejandro stood in the tarpaulin covered backyard of Dr. Sinha's home, where his last-rites ceremony was taking place. There were around twenty attendees, with Nirmala sitting right up front around the prayer area, flanked by Haresh and Dr. Sinha's domestic helper, Manubhai. A picture of the old man, bedecked with colourful garlands, was set on a small stage in front of which, a somber looking priest was sitting with the son of the deceased, chanting prayers around a small fire.

Alejandro stood at the very back, leaning against one of the bamboo posts that held up the tarpaulin. But even at this distance, his eyes were watering from the smoke that emanated from the holy fire up front. The acrid smoke drifting to his nostrils, was intermingled with other pleasanter smells—that of flowers, incense and camphor. The rhythmic sound of chanting, coupled with the myriad aromas and the heat of the midday sun, was having such a lulling effect on him that for a minute, he thought he would fall asleep where he stood.

In order to avoid creating a scene by falling flat on his face, Alejandro ventured towards one of the tables that was set under the tarpaulin, to seat the funeral attendees. He only realized that he had fallen asleep with his head cushioned on his folded arms, when the sound of voices from a nearby table awakened him with a jolt. He turned his head in that direction to see Nirmala sitting there with Haresh and Manu, speaking in hushed tones.

The ceremony seemed to have ended, with the embers of the holy fire smouldering heavily into the humid afternoon air. Alejandro rubbed his eyes and sat up. He looked up at Nirmala, but she deftly turned her face away, avoiding any eye contact. During the entire length of their grim and tedious journey to India, Nirmala had hardly spoken a word to Alejandro, choosing to sit a few seats away from him each time. Alejandro ached to speak with her. But the opportune moment never seemed to arrive.

Manu detached himself from Nirmala's table and began to hand out refreshments to the guests, as was customary. Alejandro accepted his box of snacks with a somber nod of his head. Recognizing him, Manu grinned widely and bowed.

"Thank you, Manu," Alejandro said, acknowledging the gesture. He did not think Manu would understand his words, but hoped that he would at least understand his intent. Just then, Haresh appeared by Alejandro's table and dragged Manu away for a conversation.

This was Alejandro's cue to act. He got up quickly and made his way to Nirmala, who was now sitting alone at her table. He pulled up a chair across from her and sat down.

"Hi," he said with a nervous smile.

"Hello Alejandro," Nirmala said, without smiling back.

"I ... well ... I've been." He scratched his chin searching for the right words.

Nirmala's eyes shot to his. "Been what? Bonkers?"

Her question took Alejandro by surprise. He laughed out loud in spite of himself. "I was going to say 'thinking', but yeah, you're right. That too. Also, Stupid. Stubborn. Thoughtless."

This brought a smile to Nirmala's lips. "Go on," she said encouragingly.

Alejandro chuckled. "Well, I'm pig-headed, slightly obtuse and definitely a liar," he added for emphasis.

"A liar? Wait, I didn't say that you—"

Alejandro stopped her mid-sentence. "Hear me out, will you?"

"Okay ..."

"I'm a liar, because I wasn't honest with you when I sent you away. I said that it was for your protection. But it wasn't. It was for *mine*."

"What? I'm lost now," Nirmala admitted with genuine confusion.

Alejandro sighed. "You know ... I lost my wife Maria when I was very young. I was crazy about her. She was murdered by the Aifra. I never stopped blaming myself for her death. For bringing her into the dangerous world of the Hekameses. Since then, I never allowed myself to love anyone that way. Because I was afraid. Afraid, I would drive her towards the same fate. I knew that if I lost someone I loved so dearly once more, then it would break me completely. I wouldn't be able to recover from such a loss, a second time. So, in a way, I was protecting myself from potential pain."

Nirmala shook her head incredulously. "But ... but ... what are you *saying* Alejandro?" A tepid crimson hue was rising rapidly up her cheeks.

Alejandro looked at her prim delicate hands, folded nervously on the table in front of him. He reached out and enclosed them within his own. "Do you really not know?" He asked, looking her straight in the eyes.

"I ... umm ..." For the first time since Alejandro had met her many months ago, she seemed to be at a complete loss for words.

"I cannot live without you," Alejandro simply said after a moment's hesitation. "I would have proposed, but a funeral is hardly the venue—"

"Shh!" Nirmala extricated her right hand from Alejandro's grip and placed her forefinger across his lips. "You don't have to say anything else," she said, finally finding her voice. Then, smiling meekly, "I feel the same way."

Alejandro let out a relieved sort of chuckle. "So, do you forgive me?"

"It depends." Nirmala winked, grinning playfully.

"Depends on what?"

"The size of the diamond." At this, they both laughed out loud.

* * *

Wolfgang walked to the edge of the thicket, where Alex was sitting on a boulder, blowing smoke out his nostrils. Sitting next to his friend, Wolfgang extended a small object in his direction.

Alex lowered his cigarette and furrowed his brows. "What's this?"

"Your USB. You should destroy it."

"Oh!" Alex accepted the memory device and flipped it over in his hand. "Where did you find it?"

"In the aftermath of the battle, while we were cleaning up at the Aifra camp, we found your lawyer Kevin Gao—"

"Oh! How is he?" Alex asked anxiously.

"He's dead. He had been killed and resurrected by the Aifra. But what I was saying is that, your USB was in his pocket when we found the body."

"I see." Alex looked down at the innocuous-looking object on his palm. "Well, at least we know now, that it can no longer get into the wrong hands by accident."

"Yes," Wolfgang agreed.

"What did you do with all the other bodies? The rest of the undead?"

"The Lumanians took them into their tunnels. They will be buried in a hidden Lumanian location. I figured it's best we leave it to them. They certainly know how to protect their secrets."

"And what about the other Aifra soldiers? The ones that didn't get amnesty?"

"They will be tried in the International Court. Peter and Nancy will testify. Perhaps some of them will have their sentences commuted. Others, the more hardened ones ... well, I hope they receive the severest of punishments."

Alex nodded and leaned back on his elbows. "General Sapieha just dropped dead in the middle of a drill after the Frozen Saint was banished. The army veterans think it was a heart attack." He guffawed.

"There will be others like him. The other undead Aifra goons. Although, a vast majority of them were in the main camp. So, the Lumanians were able to hide most of those bodies." Wolfgang stared into the distance, where a few Lumanians including Kazhar, were cutting and polishing stone blocks with their magic and a few others were assembling them together into livable homes.

"Wouldn't it have been better, if they'd made those out of wood?" Alex asked, noticing what Wolfgang was staring at. "It gets cold in these parts of the world."

"Oh, don't worry about that, the Lumanians have their own way of making their homes airtight and impregnable to everything including weather. They have worked with stone and magic for millennia. Besides, there's no way you would ever get them to fell a tree."

"You're right. I forgot about that!" Alex chuckled. "Do you think they're going to be comfortable with some of the former Aifra soldiers living with them in this colony?"

"Only the ones that receive amnesty, will be allowed to join them. Peter and Nancy know which ones deserve it and will testify accordingly. Also, I'm sure you're aware by now, that the Lumanians have their own procedure for newcomers. They will inspect each one individually and tamper with their unwanted memories, before admitting them."

"Ha! These folks are truly one of a kind. I hope they will grow into their new way of living."

"They certainly are unique. But I have no doubt, they will pick up our practices sooner than anyone can hope for. But what about you, Alex? Where do *you* go from here?"

Alex yawned and slid further back on the boulder. "First, I'll go back home to my wife. After that, I wish to retire from the Army. That life is no longer for me."

"I see. What do you plan to do then?"

Alex sat up and rubbed his hands together. It was nippy out here in the wild. "I want to live up here. With the

Lumanians. If they'll accept me, of course. I want to help them adjust to *our* world. And while I'm at it, there's so much I want to learn from them too."

Wolfgang smiled indulgently. "That's a great idea. You know, the Lumanians coming to live amongst us, is a blessing to us all. It could be the first signs of a new age of enlightenment."

Alex shrugged. "Could be. I know some people believe that such an age is coming."

"Indeed, they do. The Hindus for example. The Dwapara Yuga, they call it."

Alex nodded. "I certainly look forward to it." He stood up and dusted the seat of his pants. "But first, let's look forward to some dinner, shall we?"

In the distance, the last rays of the sun peeked between the wispy clouds to pour onto the ground below, as the heavenly Fingers of God. Wolfgang grinned at it and stood up. "Let's go," he said with a new hope rising in his heart.

MESSAGE FROM THE AUTHOR

Thank you for taking the time to read this book. I hope you enjoyed it as much I enjoyed writing it. If you liked it then please take a moment to leave a review for the book on Amazon (www.amazon.com) and/or Goodreads (www.goodreads.com). Your valuable opinion can make all the difference.

OTHER BOOKS BY THE AUTHOR

Colour Me Confounded
Thought Warriors: The Coming of Kalki

PRAISE FOR COLOUR ME CONFOUNDED

"Written in simple and lucid language with economic use of words, she puts forward the life of modern women as it is, minus the embellishments or the jargons of feminism and alternative living."—*The Statesman (Kolkata, December 9, 2018)*

"I applaud Poulomi Sanyal for crafting a work that captures the subtle complexities of women's lives. I look forward to reading more of this author's future works." —*J.G. MacLeod (Author)*

"Excellent work and incredible writing by Poulomi Sanyal!" —*Steven Nedeau (Author)*

ABOUT THE AUTHOR

 Poulomi Sanyal has been writing poetry since she was ten years old, and she even created her own literary magazine when she was twelve. Sanyal was born in India but has lived all over the world, including Hong Kong and, more recently, Canada. She is fluent in English, Bengali, and Hindi, and she also speaks conversational French.

Sanyal received her master's degree from McGill University in Montreal and has spent the past ten years working in engineering in Toronto. In her free time, she enjoys writing, painting, acting, and traveling.